"You don't have Leon," Sultan Petrus pointed out.

"How are you going to get him out of the Fratery?"

"Place Green Village under Al-Andalus rule, and I'll get him out!" Halvar said firmly.

"Green Village has always been under Mahak rule," Petrus said.

"If the Mahak cede their village to Al-Andalus and go upriver to their own territory, that means Green Village is no longer Mahak," Halvar reasoned. "And once Green Village is under Andalusian rule, Sharia law applies, and Leon di Vicenza must answer to it, along with everyone else on Manatas Island. I'll have him on that ship before winter!"

"Unless something else comes along to distract you," Sultan Petrus murmured.

The Afrikan servant put his head into the room to announce, "A messenger, Excellent Sultan. From Green Village."

"What does Green Village want with me?"

"Not you, excellent Sultan—the Calif's Hireling. They've just found another body."

Also By

Roberta Rogow

Murder In Manatas
Mayhem In Manatas

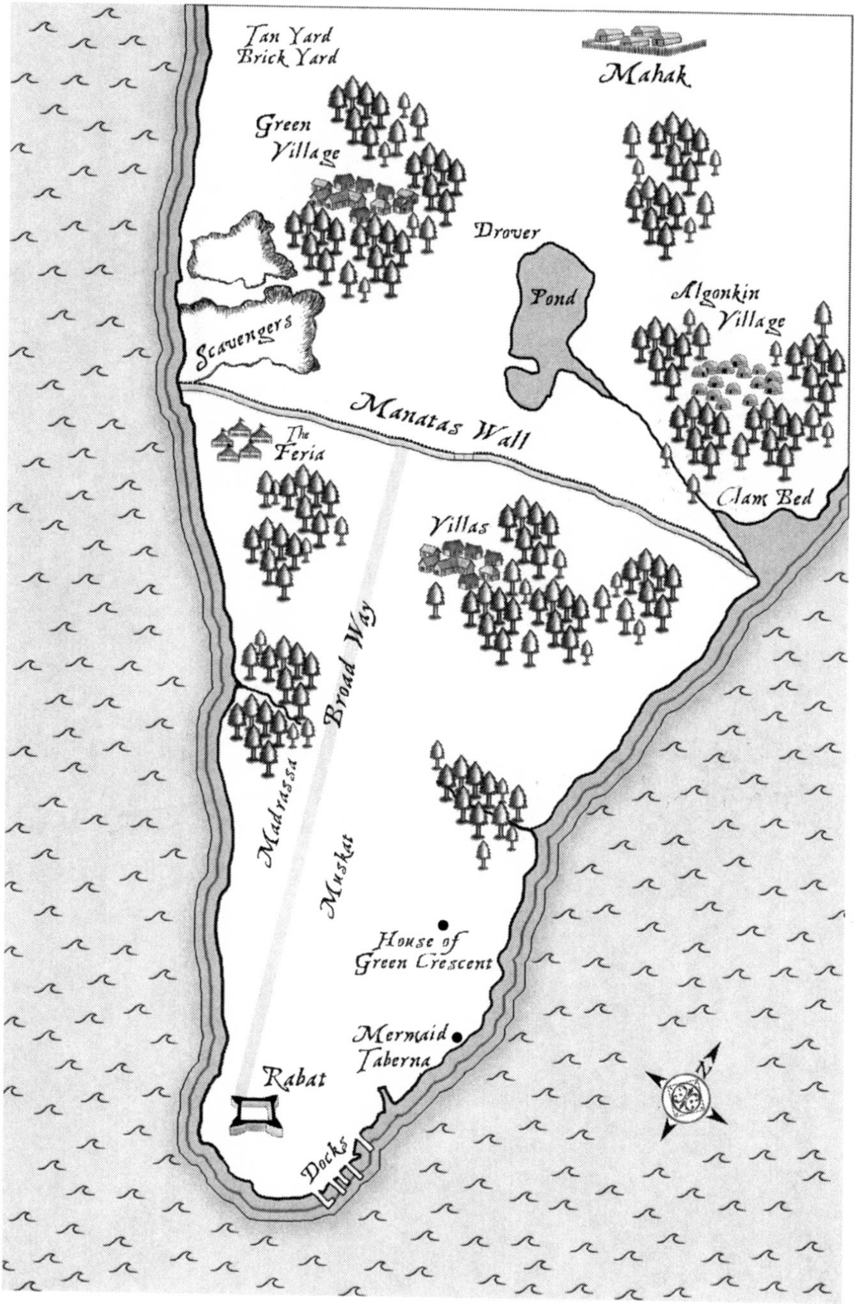

Tan Yard
Brick Yard

Mahak

Green
Village

Drover

Algonkin
Village

Pond

Scavengers

Manatas Wall

Clam Bed

The
Feria

Villas

Broad Way

Madrassa

Musket

House of
Green Crescent

Mermaid
Taberna

Rabat

Docks

N

MISCHIEF
in
MANATAS

The Saga Of Halvar The Hireling
Book 3

Roberta Rogow

Roberta Rogow

ZUMAYA OTHERWORLDS   AUSTIN TX

2015

This book is a work of fiction. Names, characters, places and incidents are products of the author's imagination or are used fictiously. Any resemblance to actual persons or events is purely coincidental.

MISCHIEF IN MANATAS
© 2015 by Roberta Rogow
ISBN 978-1-61271-285-7
Cover art and design © William Neagle

"Zumaya Otherworlds" and the griffon colophon are trademarks of Zumaya Publications LLC, Austin TX. Look for us online at http://www.zumayapublications.com

Library of Congress Cataloging-in-Publication Data

Rogow, Roberta, 1942-
  Mischief in Manatas / Roberta Rogow.
    pages ; cm. — (The Saga of Halvar the Hireling ; Book 3)
  ISBN 978-1-61271-285-7 (softcover : acid-free paper) — ISBN 978 1-61271-286-4 (electronic-multiple formats) — ISBN 978-1-61271-287-1 (electronic-epub)
  I. Title.
PS3568.O492M57 2015
813'.54—dc23
                                    2015016333

TO MY DAUGHTERS, MIRIAM AND
LOUISE: THIS ONE'S FOR YOU.

ACKNOWLEDGMENTS

I thank these people who helped make this book possible:

Lynn Holdom and Rachel Kadushin were there when Halvar the Hireling and his world were imagined.

Most of all, Elizabeth Burton, editor and publisher, who continues to support this odd mix of history and mystery.

PART ONE

A Fatality In The Feria

1

HALVAR HADN'T INTENDED TO DISRUPT THE LEADERSHIP of the Manatas Town Guard. He'd have preferred to leave the ordinary business of Manatas to its own people—Sultan Petrus and his underlings. It wasn't his fault that said underlings had tried to kill him, and he'd had to take action against them.

He had been sent by the Calif Don Felipe of Al-Andalus to this outpost settlement in the New World with orders to collect the revenues due from the fall Feria. The funds would be used to purchase arms and men to fight the incursion of the Franchen Imperator Lovis and his bloodthirsty troops, who had invaded Al-Andalus from the north. Instead, he had been inveigled into solving a series of murders.

Moreover, Halvar was supposed to find the louche artist, inventor, gadfly and pain in the bottom once called Leon di Vicenza, now known as Frater Leonidas, and fetch him home.

He had been on the island for three weeks, and in that time he had solved curious puzzles, uncovered murderers, scotched a scheme to destroy the bead currency of the island, and faced various foes with two legs and four. Now, however, he was finally free to accomplish his mission.

He strode through the Feria, a tall Dane in the green woolen coat devised especially for him by Yussuf the Tailor, adapted from the garments provided for the Town Guard. Gussets had been set into the back seams to accommodate Halvar's broad shoulders, and

1

bone buttons opened readily so that he could reach the dagger with the lump of amber in the handle, the only reminder of his youth in the Dane-March. His cap sat squarely on his head, concealing his rapidly receding hairline, although ample strands of fair hair straggled over the high collar of the coat. His jutting nose seemed to point the way through the grounds of the Feria.

His sweeping mustache had been newly trimmed, and his chin scraped clean of stubble. His booted feet scuffed among the leaves blown from the trees that stood just beyond the open space where the Feria assembled, a reminder that only the southern tip of the island had been settled. Beyond the makeshift stalls, stands and tents, oaks and maples, birches and aspens crowded the boundaries, their leaves blazing gold to yellow to russet to dark brown in the autumn sunlight.

"Business is good," he said, aloud. "The Feria should bring in a nice sum. It's too bad about the storm, but Don Felipe should be pleased."

"It's almost over," said his companion.

Sultan Petrus's daughter Salomey had insisted on accompanying him on his jaunt through the Feria. Her braids were tucked up under a turban, and she was dressed in a padded silk jacket and trousers tucked into the tops of soft leather boots. Her heavy eyebrows nearly met over her snub nose, and a few hairs on her upper lip added to her masculine disguise. To the rest of the world, she was Selim ibn Petrus, the insufferable son of the ruler of Manatas.

Halvar wished she had not taken her role as apprentice investigator so seriously. The "youth" dogged his steps whenever he left the Rabat, as if she expected him to be attacked at any moment. Not that a fifteen-year-old would be much use, except perhaps to summon help!

The Feria, occupying the space between the Mahak long-houses to the northeast and, the Algonkin wigwams on the southeast, and the collection of Oropan-style houses known as Green Village to the west was the settlement's chief reason for existence. The island of Manatas had been a focus of trade between the local tribes before the Oropans came to Nova Mundum, but when the strangers arrived, trading-ground quarrels had broken the peace, and accusations had led to bloodshed.

Then the soldiers and tally men from Al-Andalus had taken over the proceedings, imposing their regulations, checking the weights

2

and measures, and assuring the participants that all would be treated fairly. Now, Bretains and Franchen brought cloth, metal tools, finished pottery and processed foodstuffs like smoked and cured meats and dried fish to the island, where they traded for fur pelts from the west and bales of kutton, barrels of tabac leaves, and sheaves of indigo carried from the southern territories claimed by the Afrikans. The kutton would be woven in the mills of Nova Bretain and dyed with the indigo; the tabac would be sent over the Storm Sea to Oropa, where it would fetch a good price.

Overseeing every sale were the Andalusian tally men, their abacuses clicking off the percentage owed to the calif for his guidance in keeping the Feria honest and Manatas safe for traders of every nation and religion.

The Feria usually lasted the two weeks before and after the full moon of the autumnal equinox. This year, a terrible storm had disrupted the trading, and Sultan Petrus and the Mahak and Algonkin sachems had decreed the Feria would remain open for an additional week.

Daoud, the leather-lunged news-crier, marched through the Feria announcing there would be a Grand Divan in two days' time, when all claims and lawsuits would be settled. For those who needed advice, there would be tables near the tally men where advocates would offer their expertise in the intricacies of Sharia, Bretain, and Local law. What is more, Daoud announced, "The end of the Feria will be marked with sports, games, contests of strength and skill, and musical performances."

Halvar winced at this last announcement. He had already heard the buskers' rendition of "The Ballad of the Stranger and the Sekonk" repeated to the amusement of the crowd, and knew there would be more buyers for the broadsheet that depicted his encounter with the stinky creature. He was not sure whether the whispers of "There goes the Calif's Hireling" were admiring or were accompanied by a snicker and the rattle of the broadsheet with the lyrics to the ballad with its the drawing of a tall man and a small, bush-tailed animal.

He noted gaps in the lines of tables and tents. Some of the major dealers had already packed their belongings, preparing for the long trek back south or north. A few of their places had been taken by lesser vendors, who set out a cloth or mounted a small stand and announced their wares in Arabi, Erse, or Munsi, the trade language devised by the Locals. A healer touted the virtues of his herbal potions.

A woman in a gaudy red shirt and Bretain plaid skirt called out to passers-by, praising the colors of her knitted caps and scarves. A stern imam in the long dark coat and green turban that signified a graduate of the Ulema of Baghdad harangued a few listeners about the evils of gambling, which he claimed was a defiance of Ilha's word and the workings of kismet, and offered copies of his sermons.

Halvar grinned under his mustache; he had no doubt that bets were already being laid as to whether the lanky Mahak or the sturdy Bretains would win the footrace whose course was being set out around the perimeter of the Feria.

The last days of the Feria brought the residents of Manatas Town to the Feria to pick up whatever they could find at a bargain price. Yehudit in long black coats and broad-brimmed hats trimmed with fur; Afrikans in striped tunics and patterned shirts worn over loose trousers; Andalusians in robes and turbans, accompanied by women whose "modest garb" ranged from a simple hijab to cover the hair to a full burka. The air was filled with the scents of sizzling oil and meat as Local and Afrikan women hawked refreshments—the ever present hot maiz-cakes, ground-nuts called nguba, and dried berries, all washed down with sweet cider.

Halvar caught sight of a familiar face.

"*Salaam aleikum*, Firebrand. What cheer?" He accosted the Mahak warrior who had assisted him in one of his investigations.

The Mahak greeted Halvar with an upraised hand to show that he held no weapon.

"Good cheer, Hireling. As you can see, I have taken the advice of my sachem and made some of our warriors watchmen. They will see to it that there is no more fighting, no one will pass bad wumpum, and no one will sell fiery water to those who should not drink it."

Halvar noted the presence of several young Mahak among the crowd.

"Good thinking. "

"The Scavengers have grown very bold since you threw Tenente Gomez into the river," Firebrand said as they strolled along the path lined with small stalls and blankets.

"That wasn't my fault," Halvar protested. "He came at me with a halberd. Has anyone found the body?"

4

"Not yet," Firebrand admitted. "But it is possible he was swept out to sea. The river current is strong. He is surely dead by now. In a way, it was not a good thing. He kept the Scavengers in Manatas Town, would not let them into the Feria."

"You mean he paid them off," Halvar said. "And I didn't kill Tenente Ruíz. That was your doing."

"Would you prefer that he had skewered you?" Firebrand countered. "Hya!"

He stopped a pair women dressed in gaudy loose trousers and long silk tunics trimmed with glittering beads, and their male companion, a slender Andalusian with a neatly-trimmed beard, in a brightly-striped kaftan and turban.

"Are you buyers or sellers?" he demanded of the trio.

The man smirked. The women simpered.

"Just looking about, you know. Not here on business, Mahak."

"Good. Because such business belongs on Maiden Lane!" Firebrand warned the doxies and their protector.

The hubbub of the Feria was broken by the cry of the muezzin and the clang of the chapel bell in nearby Green Village. All other activity stopped as the faithful Islim prostrated themselves and the Kristos knelt for their midday prayers.

Selim obediently bowed, hands at her waist, then knelt on the grass—better than the muddy path. Firebrand stood erect and murmured something that might have been a prayer or a curse. Halvar simply gripped his amulet that could have been Thor's hammer or the Crux and recited his usual plea to the Redeemer and Mother Mara and the god Thor for protection. He hoped he wouldn't need it, but one could never be sure in Manatas.

So far, he'd been poisoned, drugged, beaten, stabbed, shot, garroted and skewered, and this was only his third week on the island. On the other hand, he'd actually been able to remove his meager belongings from the grim cell assigned to him at the Rabat to the more congenial rooms at the Mermaid Taberna formerly occupied by Leon di Vicenza without incident.

Selim said a final "Ilha is the One" and scrambled to her feet.

"Are you praying that you won't get killed today?"

"A whole day, and no one's tried. I must be doing something wrong." He stopped to admire a pile of furs on a table. He recognized the silky brown of mink and the gray-white of sable, but the bits of orange-and-black-striped fur puzzled him. He noted the distinctive black and white of sekonk fur and wrinkled his nose at the pervasive odor.

An odd item caught his eye.

"What's that?"

The vendor, a Local woman of indeterminate age in the kutton blouse and leather skirt favored by the Algonkin grinned at him expectantly.

"Araghoun," she explained, holding up the skin, which had been made into a round cap with a flat crown, decorated with the animal's tail swinging jauntily on one side.

"One string ten purple," she said in Arabi.

"Too much!" Halvar knew how the game was played. "One purple, no more. Besides, I have a hat." He patted the round cap on his head.

The Local woman wrinkled her nose.

"Too much sekonk! Better you should have this, good and warm in winter."

"You really should get rid of that awful cap," Selim commented.

"I like my cap." Halvar settled the smelly object more firmly on his head. Its boiled-leather lining had protected him from assaults for many years, and it reminded him that he was, after all, a Dane, no matter how long he had been in Al-Andalus.

"It reeks of sekonk."

All conversation stopped when the Local woman shrieked out, "Thief!"

A boy in a tattered shirt and patched trousers darted away from the furrier's table, the fur cap in one hand. He barreled into Halvar, snatched at the strings of wumpum dangling from Halvar's belt, and danced away before the Dane realized what was happening. Firebrand tried to block his path, but the the youngster veered to the left when Firebrand went to the right.

Selim pelted after him, slipping on occasional muddy patches in the grass as he darted in and out of the spaces left by the departing vendors. Firebrand shouted something in Munsi. The watchmen came together at the end of the steep path that led to the Scavengers' settlement, near the garbage pits at the end of the Manatas Town wall near the Great River.

Halvar joined the chase through the lines of stands and tents, while the vendors yelled encouragement. The young thief skidded to a halt in front of a solidly built Mahak hefting a war-club. Selim nearly bumped into him.

"Ali! What are you doing here? You're supposed to stay in Manatas Town!"

"Please!" the youngster pleaded. "He'll kill me if I don't come back with something!"

"Emir Achmet?" Selim panted. "I thought the Feria wasn't to be touched."

"That was when Tenente Gomez paid him to stay away," the boy said. "Gomez isn't here, Ruiz isn't here. Even a Scavenger's got to make a living."

"Not at the Feria!" Halvar came down the path, breathing heavily. "Gomez or no Gomez, the ruling still stands. Scavengers stay behind the wall!"

"But Emir Achmet said— " Ali whined.

"The Mahak watchmen rule the Feria," Halvar said. "What do you do to thieves, Firebrand?"

"They face punishment!" Firebrand said sternly. "Your Sharia law is too easy. What is it, to lose a finger or a hand? The thief can always use the other fingers, the other hand. We Mahak know how to deal with those who take what is not theirs. They are sent out into the forest with a knife and one day's food, and they are not to come back. Let Manitou judge them."

"And you wouldn't even get that much of a chance in Bretain or Franchenland," Halvar added as the young thief contemplated his fate. "You took a fur cap, worth at least five purple wumpum. That's a hanging offense in the Dane-March."

"Your choice, thief! Mahak or Sharia justice?" Firebrand asked the boy.

"You mean, do I want to lose a finger or try to live on my own in the forest?" The boy shrugged. "I'll take the Rabat. At least the sultan will hear me out. At the worst, I lose a finger; at the best, I get to work on the streets, and maybe I can find a better master than Emir Achmet."

Firebrand snorted his disgust at the leniency of Al-Andalus, but allowed Halvar to walk the boy back to the gate in the wall that separated Manatas Town from the rest of the island. He and his watchmen sauntered off to continue their surveillance of the grounds.

"Take this miserable thief to the Rabat for the sultan's justice. He stole a fur hat." Halvar handed the boy over to the bored guard, who grabbed the young thief by the arm, glad to have a reason to leave his post.

7

Selim coughed gently. "Haven't you forgotten something?"

Halvar realized he was holding the evidence of the theft, and that he hadn't paid for it. He found the furrier, handed her five purple wumpum beads, and placed the hat over his all-too noticeable cap.

"Not an improvement," Selim remarked with a sniff. "You can still smell sekonk."

A sudden burst of noise from a large tent ahead of them drew Halvar's attention from the virtues of fur hats.

"You must pay your share, Ochiye Aboutiye! It is the law!"

A tall Afrikan tally man in a striped kaftan and turban waved a sheaf of papers at an Afrikan man draped in the patterned cloth favored by the settlers in the southern territories of Nova Mundum.

"No! Why should I? I do not wish to support a useless cause!" The stout Afrikan waved another paper at the tally man.

"What's going on here?" Halvar demanded as he strode up to the pair.

The tally man explained.

"Ochiye Aboutiye is a vendor. He brought goods from the southern territories to Manatas to be sold or traded to Bretains or Franchen. He has made many sales, he owes the Calif his share."

"And I say, why should I pay for something that is of no use to me?" Ochiye sneered. His barrel chest, barely covered by the cloth that swathed his bulky form, heaved with indignation. The tribal scars on his broad face seemed to inflate in his wrath.

Halvar frowned at the paper thrust under his mustache with a grimace of distaste.

"What's this?" He stared at the paper, unable to read either the twisting Arabi or the rounded Erse letters.

"I'll take it." Selim scanned the front of the document then turned it over and grinned. "It's nothing. Just a news-sheet—they call it the *Gazetta*." She hurriedly folded the paper.

Halvar caught a glimpse of something that was neither Arabi nor Erse writing.

"Let me see."

He unfolded the paper to reveal a drawing of a large cow with Arabi and Erse letters on its side being milked by a person in a turban decorated with a large gem and a plume, clearly indicating someone of high rank. Two buckets alongside the cow also bore labels in the two languages.

"I can't read, but I can guess," Halvar said grimly. "The cow is the Feria? What are the buckets?"

"One is marked *War* and the other is marked *Mother*," Selim said, with a grimace of distaste.

"Meaning that the Feria is being milked to provide the calif with the wherewithal to pursue the war. And whatever is left, he gives to his mother Lady Zulaika for her pleasures." Halvar's frown deepened as he considered the implications of this silent rebellion against the authority of Al-Andalus.

"And I will not pay for a war that is lost, or for a loose woman to adorn herself!" Ochiye declared. He glared at the tally man, transferred the glare to Halvar, and turned his back on both of them to re-enter his tent.

"Ochiye is an important man among the Afrikans," the tally man told Halvar. "If he refuses to pay his tariffs, others will follow his example. Already, some are sending their kutton directly to West Caster, circumventing Manatas and so not paying any tolls to Al-Andalus at all."

"Don Felipe needs that money," Halvar said. "I'll have a word with this Ochiye and change his mind."

With that, he stepped into the Afrikan's pavilion, with Selim close behind. This revolt must be stopped before it got out of hand, and since he was the calif's man on the scene, it was up to him to do it.

2

OCHIYE'S DOMAIN WAS A CANVAS TENT WITH SIDE PAN-
els tied back to allow air and light to circulate around five trestle
tables arranged in an open rectangle around a chair from which
Ochiye held court like an Afrikan king. A smaller table next to
Ochiye's chair held a rush basket and a pottery jug and cup.

Lanterns hung from the sturdy poles that held up the tent, so
that customers could get a good look at the products laid out for
their inspection. Two Afrikan men stood behind each table, ready
to help customers decide on their purchases or to deter would-be
thieves. Two more Afrikans stood at the door, hands on their curved
swords. Ochiye was taking no chances on thieves making off with
his valuable merchandise.

This included large crocks, and wooden kegs, pottery jars and
small glass vials on the table to the right of Ochiye's large chair.
Lengths of gaily-patterned cloth were laid out on two of the three
tables in front of him. The table on Ochiye's left held the tanned
hides of large animals, and the table directly before him had a se-
lection of ornaments for body or dwelling—bead necklaces and
bracelets, elegantly embroidered cloths to be used to shade windows from the heat or wind, and most interestingly, glittering
metal bracelets and rings incised with patterns that fused Afrikan
and Local imagery.

The buyers who crowded around the tables included several
Bretains in their distinctive checkered trews and shirts, two Fran-

10

chen in tight-fitting breeches and coats with nipped-in waists, and at least one person Halvar recognized all too well.

"*Salaam aleikum*, Dani Glick!" he greeted his one-time lover and current proprietor of the Gardens of Paradise, the entertainment center of Manatas that drew revelers from all over the island to Green Village.

"*Shalom*, Halvar Danske." Dani was dressed in her "modest Yehudit" attire—long woolen skirt gathered at the waist, and neatly-fitting bodice, its low neckline filled modestly with a white kerchief. Her suspiciously red hair was tucked under a starched white cap. She wore no cosmetics, and Halvar noted the faint lines around her mouth and eyes. Except for the bracelets jangling at her wrists, she looked like any other Yehudit woman hunting for bargains on the last days of the Feria, when vendors dropped their prices so they need not carry unsold goods back home.

She stood by the side table with the jars, crocks, and vials, her Bretain bouncer Donal beside her and a halfling girl holding a large basket behind them.

"What does this Afrikan sell that a respectable Yehudit would buy?" Halvar sniffed at the crocks and wrinkled his nose at the sharp odor. "That's alcohol. I thought it was forbidden to sell it at the Feria."

"It's rhum," Dani said. "They make it in the far south from al-zucar. And it's only for sale in bulk, not by the glass, not for use at the Feria. "

"Sweet grass?" Halvar translated. "What we call sugar in the Dane-March? I thought that only grew in Afrika."

"They brought it from India," Dani explained. "It grows anywhere it's hot and wet. There are places like that along the Mechican Sea, and in the islands that surround it, and the Afrikans have started plantations to grow it here in Nova Mundum. They press the juice out of the stems, boil it down, and what comes out is sugar. Then they ferment the syrup into rhum. It's only Ochiye who brings it north, so anyone who wants it has to come to him."

"It's against Sharia to sell alcohol in Manatas," Halvar warned.

"The Gardens of Paradise isn't *in* Manatas Town," Dani reminded him. "And as long as I don't sell it to Locals, they allow me to have it in Green Village. There are some sailors who will come all the way to the Gardens of Paradise for a drink that isn't mokka or cider, and there are folks who don't like the taste of usque-

11

baugh. And I need sugar for the cakes we'll serve at the end of the Harvest Festival in three days."

She beckoned to the Afrikan standing behind the table and began the bargaining process in the jargon of Manatas—Arabi mixed with Munsi and Afrikan words, laced with slang allusions, spoken too fast for Halvar to understand more than a few words.

Halvar moved to the table with animal hides. He'd never seen anything quite like them—nearly as long as a man, with a pattern of scales that ranged from as big as his hand to as small as a fingernail. One of the Bretains grinned at his look of amazement at the size of the creature that had produced such a piece of leather.

"*Al-largato,*" the Bretain buyer explained. "Lizard."

"Biggest one I ever saw!" Halvar gasped.

"From the wetlands in the far south, " the Bretain went on. "They don't get much farther north than Powhatan territory—the winters are too cold, and there's not enough water for them to swim in. Those hides are much in demand for boots, bags, or for trimming a coat or cloak."

"When it's alive, it looks something like a crocodile," the second Bretain buyer added. "I've seen the heads. Nasty! Full of teeth! Locals use them for charms against evil. That's what those are."

He pointed to a basket of ivory-white pointed objects, some as thick as Halvar's thumb, interspersed with colored stones. Some were striped or spotted, and three or four with yellow flakes.

Selim's attention was drawn to the glittering objects on the table in front of Ochiye, where he could keep his eyes on them as he sat, surveying his kingdom.

"Look at these!"

Halvar grinned under his mustache. There was a girl under that turban after all! Then the grin faded as he realized what he was seeing.

Those bangle bracelets and bead necklaces were made from yellow metal, worked in the Afrikan technique he had seen in Al-Andalus but decorated with the linear patterns used by Locals. These were not the weirdly shaped Mechican objects that occasionally appeared in the Feria but newly made, carefully crafted pieces of very expensive jewelry.

He picked up one of the necklaces, a collection of colored stones like the ones he'd seen in the basket of teeth alternating with lumps of the same yellow metal.

Gold nuggets! The implication hit him like a blow. Somehow, Ochiye or someone he had traded with must have found found a source of gold, not in Mechican territory but in lands controlled by the Afrikans!

Gold was the great lure that had sent ships across the Storm Sea. Once it became known there was gold to be had from the Mechicans, adventurers set sail to try to find the source of it. So far, the only gold in Nova Mundum had come from the lands of the ferocious Mechicans, and it could be had only after long negotiations, and at the risk of being hauled up the steps to the top of one of their stone temples and being sacrificed to their bloodthirsty gods. If someone had found gold closer to the Afrikan settlements, men would leave their families and businesses and descend on the Afrikan farmers of the south and their Local allies, and mayhem would surely follow.

Halvar had seen what the lure of treasure could do to otherwise sane people. He'd even felt a touch of it himself in Italia, where he had been tempted to join his company in looting a Roumi Rite chapel of its gold candlesticks and silver platters. Only Old Sergeant Olaf's steady hand had kept him from stealing whatever he could carry away, and he had been spared the lashing the other thieves had received for their greed.

Halvar's eyes narrowed as he glanced at Ochiye. The Afrikan merchant was settled in his chair, a throne-like wooden object carved and padded as befitted the virtual king of the Feria merchants. He even held a scepter of sorts, a carved wooden stick with a whisk of horse's hair on the end to brush away the insects that made life miserable, even in the Feria.

"Interesting jewelry," Halvar commented.

"Very expensive," Ochiye said with a smug nod. "I only take double its weight in silver for each piece. Not wumpum."

Halvar reached out to pick up one of the bangles, but Ochiye smacked his hand away with the scepter.

"Not for hirelings," the Afrikan snarled.

"The calif might want one," Halvar said meaningfully. "As a gift, you understand."

"Your calif is a foolish boy being led by the nose by his mother!" Ochiye shot back. "I hear this from the Ashanti and Igbo when I come north. The last time anyone saw him, he was pleading with the Sultan of Tunis for arms and soldiers. He did not get them. No one will help a coward who runs from battle!"

13

"He is not a coward!" Halvar insisted. "He's outgunned, and he needs every ounce of silver or gold you've got to get his land back!"

Ochiye stood up, radiating fury, waving his staff.

"He will not get it from me! And I will tell my brother merchants. We will not pay tolls to someone who will only waste them in this useless attempt to turn a tide that is against him. Ilha has turned his back on this calif!"

He took a deep breath then gasped and sagged into the chair. A slender girl darted from where she had been cowering behind it, holding out a small basket. Ochiye reached behind him, found something and popped it into his mouth without inspecting it.

Immediately, he knew he had made a bad mistake. He let out a roar of anguish and tried to spit out what he had just put into his mouth.

"What's wrong?"

Ochiye gagged and fell into his chair. Halvar stared wildly about.

"This man is ill! Fetch a doctor!"

Selim shoved the curious onlookers away as she ran in search of medical help. Dani shoved the basket-toting serving-girl out of the tent to follow her.

"Fetch Frater Iosip from the fratery!" Dani shouted.

"And have him bring Frater Leonidas with him!" Halvar added. "This looks like poisoning, and he's an apothecary's son. He knows poisons."

He noticed the pitcher and cup on the table next to the chair and took a step towards it but the girl had already poured liquid into the cup, and held it to Ochiye's mouth. The man swallowed one sip, roared again, spat the liquid out, and pushed her hand away.

"Mmmmmaaaaa.... "

"What are you trying to tell me?" Halvar leaned closer.

"NNNNNNooooooommmmmaaaa......" Ochiye's mouth could not bring sense to the sounds. His dark face took on a deep maroon hue. He struggled to breathe while his bodyguards stood, helpless, unable to rescue their master.

"AAAAAhhhhhhhhh!" Ochiye gasped, and screamed, then let out a very long sigh.

Selim popped her head into the tent.

"I've got medicals!" she announced.

Halvar eased Ochiye to the ground and looked at the new arrivals.

"Too late," he told the doctors. "This man is dead."

14

3

THE AFRIKAN SERVANTS HUDDLED AT ONE END OF THE
tables. The young girl shrank back into her place behind the chair.
The customers were torn between morbid curiosity and fear of possible contagion from whatever had killed Ochiye.

Halvar solved that problem.

"Selim! Get Firebrand! He should be somewhere nearby—look
for the watchmen. You!" He turned to the customers. "As soon as the
watchmen get here, you tell them exactly what you saw." He glared
at the two men approaching Ochiye, one in an elegant green kaftan and high tarboosh, the other in a short jacket, baggy pantaloons,
and turban. "Who are you?"

"I am Doctor of Medicine Georgi di Athens. I have studied at
the Madrassa in Corduva, also the Ulema of Stamboul, also the medical schools of Parma and Napoli in Italia," the tubby man in the
kaftan and tarboosh announced. "I bring my knowledge and expertise to this miserable place only because ill-natured gossip destroyed
my reputation in Savilla."

"He means too many of his patients died of his hasty diagno-
ses," the taller man in the turban snarled. "This man still practices
the ancient arts of the Greco and Roumi, who have long been found
to be mistaken in their beliefs, and who are pagan into the bargain.

"I am Caroli, once surgeon to the Free Company of Genoese, an
apothecary and dealer in herbal preparations that are far more ef-

15

fective than this charlatan's preposterous potions, based as they are on the theory of humors. I also draw teeth and set bones."

"A mere surgeon!" Georgi sneered. "You think your cures are better than mine? I, who have studied under the greatest minds in Baghdad and Corduva!"

Caroli shouted him down.

"At least my patients have a chance of living! You medicos are too proud to look at what is in front of you! You do not wish to dirty your hands with the real world, your head is in Cloud-Cuckoo-Land!"

Halvar stopped the argument.

"Thor's Hammer! Both of you, shut up and take a look at this man! He was alive a minute ago, and now he's dead. Why?"

The two medical experts peered at Ochiye in fascinated horror.

"His humor was hot, choleric," Georgi said. "I have heard him bellow for the last week. My tent is in the row behind this one," he explained.

"Next to mine," Caroli groused. "This charlatan takes away my patients with his hifalutin talk of humors and such nonsense. And he casts horoscopes, too, for all the good that does."

"Our kismet is written in the stars," Georgi told him. "And your potions are worthless in the face of disease. All they do is alleviate pain and reduce fever."

"Your wordy babble doesn't even do that much!"

While they argued, an Algonkin woman crept into the tent. Halvar tried to block her entrance, but she ducked under his arm and knelt beside the dead Afrikan.

"What are you doing?" he demanded.

"I am Corn Woman, I know herbs. I sell good medicine, not like silly men. I am shaman."

She ran her fingers into Ochiye's mouth, frowned, looked around, spotted the rush basket on the table, and pointed to it.

"He eats from this this?"

Halvar shrugged.

"He put something into his mouth, that I saw. As soon as he did, he started choking. He tried to drink, choked again."

"Not water." The Local woman sniffed at the cup and grimaced. "Bad stuff. Fiery water!"

"Alcohol?" Halvar dipped a finger into the cup, touched it to his tongue and spat. "What's that stuff? Sweet and hot at the same time?"

"Rhum." Dani Glick pronounced. "It looks like water, it's clear, not tinged with red like wine, or yellow like cider, or brown like ale or usquebaugh."

"What's in this basket?" Halvar peered into the woven rush receptacle, a match for dozens of others used to carry small items in Manatas.

The Algonkin woman poured the contents onto the table. She and Dani carefully sorted out bits of fruit and nut-meats.

"That's crane-berry," Dani said, as she separated a small red object from the rest of the bits of fruit and explained the contents of the basket to Halvar. "It grows in wetlands, the Bretains dry the berries and save them for the winter. Same with these blue berries, and these—they call them huckleberries."

She pointed to a crescent-shaped sliver of something orange.

"This is from the south, they call it persimmon. Locals dry them, like the crane-berries, for the winter, and merchants carry them here to the north. Sometimes they mix them with sweet cider to make a preserve; sometimes they use them to make a kind of cake with animal fat, dried meat and berries pounded together."

"Pemmican," the Local woman added.

Dani nodded. "It's not very tasty, but it's enough to keep a body going until spring planting if the winter is very long."

"You've eaten it." Halvar judged, by the look of distaste on his old friend's face.

"I have. I'd prefer not to eat it again."

Halvar frowned at the basket of dried fruit.

"No apples? No pears?"

"Apples are used for cider," Dani said. "The Bretains grow them. They don't do well in the south—they need a cold winter to rest before they put out fruit. No one's managed to grow pears in Nova Mundum yet, but I hear someone brought peach trees to the Afrikan territories, and the orange fruits from India that need a long, hot summer to ripen. This doesn't look like either of those."

She reached for a round flat piece of pale greenish-white fruit. The Algonkin woman gasped and batted Dani's hand away from the fruit.

"No touch! Bad, bad, bad! Mal-chinee!"

"What's that?" Halvar sniffed at the fruit. It smelled faintly sour.

"That," said someone right behind him, "is something I've only heard about until now. That is the fruit of the most poisonous tree on earth, and if he ate it, it is undoubtedly what killed this Afrikan."

17

Halvar turned around.

"I wondered how I could get you out of the Green Village Fratery, Leon, but I never expected it would be a corpse that did it."

4

LEON DI VICENZA, KNOWN TO THE GREEN VILLAGE FRA-
tery as Frater Leonidas, swaggered into the tent, followed by Frater Iosip and two of the brawniest clerics Halvar had ever seen. The
painter wore his shabby woolen frater's robe as if it were the most
elegant of kaftans. His fair hair had been cut short, and a tonsure
shaved front to back, as a sign of humility; but his delicate features
were set in his usual expression of hauteur, and his bearing was that
one of one who knew his own worth—and valued it higher than anyone else's.

Behind him Frater Iosip, short and stout, a pair of lenses perched
on his bulbous nose, fussed and fretted.

"What is all this about? We were just starting our mid-afternoon
prayers when a girl came pounding on the door saying there had
been a death at the Feria, and that we should come immediately. Abbas Mikhail would not have allowed it, but Frater Leonidas insisted
this was something that must be looked into. Especially when your
name was mentioned, Don Alvaro."

Halvar eyed Leon sourly.

"You came because of me? You weren't looking for an excuse
to get out of the fratery?

"Never think it," Leon protested. "Where is this dead man of
yours?"

Halvar indicated the body of Ochiye.

"Here he is, and he's not mine—he's Afrikan, not Andalusian.
According to this Local woman, he's been poisoned."

19

He turned to look for her. The woman had been stopped at the entrance to the tent by one of the Afrikan bodyguards, who thrust her back into the center of the circle around the dead man.

Leon smiled winningly at her.

"You are Shaman Corn Woman. You know all the herbs and medicines on Manatas. Why do you say he was poisoned with mal-chinee? That is not common here."

"You know this stuff, this mal-chinee?" Halvar asked with a suspicious frown.

"Not really. Poisons are more my sister Eva's specialty. I am a maker of scents, so I am familiar with certain odiferous plants, some of which can be nasty if taken internally. I know the minerals to grind for colors, some of which are extremely dangerous if ingested, but I don't think this fellow ate one of my pigments."

Corn Woman looked around for support and found none. She muttered to herself in Munsi.

"What do you know about this mal-chinee? I can't make out what this Local woman is saying."

Leon wrinkled his nose as he observed the mess that Ochiye had spat up in his last moments of life.

"She's saying that it's so evil no one can even touch it. There are sailor's tales of the stuff, They say the tree's sap is so venomous that breathing it is deadly. Something like having burnweed go into one's lungs."

"Ugh!" Halvar grunted. "Nasty indeed!'

"The runner has brought Dr. Moise," Selim called out from the door of the tent. The place was getting crowded.

Halvar looked at the assorted customers and vendors.

"All of you, outside. You will tell this lad exactly what you saw, and he will write it down. Then you may all be on your way. One more thing: you will not discuss this with anyone until the news-criers make the official announcement of Ochiye Aboutiye's death."

He only hoped the gossip chain would not start until the doctors left the tent.

Dr. Moise, the tall, slender Afrikan doctor who served at the Rabat, stepped aside as Halvar herded his witnesses out. Dani Glick joined Halvar and Selim.

"These two are staying at the Gardens of Paradise," she said, indicating the Bretains. "I can vouch for them. They haven't been anywhere near Ochiye until today. They sell boots and shoes and buy hides to make them."

20

"What did you see?" Halvar asked the two Bretains in Danic-accented Erse.

"He put something in his mouth and choked on it," the taller Bretain said with a shrug. "Don't know what it was. Was that what killed him? Don't want to bring home some plague or pestilence."

"Whatever killed him, I don't think it's contagious," Halvar assured him. "He was roaring with anger a minute ago, and he wouldn't have been so lively if he'd been sick. You may go, but keep yourselves available. You may be asked to give evidence at the Grand Divan."

The Afrikan servants, each with the gold ring in his ear that denoted a slave, were of little help. They, too, had seen nothing amiss. Ochiye was angry, but he was often angry. They could not say who would be angry enough with Ochiye to put poison in his fruit or alcohol in his drink.

The two doctors fussed at Halvar while he tried to question the servants.

"We know nothing of this man," Caroli told him.

"Except that he was of a hot and choleric nature," Georgi added. "One could hear him venting his wrath at the calif and his tolls all day long."

"Rebellious, was he?" Halvar frowned.

"He turned the tally men away from his pavilion," Caroli said. "I, on the other hand, am grateful for the protection of the calif at the Feria."

"So that you can peddle your worthless potions and powders!" Georgi snarled.

"Get back to your stands, but hold yourselves in readiness to give evidence at the Grand Divan." Halvar dismissed the doctors and re-entered the tent. He spotted the slender girl with long black hair and blunt features, dressed in a simple kutton tunic, who had handed the basket of fruit to Ochiye.

"Come here, girl," he ordered.

She shrank away from him.

"What's the matter with her?" He turned to the Afrikan men. "Who is she? What's her name?"

"Maya," the largest of Ochiye's bodyguards spat out.

"I don't think that's her name," Leon put it. "Maya is the name of a tribe of Locals far to the south. The Mechicans conquered them before the Oropans and Afrikans got to Nova Mundum. She must be one of their slaves."

Halvar glared at him.

"I suppose you know everything about these Maya."

"There's not much anyone knows about them," Leon admitted. "There aren't many of them left. There are rumors of vast temples and palaces in the middle of the jungle, and stores of gold and silver and precious stones, but so far, no one has found any of them. Tales of huge cats like leopards, and snakes that will squeeze the life out of a man, are matched only by the reputation of the Mechicans for slaughtering anyone who dares to encroach on their territory. As a result, no one has been foolish enough to venture into the forests barring a few adventurers who tried to chop their way through the vines and trees. They never came out of the jungle.

"There are also rumors of flesh-eating ants, and fish that chop anything that enters their waters into shreds in minutes." Leon grinned with delight. "I'd love to go and see for myself!"

"I don't suppose your studies in Local culture have included languages. Can you talk to this girl? Find out what she's doing here?"

"Concubine. Whore." The second Afrikan bodyguard sneered. "Ochiye Aboutiye brought her with him from his last trip, when he went to buy from the people by the Mechican Sea. He came home with hides, sugar, and Maya."

"That should have pleased his wife," Halvar remarked.

"Wives. There are two of them."

He had forgotten Dani Glick was still there.

"One is Afrikan," she continued, "and stays here in Manatas all year around, selling Afrikan beads and cloth in the souk when the Feria is over. She also arranges the shipments of Ochiye's goods during the year. I've bought some very nice pieces from her." She arranged the bracelets jangling on her wrist. "The other wife is a Local—I think her people are called Cherokee.

"From what Tekla says of her, I assume the Afrikan wife doesn't think much of the Cherokee one, but Tekla lives in Manatas and the other stays in Savana Port, in Yoruba territory in the south, which suits both of them."

"Cherokee Yona is here," the Afrikan bodyguard said. "She came with Ochiye to Manatas for the spring Feria. She brought Cherokee guards with her. She stays to look after her son, who is at the Madrassa."

"An interesting household," Dani commented wryly.

Halvar ignored the snide remark.

"Selim, we have to get Ochiye's body back to Manatas."

"I came with a donkey-cart," Dr. Moise stated.

"And I sent a message to Tenente Flores to meet us at Ochiye's villa with a squad of guards. You'll want to question the household." Selim added perkily.

Halvar nodded. The lass was getting too full of herself. But it was what he'd have done, and he couldn't fault her reasoning. No one at the Feria could have introduced poisonous fruit into Ochiye's basket. It had to have been someone in his household.

Halvar bowed his head in respect as the body of Ochiye Aboutiye was carried out of the tent to be placed in the waiting donkey-cart.

Dr. Moise turned to him.

"I am not sure about this mal-chinee. It is possible that it is the primary cause of this man's death, but there may have been other factors. I prefer to defer judgment until I have examined him more closely. I will also consult Eva Hakim about this mal-chinee fruit."

"Leon says she is the expert," Halvar admitted, glancing at Leon, who was sniffing at the vials and jars on the table in front of him.

"Eva Hakim has been working with Local women, learning their secret cures. She may know more about this mal-chinee than I, particularly if it is used by the Locals. As for Ochiye, I suggest that the effects of the poison, if any, may have been exacerbated by some other physical condition. I will not know until I conclude my examinations. I only wish I had been called here sooner. A sample of his urine would be helpful."

The girl, Maya, looked from one medical man to the other as if trying to make out their rapid Arabi. Leon smiled sweetly at her. He mimed urinating.

She nodded. "Pissy."

She pointed down at a jar placed under Ochiye's throne.

"I think you have your sample, Doctor." Leon smirked. "It would seem our Afrikan is so careful of his goods that he won't even leave his tent for the most basic of reasons. Typical Afrikan merchant mentality."

Dr. Moise sniffed at the jar and frowned.

"I will take this with me," he announced. "I will perform the autopsy at the Rabat. Frater Iosip, I do not think your services will be required."

"What about Frater Leonidas?" Halvar laid his hand on Leon's sleeve. "He's the expert on poisons. You'll come to the Rabat, won't you?"

"That I will not, Halvar Danske." Leon picked Halvar's hand between thumb and forefinger and removed it from his arm. "I am a faithful Kristo frater. These two fraters have orders from Abbas Mikhail to bring me back to the fratery, with or without your goodwill. I have a painting to complete, prayers to say. And you can't take me by force."

"You're still needed in Al-Andalus," Halvar stated.

"Not if what I hear is true," Leon sneered. "You're too late, Halvar. There is no more Al-Andalus, and no need for me to cross the ocean and waste my time there. There are other things I want to do, here in Nova Mundum, and I'm going to do them!"

"Only if you get off this island," Halvar reminded him. "Go back to your fratery. Hide your face under a woolen hood. Let Al-Andalus be swallowed up into Lovis's Kristo Imperium."

"Why does it matter so much to you?" Leon asked. "Al-Andalus isn't even your home."

"It's the only country I know of where folk don't give a blank bit what you think so long as you pay your tolls and keep the peace."

"There's one other," Leon said with a nasty grin. "And you're standing right in it."

With that, the alleged frater swaggered back down the path to Green Village, leaving Halvar fuming beside the donkey-cart.

Selim jogged his arm.

"What next?"

"Back to Manatas," Halvar said, getting into the cart beside Dr. Moise. "I hope Flores has more sense than either Gomez or Ruiz. It'll be hard enough getting information out of those Afrikans. If he menaces them, we'll never learn which of them poisoned Ochiye."

5

THE DRIVER PICKED UP HIS WILLOW SWITCH TO URGE THE patient donkey into movement. Before the animal could lift a foot, Firebrand and two of his watchmen stepped onto the path, emerging from the crowd.

"You sent for me?" Firebrand grabbed the bridle of the donkey cart.

Halvar spoke from his seat in the cart, nodding toward the bundle under his feet.

"I did. There has been a death at the Feria. An Afrikan merchant had a seizure, and these eminent medicos suspect some kind of poison. We're taking the body back to Manatas Town so that Dr. Moise can examine it and find the cause of the death.

"Since you and your watchmen are supposed to be guarding the Feria from harm, I thought you should be notified. You can question all these people—they saw it, too." He indicated the bystanders, who began to protest that they had nothing to do with Ochiye's death, that they were busy people, and that they had to get back to their stalls.

"This Afrikan merchant... was he killed in a fight? Was a Mahak involved?" Firebrand peered at the body, which had been covered with one of the lengths of cloth from Ochiye's stock.

"No steel involved. He ate something and choked. No Mahak anywhere near him."

Firebrand sniffed disdainfully.

25

"A cowardly way of killing, poison. What has this to do with me?"

"I thought it a courtesy to tell you, since you and your watch-men are supposed to be guarding the Feria," Halvar repeated. He nodded to the driver. "Get on , man. this Afrikan's not getting any sweeter." The Mahak gripped the edge of the cart.

"Not so fast," Firebrand said. "I was coming to see you when your messenger found me. You must come with me to the council fire. The sachems want to speak with you."

"About this death?"

"Another matter entirely." Firebrand again surveyed the cart and its contents. "You may take this Afrikan where you will." he told the driver. "We do not want him in Mahak territory. Make sure you find out who did this; otherwise, his ghost will come here, and we do not want any Oropan or Afrikan ghosts in our territory. Let them haunt Manatas Town.

"As for these people, they may go about their own affairs. You are the one who knows how to find murderers. I will let you get on with it, as soon as you have finished at the council fire."

"I'll find the killer, because I'm here to oversee the Feria," Halvar promised him. "The calif, may he rule long, sent me here to do that, and that's what I will do."

"And that is why the sachems want you to come to the council," Firebrand said. "You speak for your calif. You know his mind."

"I've *served* him for seven years," Halvar said carefully, mind-ful of the listening crowd that had gathered around the cart and the presence of two members of Sultan Petrus's household behind him. "I last saw him three months ago when I set sail from Al-Andalus.

"I have only heard what everyone else has heard since then. I cannot tell you what he is doing now, or where he is. And I must remind you that Sultan Petrus is the official representative of Al-Andalus in Manatas. I am only a Hireling. I answer directly to the Calif Don Felipe, but I can't speak for Al-Andalus, or for Manatas."

"But you know how this calif thinks. You can tell the sachems what he will do."

"Old Sergeant Olaf used to say, 'You want to know how a man thinks, ask his mother or his teacher.' You have his teacher right here." Halvar pointed to Leon, retreating down the path to Green Village. "Leon di Vicenza, the one they call Frater Leonidas—he was the one Don Felipe followed when he was at the Madrassa in Corduva."

Firebrand's impassive expression hardened to one of distaste.

"It is too soon after the death of my cousin Otter Tail for my father to look on the face of the one who caused that death. You must come to the council now."

The two watchmen stepped forward, hands on the tomahawks thrust into the waistbands of their breech-clouts, to emphasize the urgency of the request.

There was no backing out of it. Halvar mentally shrugged and heaved himself out of the donkey-cart.

"Dr. Moise, take this Afrikan back to the Rabat. Do what you must, and let me know the results as soon as you have them. Selim—"

Before he could give any more orders, Selim stood beside him.

"You need an interpreter," she stated. "I know Munsi. Otter Tail taught Leon, and I've picked up some more." She glared defiantly at Firebrand.

Halvar heard echoes of the strident tones of the woman who had taken charge of the wounded on the battlefield where he had years before been picked up half-dead. Lady Fatima, the wife of Sultan Petrus, had assumed the duty of caring for anyone on that battlefield who still breathed, including the enemy.

Selim was her daughter, and every bit as stubborn as her mother. If she wanted to dress as a boy, she would; if she wanted to learn Munsi, she would; and if she wanted to follow Halvar like a puppy, there was nothing he could do to stop her.

Halvar told Firebrand, "If I'm going to address the sachems, I should have someone with me who can speak Munsi. This lad will act as my translator."

Firebrand made a noise of reluctant agreement.

"We have visitors who do not know Arabi," he admitted. He regarded Selim sternly. "Come with us, then, but only speak when Don Alvaro needs to know what is being said. Otherwise, stay silent!"

Selim nodded back. The donkey cart went south, and the Mahak party headed east to the palisade of upright logs behind which the Mahak had built a small village of longhouses.

The council sat on stumps arranged around the central fire. Halvar salaamed to the two Local chiefs he knew—the Mahak Gray Goose-Feather and the Algonkin Mahmoud. The Mahak retained his traditional garb of leggings, breech-clout, and breastplate of animal bones, his hair covered with a small turban of simple cloth. Mahmoud, who had adopted the dress as well as the religion of the newcomers, wore a woolen shirt and loose trousers, and a more elaborately tied turban.

Next to Mahmoud were two sachems Halvar did not recognize, dressed in a combination of Afrikan and Local garments. Their leggings were of deerskin, but instead of the leather shirt known as a *wamus*, they wore Afrikan kutton shirts cut to the same pattern as the woolen hunting shirts favored by their northern cousins. Their heads were covered in twisted cloth trimmed with feathers from exotic birds. One had a necklace of gold beads; the other carried a staff with a gold knob on the end.

Behind the sachems stood a line of women, arms folded, faces grim. Halvar salaamed toward Nokomis, the mother of Otter Tail, who worked at the House of the Green Crescent and was considered as important as the sachem in the day-to-day running of the Mahak community on Manatas.

Firebrand stepped forward.

"Good cheer, sachems. I bring you Don Alvaro, who speaks for his master, Calif Don Felipe of Al-Andalus," he announced in Munsi.

Halvar salaamed again.

"I bring you greetings, noble sachems of the Mahak and the Algonkin," he said in Arabi. Selim repeated it in Munsi.

Sachem Gray Goose-feather spoke in Arabi.

"Good cheer, Don Alvaro. We ask you here to speak for your calif to our brothers from the south. This is Se-Kwa-ya, of the Cherokee, and Te-Kum-Se, of the Choctaw. They come from the Five Nations of the South—the Choctaw, Chickasaw, Creek, Seminole and Cherokee, who have united, as have we Mahak, Seneca, Cayuga, Oneida and Onondaga, who are the Five Nations of the North.

"They do not know of Al-Andalus, or Bretain, or Franchenland. They only know the Afrikans who have settled in their lands. The Cherokee language is much like Munsi, so Se-Kwa-Ya can speak to us for the Five Nations of the South."

"This is Selim, who speaks both Arabi and Munsi," Halvar introduced his interpreter. "Selim is the child of the sultan who rules Manatas Town and can speak for him as well." Halvar could only hope the sultan would agree with to what his wayward child might say on his behalf.

"We will smoke tabac," Sachem Gray Goose-feather ordered.

28

This was the one formality Halvar dreaded. He had never liked tabac smoke, had never acquired the habit, and hoped he would not choke on it when the pipe was passed to him. He managed one puff, passed over Selim, and handed the pipe to Firebrand. Then he waited for the next piece of business, wishing he were back in Manatas Town.

Whatever was happening here could not be as important as staving off a revolt among the merchants that would lead to a disastrous drop in the revenue needed to pursue the war in Al-Andalus.

Gray Goose-feather rose to address the gathering in Munsi.

"My people, my allies. This is a very serious matter. Our brothers of the Five Nations of the South have asked for our support in their undertaking. They wish to go on the warpath, to dig up the tomahawk they buried when the Afrikans first came to their lands. They want us to join with them."

Halvar was jolted out of his musings as Selim translated. There had been sporadic skirmishes with Locals ever since the Oropans and Andalusians first came to Nova Mundum, but for the most part all had lived in relative peace for many generations. The last thing Don Felipe needed was a war in Nova Mundum while he was fighting for his life and lands in Al-Andalus!

Sachem Mahmoud had his say.

"My people have no quarrel with the Afrikans or Al-Andalus. Some of the Bretains have come to live among us, to grow their crops with us and trade with us. They bring us good tools of iron, fine cloth for warm clothing, metal pots that do not crack.

"Their gods are good gods. Our women ask Mother Mara and her son, the Redeemer, for blessing, and Mother Mara and the Corn Mother give us good harvests. We men follow the Prophet, who was a warrior and a law-giver. The Prophet's laws of Sharia are just. When we go to the Grand Divan, Sultan Petrus gives fair judgment. I can attest to this, because I had a dispute with my kinsman Kanarsee on the Long Island, and Sultan Petrus settled it to both our satisfaction, and there was no blood shed, no blood-vengeance taken.

"I speak for the Algonkin when I say we do not follow the warpath unless we are directly attacked. This has not happened. Al-Andalus rules justly, the Bretains trade well, we have no quarrel with Sultan Petrus. I say the tomahawk remains buried." He sat down to murmurs of assent from the Algonkin standing behind him.

The Cherokee with the gold-topped staff stood up.

"I am Se-Kwa-Ya, of the Cherokee. I lead the Five Nations of the South," he said slowly, in oddly-accented Munsi. "I have seen many winters. When I was a boy, an Afrikan came to my father's village. He wanted to plant kutton where we hunted. He told us his people would cut down trees, clear the brush, and plant a crop that no one could eat, but that would be taken away to be made into cloth.

"He wanted the land, but he also wanted our food. We were to grow food for him and his people, and in return, he promised to care for us, to allow us to hunt and to grow maiz as we always had. The only thing he insisted on was that we worship his gods, Ilha and the Prophet, and follow his laws. Many of my people found no difficulty in this, but some of the women disliked the strictness of Islim ways and remained true to our own spirits.

"Then he brought more of his people to our lands, and cleared out more of our forest, so we could not hunt. His soldiers took our children to work in his fields, to plant maiz for him but not for us. He would not let my father's hunters into the fields that he had planted.

"When my father and cousins tried to take back what had been theirs, the Afrikan brought his men to my village, set fire to it, killed the men with fire-sticks, took all the women to be concubines." Se-Kwa-Ya's voice shook with rage. "This has gone on and on and on. We of the South have had enough of this! We will do as our brothers in Mechico have done. We will sweep these Afrikans and their kutton away, back to the sea from which they came!"

He sat down to a chorus of muttering.

Halvar tugged at his mustache. The southern territories of Nova Mundum had been settled by Afrikans from Mali, Ashanti, and Yoruba territories many years before Al-Andalus had established the sultanates in Powhatan and Sequannok territories and taken over the trading at Manatas. They were allies of Al-Andalus, united by religion and trade, but the calif could not control what the Afrikan settlers did or did not do.

Apparently, what they were doing was what they did in their Afrikan homeland—raiding neighboring settlements for slaves to produce more kutton and tabac and indigo and, now, sugar. And just as obviously, the Locals didn't like it.

The second visitor stood up. He spoke slowly, translating from his own language into unfamiliar Munsi, punctuated by gestures to accentuate his words.

30

"The Afrikans bring many, many of their own people into our territory. They raid each others villages. They send men to our villages, to take prisoners to work in their fields as slaves. We follow the Cherokee into battle to take our people back."

Selim's voice shook as she translated.

"I know that the Afrikans capture slaves from each other," she murmured. "I didn't know they capture Locals."

"It's what Afrikans do," Halvar said, in the same undertone. "Now that the wars in Oropa are ending, the soldiers have to find work where they can. They're being paid by the Afrikan traders to go into the forests in Afrika, to grab whoever they find and bring them to the port, so they could be sold and brought over to Nova Mundum. I met one of my old comrades, from one of the Italian companies, in Corduva. He wanted me to join his band, said they'd be paid in gold, and in land when they got to Nova Mundum."

"What did you tell him?"

"That I already had a job."

But that was only because I've had the Redeemer and the god Thor on my side, Halvar thought. And he had to admit that, even though he found capturing unwitting farmers distasteful, there were plenty of men who had no qualms about doing it, especially if they were well paid.

There was a lull in the orations. Halvar realized that the pipe had come around the circle, and all eyes were now on him.

Selim nudged him.

"They're waiting for you to speak, Don Alvaro."

Halvar stood up, conscious of all the weapons so close at hand. The Cherokee and Choctaw sachems regarded him with suspicious stares; the Mahak and Algonkin impassively.

Selim scrambled to her feet, standing next to him, fairly radiating the importance of her task. One word out of place could ignite a war!

"Forgive me, Noble Sachems, if I speak Arabi," Halvar began. "It is not even my own tongue. I rely on this youth, Selim, to repeat these words to you." He stopped to let Selim translate then went on. "You do not know my speech, nor I yours, and yet we are all here, on this island of Manatas. We come here in peace to trade. When there is a dispute, we do not resort to fighting with knives or tomahawks, we take our dispute to a person who is not related to either party, and he judges according to the laws set down by the Prophet, which we call Sharia. When there is a problem that is

31

not covered by Sharia, we have a set of rules—laws—to guide the sultan, who judges fairly between claimants.

"The Calif Don Felipe, may he rule long, is now engaged in a struggle with those who would take his lands and force the people in them to obey a religion and a ruler they do not want. He is not responsible for the actions of Afrikans who take lands that are not theirs, or who enslave their workers. I am here only to collect the tolls due to the Calif Don Felipe. I cannot read what is in his mind or his heart."

"And this Lovis has already beaten this calif of yours," Te-Kum-Se stated. "This is what we hear from the Oropans who fight for the Afrikans."

"Don Felipe is down, but he's not finished," Halvar said, hoping it was true. "That's why he sent me here. I am to take the silver and trade goods back with me. They will be used to get men and guns, to fight Lovis in Al-Andalus.

"If the Five Nations of the South wish to follow the warpath, that is their folly. The Afrikans are hiring soldiers who are without work in Oropa. They will bring them to Nova Mundum and set them loose, with their guns. to fight against you, as they do in Oropa. I have seen what happens when soldiers are turned loose without a guiding hand. You will not like it, sachems of the south."

"Do you see into the future? Are you a shaman?" Te-Kum-Se challenged him with a sneer.

Halvar said grimly, "I know what I have seen with my own eyes." He hesitated, swallowed the bile that rose in his throat as he remembered the scene that haunted him in nightmares.

"There was a town—just a way-station on the road between Franchenland and Helvetia. They ruled themselves, did not owe allegiance to any lord, but kept their own laws. They would not accept Lovis as their ruler when his army passed through.

"He decided to punish them, to show other places what he could do if they did not obey his rulings and pay tolls to him. The town put up a good defense, and sent for the Free Danes to help them in their fight. We got there too late."

He swallowed hard again, trying to find words in Arabi that could be put into Munsi that would not shock his juvenile translator.

"Lovis hired another free company, one that had a reputation for brutality. He told them to 'have some fun.' They took the town… and destroyed it. They killed as many men as had survived the

32

siege, took away the women, killed any children who might have witnessed the event. Then they fired the town.

"We arrived to a smoking ruin. We would not have known what happened, but we found three children who had been locked in a cellar. The oldest was twelve, a brave lad who was ready to kill me when I opened the cellar door. The youngest was not able to speak, too shocked by what she had seen."

"And you say this will happen to us in Nova Mundum?" Se-Kwa-Ya sounded skeptical.

"I repeat—I don't know it will happen. But reason tells me that someone who has done something and profits from it will keep on doing it. Imperator Lovis hires men to fight for him in Oropa. Who is to say that he does not have his eyes on Nova Mundum? His people are already arming the Huron with guns in Kibbick. If the Huron come south, who will defend Manatas?"

"Your calif is supposed to do that," Mahmoud said.

"Will your calif help the Afrikans?" Te-Kum-Se asked.

Halvar shrugged. "They didn't help him. His fight is with Imperator Lovis, not with you. That's all I know."

The Cherokee and Choctaw sachems muttered together, while Gray Goose-feather and Mahmoud's expressions grew grimmer as they considered what Halvar had told them.

"Then you tell us we should let the Afrikans take our lands and sow their plagues among us." Te-kum-Se said bitterly. "Many people have died of the spotted sickness, and the blister sickness, and the sickness that makes a man a woman."

"I can't tell you what to do. I don't know anything about plagues or sicknesses. Al-Andalus rules the territories known as Powhatan and Sequannok and Manatas, between the long bay and the Great River, and there has been peace between Al-Andalus and the Locals since they came. I hope that the noble sachems of the Mahak and Algonkin will keep the peace they have maintained for so long, and that they will not dig up the tomahawk here in the north.

"There is a danger here, but it is not from Afrikans. It is from Imperator Lovis, and his Franchen in Kibbick, and their Huron allies. If the Five Nations of the South draw the young Northern Nations men away to fight Afrikans, there will be no one here to fight the Franchen and Huron but a few Andalusians and Oropan settlers."

Halvar stopped to let Selim put this into Munsi. There was more muttering from the women behind the sachems.

Gray Goose-feather rose.

"You have given us much to think on, Don Alvaro. For now, the Mahak will wait and see what happens at the Grand Divan."

Firebrand whispered something to him.

"My son tells me you have another murder to solve. You are better at solving murders than you are at arranging peace. Good cheer, Don Alvaro." He glanced at Selim. "And tell your sultan that we, too, have rebellious children who do not behave as their parents would have them do."

Firebrand set Halvar and Selim on the path back to the Feria.

"Do you think they know that I'm not a boy?" Selim whispered as they headed back towards the bustle of the market.

"Keep wearing that thin shirt, and everyone will know," Halvar replied. "We have more important things to worry about than whether or not the Mahak know that your father isn't exactly truthful about whether his children are boys or girls. We've got an Afrikan's murder to solve, and a Local war to stop. Let's hope we can do both before more blood gets shed in Manatas."

6

A BRISK WALK TOOK HALVAR AND SELIM THROUGH THE
Feria, back to the Manatas Town wall, where they found a donkey-
cart and driver to take them to the Afrikan quarter. The Street of
Afrikans stretched eastward from the Broad Way towards the East
Channel. It was a street of separate villas built in the Andalusian
style—square frames filled with brick, covered in plaster, the narrow windows shielded from the outside by wooden shutters and iron
bars.

A few Local women sold vegetables, fowls and other oddments
in a small market at the Broad Way end of the street; a muskat marked
the end of the line, its minaret and dome marked with Afrikan designs There the Afrikans could listen to their own mullah exhort-
ing them to follow the strictest interpretation of the Holy Books
and the Prophet's teaching, scorning the more relaxed ways of Andalusian mystics and philosophers.

Ochiye's villa was in the middle of the line, dominating its sur-
roundings. The Afrikan had decorated his outer walls with elaborate designs,—zigzags of contrasting yellow and brown, with dots
of red between the zigs and zags.

Halvar and Selim descended from the donkey-cart to where
Flores, now wearing the braid of a tenente on his sleeve, was waiting with four of the Town Guards.

"*Salaam aleikum*, Don Alvaro, Selim ibn Petrus," he greeted the
pair.

At least the new tenente is polite, Halvar thought. Aloud he responded, "*Aleikum salaam*, Tenente Flores. Has the household been informed of the death of the master?"

"I thought you'd better do that when you got here," Flores said, with a grimace at the door to the villa, which was studded with spikes. "The doorkeeper's a nasty one, and there's an old geezer inside who's up on his dignity. These Afrikans, they think because they're rich they own the world."

"Some of them have enough gold to do it," Halvar muttered. He knocked on the door.

A small panel opened wide enough for a pair of suspicious eyes to peer out.

"What do you want?"

"We must speak with the mistress of the house," Halvar said in his most careful Arabi. "We have sad news of the master."

`"I will get the vizier." The panel closed.

"Vizier? Who does this Afrikan think he is, the calif?" Flores snapped scornfully.

"He called himself Aboutiye, which means 'ruler' in the Afrikan tongue," Selim put in. "Or maybe...'father of his people'?"

"Something Leon taught you, no doubt," Halvar said.

Selim pouted. "I learned a lot from Leon. He was interested in all kinds of things. Languages was one of them. I know Arabi, Erse, Munsi, some Franchen, and some of the Afrikan speech. It's not easy, though—they have a lot of odd sounds in their languages that don't make much sense to anyone else."

The discussion on linguistics ended when the door panel opened.

Halvar approached again.

"We have sad news from the Feria," he told the pair of eyes behind the panel. "Your master, Ochiye Aboutiye, suffered a seizure, and is now with the Prophet, may his name be blessed, in Paradise." *Or in Sheol*, he added silently, considering what little he had seen of the Afrikan's attitude and demeanor.

The door opened to reveal an Afrikan, ebony skin stretched tightly over his face, clad in a long striped kaftan and small knitted cap. He looked Halvar up and down with an expression of disdain.

"I am Noam, vizier of the household of Ochiye Aboutiye. What has happened to the master?"

"We don't know yet," Halvar told him. "May we come inside? We must make certain inquiries."

Noam peered past the guards to the waiting donkey cart.

"Is that ...?

"No. The body of Ochiye has been taken Rabat for further examination," Halvar explained. "We don't think that what killed your master was contagious, but if poison was used, we must find out what it is, where it came from, and who gave it to him."

"Most of all, who gave it to him," Flores growled. "Move aside, old man. This is Town Guard business."

"Town Guard?" Halvar intercepted Flores's attempt to brush past Noam. "You forget, Tenente, that the death occurred at the Feria. I made it clear the first day I got here, when we found the body of the frater, that anything that happens at the Feria is my concern, not yours. I will conduct this investigation, Tenente Flores."

"He may have died at the Feria, but he lived here, in Manatas Town," Flores countered. "I've been appointed to head the Town Guards, and we're responsible for what happens in this town."

"Why don't the two of you question the members of Ochiye's household together?" Selim suggested.

Flores scratched at his bristly beard and nodded.

"That makes sense." He turned to Halvar. "I've seen enough on the waterfront and the souk to know that these things aren't always as simple as they seem. Still, when a man's been poisoned, the first place to look is the kitchen."

"True, the most likely one to poison him is his wife," Halvar agreed. "We'll have to question her. Them," he corrected himself, recalling Dani's gossip.

"You'll have to do it in the harem," Selim reminded them.

"I don't think Afrikans are so particular," Flores sniggered. "They let their women run loose all over the souk and the Feria."

Noam regarded the minions of the Law with the air of one who has found vermin in the larder.

"You will not approach the Lady Tekla," he ruled. "You will not approach the Lady Yona."

"We have to question everyone in the household," Halvar explained. "Don't you want to find out what killed the master?"

"If it was his kismet to die, then so it was," Noam said piously. "There is no more to be said."

"Someone surely hastened the day," Flores said rudely.

"Don't you want to find out who?" Halvar added.

While Noam considered this, a large Afrikan woman swept into the foyer. Dark-skinned, broad-nosed, and wide-mouthed, she was swathed in Afrikan cloth, elaborately draped around her generously proportioned figure. Her headdress added at least a handspan to her height, and she fairly clanked with gold bracelets and necklaces.

Behind her cowered a smaller, lighter-skinned woman in a Local-style dress of Afrikan cloth, her braids held in place by a beaded headband. Unlike the Afrikan, her only ornaments were a simple bead necklace and long beaded earrings.

"What is this disturbance?" The African woman regarded Halvar and Flores with as much disdain as Noam.

"*Salaam aleikum*, Lady Tekla," Selim said with a bow. "We have sad news. Your husband, Ochiye Aboutiye, was struck down in the Feria, and is dead."

"That is not possible!" the woman behind Tekla gasped. "He was well enough this morning. He took his morning meal with me."

"What did he eat at this meal?" Flores jumped in. "When was it? Who served it?"

"What are you implying?" Tekla glared at the intruders into her home. "Noam, who are these people?"

Selim made the introductions.

"I am Selim ibn Petrus, from the Rabat. This is Don Alvaro, the Hireling of the calif, and this is Tenente Flores of the Town Guard. And I saw your husband when he fell, so I can tell you that it is true, that he is, indeed, dead, and I am very sorry for it." She stopped for breath.

"May we come into your house, Lady Tekla?" Halvar asked. "Tenente Flores is right to ask these questions, but do we have to do it here, where everyone in the street can hear us?"

"It is not seemly—"

"Oh, stop fussing, Noam," Tekla scolded him. "This is my house, and I will decide what is seemly in it." She regarded Halvar and Flores regally, then stood aside. "You may enter."

She led the party to an entry-room to the right of the door, a small square chamber furnished with two benches, a small table, lamps in sconces, and three backless stools. Tekla sat on one stool, ignoring the other woman, who stood beside Noam. The vizier glared at the men who had dared intrude into his domain.

Halvar, Flores and Selim sat on one of the benches, while Flores's squad remained by the door, propped on their halberds. Selim pulled out her notebook and pen case before Halvar had the chance to tell her to take notes on what was being said.

"Now," Tekla said. "Tell me again. What has happened to Ochiye Aboutiye?"

"We are not sure," Halvar said before Selim could launch into a vivid description of Ochiye's last agonies.

"He ate something from a basket." Selim said. "A Local woman said it was something called mal-chinee, and that it was poison."

"And after he ate it, he died. But the physician does not think that was the direct cause of his death, and so, Lady Tekla, we must ask once again, what did Ochiye eat this morning?" Halvar cut his eager student off.

Tekla frowned.

"He did not take his morning meal with me," she admitted. "He was in the other part of the house, not mine." She glared at the smaller woman. "Yona, you said he took his morning meal with you. Was he alone with you?"

Yona, the Cherokee wife, met Tekla's look with a bland one of her own.

"There were my servants, the ones I brought with me from Savana Port, and the Maya girl."

"Bodyguards!" Tekla sniffed. "As if you needed protection in Manatas! We are not like the uncivilized folk in the south, always fighting. We do not need to keep an army in the house."

"My people were needed on the trip north. We will need them when we go back. There are pirates, bandits." Yona's voice was soft but firm. "Ochiye understood this."

"He didn't take them when he went to West Caster," Tekla huffed.

Halvar ignored the argument.

"Where is the Maya girl?" he asked Selim.

"I saw her in the cart that took the body...Ochiye...to the Rabat."

"Very loyal of her," Halvar commented.

"She knows she is not welcome here," Yona said bitterly. "Now that Ochiye is gone, she will leave this house. We do not want her here."

"Oh, she'll find someone to care for her," Tekla sniffed. "Look to your son, Yona. He's ready for a woman."

"To take his father's concubine?" Noam sputtered. "Unthinkable!"

Yona agreed. "He will not do that. He will take a wife from a good Cherokee clan. I will see to it." She smiled smugly. "I have taken steps. If he will not have a Cherokee, there are others he can take."

"So, that is why you spent so much time with the Locals here!" Tekla smiled scornfully. "To make an alliance with the Mahak? The

Mahak only marry within their own clans. And the Algonkin are not worth bothering about."

Halvar wrenched the interview back to its purpose.

"Lady Tekla, Lady Yona, can either of you tell me who made up the basket of fruit that Ochiye had with him at the Feria?"

Tekla said, "I told the cook to make up the basket. I do not know where she got the fruit, but I trust her—she has been with me for many years. She buys food at the souk or at the corner market and spends only what I give her on it."

"I'd better question the cook," Flores decided.

"Do it gently," Halvar warned him. "Torture doesn't work, not even on slaves. And we don't know yet what poisoned Ochiye. It might have nothing to do with the stuff in the basket."

"It was the concubine who carried the basket," Tekla said. "Look to her!"

"Be sure of it," Halvar said. "And now, with your permission—"

Two young men burst into the entry-room.

"What is this I hear about our father?" The taller, darker one ran to Tekla.

"Ask these people," Tekla said bitterly. "This Dane says he was there when Ochiye Aboutiye breathed his last."

Noam made the introductions.

"Don Alvar, these are the sons of Ochiye Aboutiye, Yakub and Isai."

Halvar took a deep breath and prepared to deal with the sons of the household. The wives were bad enough; the sons would be at each others' throats. He would prefer to face the tomahawks of the Cherokee.

40

7

OCHIYE'S SONS WERE A STUDY IN CONTRAST. THE ELDER, Yakub, stood beside Tekla, his head higher than hers, his shoulders as broad as his father's. His pure Afrikan heritage was manifested by his dark skin and tribal scars, broad nose and wide-lipped mouth. What hair was not covered by his round cap was twisted into small knots.

He wore the clothes favored by the younger Afrikans in Manatas—a gaily patterned loose shirt draped over indigo-dyed kutton trousers—rather than the constricting, toga-like draperies of the elders. Halvar judged him to be in his mid-twenties, old enough to consider setting up his own establishment but still young enough to be guided by his domineering mother.

Much like Don Felipe, he thought suddenly.

His younger brother, Isai, had inherited the reddish-copper skin of his mother Yona, as well as her dark eyes and narrow nose. His straight hair was twisted into two braids, held in place with a single leather headband. Like his brother, he wore the colorful shirt called a *dashiki*, but he preferred Local leggings and breech-clout to kutton trousers. Halvar noted that Isai's fingers were stained with ink, and he carried at pen case at his belt, the sure sign of a student at the Madrassa.

Halvar took another breath.

"I bring very sad news," he said "It is true that your father, Ochiye Aboutiye, died in the Feria. And it is also true that it was not a normal death."

41

"He was healthy enough this morning," Yakub said. "He came from his rooms and joined my mother and me for our morning meal… after he had been with Yona." The sneer in his voice indicated what he thought of that arrangement.

"What did he eat? Who prepared it?" Flores asked.

Yakub frowned. "Maiz porridge, made in the kitchen by our cook. And before you ask, it was served in a large bowl. I ate some, and so did my mother. Ochiye didn't eat it. Are you well, Mother?"

"I am well," Tekla said serenely. "As you can see, Don Alvaro, whatever killed my husband, it was not served at my table."

"Who else ate with you?" Halvar asked. "Lady Yona? Isai?"

"I eat at my lodgings," Isai said. "I have not seen my father since he returned from his trading trip north. I've been busy at madrassa."

"Busy playing stick-and-stone!" Yakub snorted. "Lady Yona is well enough. She eats in her own rooms. Was this poison given to him there? How?"

"We're almost sure that it was a kind of poisonous fruit introduced into a basket that he took with him to the Feria," Halvar said.

"I supervise all the food that comes into this house," Tekla stated imperiously. "It is my house!" She glared fiercely at Noam. "I do not need a vizier to run my household. I have done it quite well myself, ever since Ochiye left me here alone to run his business for him in Manatas."

The Cherokee wife smiled sweetly.

"Ochiye preferred that you remain here, with your son, to run his business. He returned to me in the south, where the winter is not so harsh. I only accompanied him to Manatas this year to see that my son was properly situated at the madrassa," she explained to Halvar. "Ochiye was very proud of Isai. He wanted him to become a scholar, to bring honor upon his name."

"Yakub was his father's right hand!" Tekla protested. "He maintains the business here in Manatas. There could be no House of Ochiye in Manatas without Yakub! And you spent more time with the Mahak women than you did at the lodgings near the madrassa. You only came north this year because you were jealous of the Maya girl."

"It was Isai who traveled with Ochiye across the south before we came north for the spring Feria," Yona countered. "There would be no sugar, no al-largato hides, if Isai had not bargained so cleverly with the Mechicans and the Seminole. Your Yakub would have nothing to sell were it not for my Isai. And the Maya girl is noth-

42

ing to me. Ochiye would have tired of her soon enough. He always came back to me," she concluded, with another smug smile.

Halvar put an end to the spousal sniping.

"With permission, ladies, I must ask is there anyone who wished Ochiye harm? A rival in business? Someone who felt ill-used?"

"Ochiye Aboutiye was a hard bargainer, but a fair one," Tekla said. "We have many rivals. Of course, there is the Igbo in the next villa, who thinks he is more important than a Yoruba, but that is of no matter. He and his daughters are not to be considered alongside Ochiye." She glared at her son, whose face darkened under her gaze.

"Differences between Igbo and Yoruba mean nothing here in Manatas," Yakub said, more to his mother than to Halvar. "Samuel Igbo did not like my father, but he would not kill him with poison. How could he? He does not come into our house, nor do we go to his."

"Servants go between houses," Halvar noted.

"What about that Maya girl?" Flores took the questioning in another direction. "Where did she come from? What do you know about her?"

"She has nothing to do with this," Isai said quickly. "My father got her on our last journey in the south. Ochiye wanted her because she spoke the Seminole language and could translate for us when we bargained with them."

And because she's a very pretty girl, and he was a randy old man, Halvar thought. Aloud, he said, "What about Ochiye's ranting against the calif and the wars in Al-Andalus? He said he would not pay for a lost war. Did he mean to make a revolt in Nova Mundum?"

Tekla snorted her derision.

"Of course he did not want to pay the tariffs at the Feria. No merchant does. They all make noises about it, but they pay anyway. Far better to have the calif's laws than for things to run wild, as they do in the south, where no one regulates weights and measures and you can't be sure you're getting what you paid for."

"My father would not pay if he thought he was being cheated," Yakub said, with the confidence of one who knows his subject well. "I heard him say many times that the Calif Don Felipe was a weakling, nothing like his grandfather Don Carolus, or his father Don Fernan, who was killed fighting the Franchen. He hated the idea of wasting money. But he would pay, in the end."

"You Afrikans keep up with what's happening in Oropa," Halvar commented.

43

"We are not ignorant savages, as the Oropans claim," Isai said indignantly. "The round ships carry more than just slaves to our territories. The Oropan soldiers who have been left without their livelihood now that Lovis has imposed peace on his conquered lands come to Nova Mundum, and are hired to protect the holdings of the great kutton planters. They have stories to tell of battles fought—and lost—by this calif. I heard many of them on the journey north this year."

Halvar digested this information, then said, "Did Ochiye have friends with like views? Did they meet here, or anywhere else?"

"Don't you mean, did my father conspire against the calif?" Isai's voice dripped scorn. "There may be others who feel as he did, but I will not give you their names, nor will I betray them to the Town Guard." He took a noble pose, chin up, shoulders back.

Yakub snorted derision. "You are too busy drinking mokka and arguing nonsense with the scholars in the madrassa to know what was in our father's mind. And when you are not doing that, you are running about with sticks and stones. It was up to me to make this business run, so that you can have the money to waste your time listening to air-dreamers and playing foolish games."

He turned to Halvar.

"My father blustered about paying the tariffs, but he was no fool. He would have paid what was asked. He simply had to put on a show, to make people believe he was stronger than he was."

Tekla laid her hand on her son's arm, but he went on.

"There was something wrong with his health. I could tell he was pretending to be fierce and strong, but he would get weak and have to sit when he used to stand. He had a chair brought from his house to the pavilion in the Feria so that he could sit down. That's why he had the fruit with him. It was my mother's idea.

"Not only mine," Tekla said. "It is true, I worried about Ochiye's health. I noted the difference in him when he came here for the spring Feria. He was strong when he left after the fall Feria last year, to go back to the Cherokee woman and her brood. When he came north for the spring Feria this year, he was thinner, and he complained of having a pain in his belly.

"I told him to consult a doctor, but he would not hear of it. I went to the House of the Green Crescent and consulted the knowledgeable Eva Hakim. She suggested that I provide Ochiye with a basket of dried fruit, to eat if he felt weak or ill."

"Fruit! Never!" Yona sniffed. "I, too, noticed that he had periods of weakness, especially after a meal, when he came to our house in Savana Port after last year's fall Feria. I made up herbal tea from roots found in Cherokee territory. I gave it to Noam and told him to make sure he drank it when he went on his buying tour with the caravan this winter."

"He did not need your tea!" Noam snapped. "Ochiye was strong! He was not sick or weak."

"Not so," Tekla said. "He would eat, and then use the pot over and over. Yona dosed him with her tea, but it didn't help him."

"Better my tea than your silly fruit," Yona said. "And that Maya girl was always hovering over him. Ask *her* what was in that basket!"

"I want a sample of that tea," Halvar ordered. "Tenente Flores, go to the kitchen, and talk to the cook. And I want to see Ochiye's private papers, his accounts."

"To make sure that the calif gets his last white wumpum?" Yakub snapped. "You may look all you wish! I keep the accounts for my father's business, and I assure you, I may not be a madrassa lad, but I can do numbers! Every transaction is listed, all the silver is accounted for, and the calif may seize what he will for his useless wars. Assuming he is still alive to pursue them," he added bitterly.

With that, Yakub led Halvar across the entryway to another small room facing the street.

"This is where the business of the House of Ochiye is conducted," he said. "And now I must make arrangements with the imam. When will my father be ready for burial?"

"When we've found his killer," Halvar said.

8

HALVAR EDGED CAREFULLY INTO THE SMALL ROOM THAT
served as Ochiye's private study a square cell filled with paper. It
covered the top of a table placed so that light from the small window would fall on it; it filled the set of shelves against the wall
opposite the table; and it was even stacked on the stool on one
side of the table. There was barely enough room for himself and
Selim. Flores had to remain at the door with his guardsmen.

"There should be a chair," Halvar murmured.

"Probably the one Ochiye had at the Feria," Selim said, raising
an eyebrow in silent question as she looked at the papers.

Halvar wished he could make sense of the twists and swirls of
Arabi writing. He would have to rely on the wit of this youngster
to deal with these business dealings and hope that Selim could
understand what she read. Meanwhile, there was one chore that
could be done better by someone else.

"Tenente Flores," he said, "you go to the kitchen. Question the
cook and the other servants. Find out who prepared that basket of
fruit, where they got the berries and other bits, and take the measure of the household."

Flores grinned nastily. "Don Alvaro, I don't know why you're
even bothering with this business. It looks to me like a typical harem
intrigue. Two wives, two sons, one inheritance. The cook's been paid
by one or the other of the wives or the sons—it's nothing to do with
the calif or the wars, or the tariffs. And I don't like the looks of that

vizier, or whatever he calls himself. He's got to be tied up in this mess, one way or another. Just a domestic dispute."

"You may be right," Halvar said. "But anyone who threatens to withhold tariffs is a danger to the calif. If there is a conspiracy here, I'll find it."

Selim piped up, "There's always accident. If this mal-chinee stuff is so rare, it's possible that it got into the basket by mistake, and whoever put it there didn't know how nasty it was, only that it was expensive. Or maybe someone told Ochiye that it would be, um, good for him? I mean, he was old, and he had a young concubine…"

Her voice trailed off as two sets of older masculine eyes drilled into her.

"I hadn't thought of that," Halvar admitted. "You'd be surprised what a man will swallow if he thinks it will add to his, um, powers."

Flores nodded. "I'll see what I can find out, but you mark this, Don Alvaro. I'm sure this murder is a family matter, nothing for your calif to worry about. Once we find out which of the wives put the stuff into the basket, we can take her to the Rabat, and the sultan will deal with the business at the Grand Divan."

Flores stamped off, leaving Halvar and Selim alone under the disapproving eyes of Noam.

"You must not touch the master's papers!" The vizier stood beside the desk and its tempting contents, arms folded, daring the intruders to advance.

Halvar was not to be deterred.

"Ochiye Aboutiye stated in my presence that he would tell other merchants not to pay their tariffs to the Calif Don Felipe, may he rule long. I want to know if this conspiracy went further than bluster at the Feria. I have no interest in any of Ochiye's business dealings, how much he did or did not get for his hides and his sugar and his other goods. This lad…" He thrust Selim forward. "…will scan some of these papers to see if any of them are threats against the calif. If they are not, then we will leave the household to mourn their dead master. If we find out instead that Ochiye Aboutiye was engaged in a conspiracy, we will take action accordingly. Do you understand me, old man?" Halvar loomed over the vizier.

Noam stood his ground.

"I will remain here. You will take nothing from this room."

"We're not thieves!" Selim said indignantly. "Don Alvaro is the personal hireling of the calif, and I am the child of Sultan Petrus."

She looked around for something to sit on, found a small stool, and sat as she proceeded to sift through the papers on the table. Noam glowered over her shoulder, taking each paper as soon as she laid it down, placing it neatly into a pile.

"These are lists of merchandise," Selim reported after checking several of the sheets. "Cloth, hides, sugar, jars of some kind of preserves. I don't know some of these words—I think they're a Local language—but they're on this list, so they must be some kind of trade goods."

"That is Ochiye's business!" Noam protested. "Not for the calif's Hireling to know!"

"No personal letters?" Halvar sounded disappointed. "Nothing about the calif, or the tariffs?"

"Just the sort of thing someone buying and selling would have. How much of something someone had, how much he wanted for it, how much he thought it could be sold for."

"As I told you," Noam said.

"Who are these lists from?" Halvar's frown deepened. Lists of goods for sale could be a coded message, indicating who was interested in conspiring against the local authorities, how many men they could muster, what arms they had, and how much money they were willing to contribute to the cause.

"Customers," Noam said.

"What kind of customers?" Halvar was relentless.

Selim frowned in concentration.

"I'm not sure—some of these are really badly written. The Arabi is terrible, all mixed in with Afrikan and Local words for things I don't understand. And the handwriting is almost unreadable. But the numbers are easy enough. They're the ones every merchant uses in Al-Andalus, not the Roumi figures that don't really work well for calculations."

"I suppose Leon taught you numbers," Halvar groused.

"No, I knew that before Leon became my teacher. My mother made me learn, said I'd need to know my numbers so I wouldn't be cheated out of my inheritance if she wasn't there to fight for it." She sighed. "This is useless, Don Alvaro. There's nothing here about tariffs, or how much the calif gets, just lists of stuff for sale."

"Sometimes what's missing is as important as what's there. And what's this?" Halvar picked up a paper that stood out from the other correspondence, of a heavier, rougher texture and darker color. Noam tried to snatch the paper out of his hand. Halvar held it away from the agitated Afrikan to examine it more closely.

It was a crude drawing, a jagged line with a curved line bisecting it. Above the line were four dots forming a rough square, with three more dots across the center. On the upper left was a crescent; on the upper right, a series of Indian numerals.

Halvar turned the paper over. On the other side were a series of weird symbols he had never seen before.

Noam muttered something that sounded like a curse.

"That fool!"

"I will take this to the Rabat," Halvar insisted. "It will be returned soon enough. Selim, I think we've found what we're looking for. Noam, you may show us to the kitchen. We will join Tenente Flores. I only hope he hasn't scared the cook too badly."

He folded the paper and inserted it into the front of his jacket, where Yussuf the Tailor had sewn a small pocket.

"To keep your wumpum safe," the tailor had explained, proud of his innovation. Halvar agreed—much better to keep the strings of beads close to his body than dangling from his belt where a nimble-fingered thief could grab them.

Noam watched the paper disappear into Halvar's jacket, his face twisted with fury. There was nothing he could do about it.

Halvar turned to him.

"Now, vizier, or whatever you call yourself, show me the kitchens."

Noam plodded through the house, leading Halvar and Selim across the open central courtyard to the back of the house, where Flores and his men had assembled the rest of the servants, muttering to himself in an Afrikan dialect with many clicks and grunts.

One of those old servants who consider their masters' lives more important than their own, Halvar thought. *I'll have to have another chat with him.*

First, though, he'd question the kitchen staff. Someone had put the poison into Ochiye's basket of fruit or his sweetened drink. If not the Maya girl, then who? Someone in that kitchen *must* know.

9

FLORES'S RASPING VOICE COULD BE HEARD THROUGHOUT
the house as Halvar and Selim followed Noam to the kitchen, a
large room at the rear of the villa. It was a spacious area with an open
fireplace at one end as well as a small closed oven built into the
wall. A large table filled the center of the room, where the midday
meal was already in preparation. Two Afrikan girls were shredding
various vegetables, while a Local woman stirred a pot of grain porridge bubbling on a ledge just inside the fireplace.

The chief cook and the guardsman faced each other belliger-
ently. They seemed to be evenly matched—Flores, stocky and swarthy,
marked with smallpox, dark eyes glowering over a bulbous nose,
and the Afrikan cook, a muscular woman in the typical Afrikan
tunic and twisted headdress, her broad face suffused with fury.
The gold earring that marked her servile status shook to punctu-
ate her tirade.

"You say I poisoned the master? Why should I do so? I am a good
cook, he was a kind master. My food is good food, I would not add
poison to it!" She spoke stilted Arabi with the singsong accent of the
Afrikans.

"It's not your cooking that's in question." Halvar stepped into
the kitchen, putting an end to the argument. "Who is this woman?"

"She's called Sanya, and she says she didn't poison Ochiye,"
Flores said.

"I heard her. I think everyone within earshot heard her."

Selim looked over the ingredients of the meal under preparation that had been laid out on the table in the middle of the room.

"You've got vegetables, porridge, some kind of spice in a jar," she observed. "When was this going to be served?"

"We eat at sundown, when the master comes from the Feria." Noam took a place beside the cook, trying to exercise his authority over the household. The cook ignored him.

"I cook for the mistress, as she tells me," she declared. "We eat here twice. Break the night fast, dinner at sundown after evening prayer. I cook to the mistress's orders."

"Ochiye didn't come from the Feria for a midday meal?" Halvar strolled around the kitchen, sniffing at the jars ranged on shelves next to the oven.

"He took food with him," Sanya said. "We make up a basket every day. A pot of maiz porridge, a piece of cold fish from last night's dinner. A bottle of water, sweetened with sugar. The mistress told me to include a basket with bits of dried fruit, raisins and dried berries from the souk."

"And where did all this stuff come from?" Halvar continued. "Do you bring it with you from the south, or do you buy it here in Manatas?"

Noam began to speak, but Sanya interrupted him.

"Mistress Tekla tells me what she wishes to serve, and I order the provisions from the souk. Sometimes vendors come with fish from the waterfront, sometimes Local women bring fruits and vegetables, sometimes we go to the small market at the end of the street if we run short.

"For meat, we go to the Yehudit *shochet*, who follows *halal*. He kills the fowls and dresses them, and brings good cuts of meat to the house. There is nothing in this house that is not halal. We are good Islim here. I know the laws, I do not give the master or the mistress any but the best food!"

She glared at Noam, daring him to contradict her.

"The small basket of dried fruit at the pavilion," Halvar went on. "Who put it together? Who bought the fruit?"

Sanya shrugged dismissively.

"I bought the dried berries myself, from the Algonkin woman in the market at the end of the street. The raisins, the persimmon, they were brought by this man..." pointing to Noam "...when he came with the master from the south. Our food was not good enough, he said."

She glared at Noam again, who returned her look with one of his own.

"Ochiye was fond of dried persimmon, which is not grown here in Manatas," he explained. "I brought some with us when we came for the spring Feria. There is not much left of what I came with."

"Where is this fruit?" Flores asked. "This persimmon? What does it look like?"

"That was the orange slices in the basket," Selim explained. "The Local herb-woman pointed it out. The mal-chinee was pale green, not like persimmon at all, and not round like a berry but more like the dried apple slices the Bretains bring with them to Green Village." Her voice quavered under the scrutiny of many eyes. "Padraig likes dried apples," she added, as if that explained her knowledge of local delicacies.

Sanya pointed to the pantry, just outside the kitchen door.

"Mustafa, show them what came with the master. Not much left," she added. "He brought just enough to last until he went back to Savana Port."

Selim followed the servant to the pantry.

"He didn't plan to stay after the fall Feria?" Halvar observed.

"The master always came in the spring and left in the fall. He did not like the winter." The cook sniffed her disdain. She was well-padded against the chill.

"What have you got there?" Halvar asked as Selim and Mustafa emerged from the pantry carrying a crock, a basket, and a small wooden box.

"This had raisins in it," Selim said, sniffing the frail box. "And this crock had some kind of preserved fruit coated in sugar." She carefully withdrew one orange-colored object. "Persimmon, I think. There was something like this in Ochiye's basket." She peered into the crock. "Not much left of it, though."

"What about this stuff?" Flores fingered the items in the basket.

"Local stuff," Selim said. "Blueberries, huckleberries, craneberries, and the kind of nuts they call hickory. The Algonkin women pick them and dry them for the winter. The same mixture we saw in Ochiye's basket at the Feria."

"No mal-chinee," Halvar observed.

"Not in this mixture," Selim admitted. "It's a sickly green color, and there's nothing like that here."

"It had to have been added to Ochiye's basket after it left this kitchen," Halvar stated.

"By who?" Flores demanded. "One of the wives? Or one of the sons? One of the servants?"

"It had to be someone who knew what mal-chinee is, who could get it and could introduce it into that basket," Selim said slowly. "Because it's not common hereabouts. Leon would have known all about it if it were—he was always asking Locals about their plants and how they were used."

Halvar nodded briefly. "Tenente Flores, you and your men will search this house for more of this mal-chinee."

"What if the poisoner used it all up?" Selim objected. "I mean, it might have been in one of these jars, or baskets, or boxes."

"It's not in the basket," Halvar said slowly. "Bring that crock along to Dr. Moise at the Rabat. There may be something left of the mal-chinee at the bottom of it. While I'm doing that, Tenente. You and your men search this house. If there's any mal-chinee here, I want you to find it."

Flores nodded. "I'll do that!"

Noam started to protest, but Halvar cut him off.

"This is the calif's business. You will give Tenente Flores all the assistance he needs, and he will, in turn, respect the people of the house. Selim, you come with me. We have to get this stuff to someone who can tell us what it is."

Before they could move, there was an agitated squawk from the direction of the pantry. Halvar's head jerked around.

"What's that?"

"There's a door that leads out of the pantry into the alley" Selim said.

"It's where we put out the basket for the Scavengers to take," Sanya added. "And the necessary."

An Afrikan boy ran into the kitchen.

"Come quick! There's a stray dog, I think he's gone mad!"

"Mad dog? Here in Manatas? Never!" Flores scoffed.

"He's shaking his head, he's howling," the servant insisted. "He's mad, I tell you!"

Halvar shoved through the narrow door into the alley. Sure enough, a scrawny dog was leaping about, shaking his head, slavering, giving every sign of a creature afflicted with the terrible disease for which there was no cure.

"He's eaten something." Selim pointed to an overturned basket in the middle of the narrow gap between the villas.

The dog gave one last despairing howl and expired.

"I think we just found our poison," Halvar said in the grim silence. "Mustafa, you get this poor creature out of the road, and be very careful how you touch him. We don't know how powerful this poison is. Tenente, search the house for more of this poison. Then rake up whatever you can find of what the dog ate and get all of it—the dog and the garbage—to the Rabat for Dr. Moise to look at. Selim, you come with me."

Halvar strode back through the house, Selim pattering behind him. Flores is right, he thought. Someone in that house is a murderer. The only question was, which of the wives, sons, or a combination of the two was the guilty one.

He would leave that to Flores's skills. *His* only concern was how much influence Ochiye had on his fellow-Afrikans, and whether it would impact the revenues from the Feria.

10

HALVAR EMERGED FROM OCHIYE'S VILLA TO FIND A CROWD
of Afrikans waiting in front of the next house, led by a tall man
whose arrogant attitude marked him as the leader of the pack. Halvar reasoned he must be one of the many wealthy Afrikan merchants who remained in Manatas after the Feria had dispersed. His
elegant kaftan was edged with a silk-embroidered border and neckline; his turban was green, indicating he had made the hajj to Mecca.
He was ebony-dark, with a narrow nose and thin lips; his small
chin-beard had been cut to a point in the latest Andalusian style.
He had no obvious tribal scars. Clearly, this man considered himself more Andalusian than Afrikan.

He accosted Halvar as soon as the Dane stepped into the street.

"*Salaam aleikum*, Don Alvaro."

Halvar looked him over, trying to recall whether he had met
him at the chaotic banquet given by Sultan Petrus to introduce the
Calif's Hireling to the notable persons of Manatas Town.

"*Aleikum salaam*." He looked around for Selim, but the youngster was already at the intersection of the Afrikans' street and the
Broad Way, looking for a donkey-cart that would take them back
to the Rabat. "I ask your pardon, noble sir, but if we met at the
banquet it was briefly, and I cannot recall your name."

"You may have been distracted by other things. You have been
looking into the matter of the false wumpum, and the shocking
death of the Franchen assassin." The Afrikan smirked. "It was written in the Gazetta from Green Village."

55

I am going to destroy Dani Glick's printing-press, Halvar told himself. News-sheets, broadsides, what would that Yehudit houri think up next?

Aloud, he asked, "May I ask that you repeat your name for me? My memory is not what it should be."

"I am Samuel the chief broker for the Igbo, who plant kutton and indigo in the Ashanti territories of the south. I speak for all the Igbo in Manatas."

Apparently, this made him more important than the rest of the crowd, who murmured their consent for him to speak for them, in precise Arabi with no trace of the lilting accent of the Afrikans of the south.

"But you do not speak for the Yoruba, or other Afrikans?" Halvar tried to grasp the complexities of the Afrikan community in Manatas. "Ochiye Aboutiye said that he spoke for *all* the Afrikans, that they would follow where he led. Is this true?"

"Certainly not!" Samuel sniffed his disdain. "The Yoruba are low persons, they do not keep all the Prophet's teachings. Ochiye called himself *Aboutiye*, but he was no more than a trader, a traveler through the southern territories. Is it true that he died in agony?" His voice took on a vindictive edge.

"It's true. I witnessed his death. He put something into his mouth and died. The doctor thinks it was some kind of poison. There was a dog who ate something in the basket left for the Scavengers. It died as well, so you may put worries of disease out of your mind. Whatever killed Ochiye, it is not contagious."

"I am not surprised that Ochyiye died from overeating. I told him Ilha would punish him for his greed." The man fairly oozed smug satisfaction.

"It wasn't Ilha who put poison into his food," Halvar said. He looked at the crowd behind Samuel. "This isn't the place for a chat, but if you will come with me to the Rabat, I would like to hear what you can tell me about Ochiye."

"I can tell you right here, before my people, what I thought of that boor. Ochiye may have called himself 'father of his people,' but he was an empty braggart. He did not live here in Manatas, but only came for the ferias. He traveled in the southern territories, buying and selling and carrying messages from one settlement or farm to another. He did not obey the Prophet's laws, did not come to muskat, did not keep halal in his kitchens. He sold

56

alcohol, against the Prophet's direct commands!" Samuel stopped his tirade to catch his breath

"Did you buy goods from him?" Halvar kept his voice even. He had already assessed Samuel as a pious prig, obviously envious of Ochiye's wealth and influence. This did not mean the man would lie, but Halvar would not take what he said as total truth without further evidence.

Samuel grudgingly admitted, "My wives and daughters wished to buy his gold ornaments. I bought bracelets and rings that Ochiye had at his pavilion in the Feria, and sometimes went to the stand his son Yakub keeps in the souk. I can afford such things. I am the chief of all Igbo on Manatas Island."

Behind him, the Afrikans muttered their agreement with his personal assessment.

"Then you would have no reason to remove Ochiye from this earthly realm?" Halvar asked casually.

"I would not bother to notice that Yoruba lout were he not so loud, bellowing his opinions to anyone who would listen, or even those who preferred not to listen." Samuel sniffed. "I would not speak to him at all, except that his wife and my chief wife thought that it might be useful for his son Yakub to marry my daughter Rahel. He brayed his opinion of that all over Manatas, too! I had enough of him and his opinions, and I told him to his face."

"Opinions about the Calif of Al-Andalus, for instance?" Halvar hinted. "And the necessity for paying the tariffs at the Feria for the shipment of kutton and tabac and indigo?"

"One accepts such things as the price of doing business," Samuel said loftily. "As for Ochiye, he may have regarded himself highly, but I can assure you, Don Alvaro, he did not speak for the Igbo on Manatas. We are loyal to Al-Andalus. We follow the Prophet's teachings. We do not marry our daughters to Locals, nor do we take them as wives or as concubines."

"Keep to yourselves, then?"

Samuel's voice took on a bitter edge. "Ochiye bragged about his connection to the Cherokee, flaunted his Maya girl before his true wife." He fairly radiated disgust. "I did not wish to listen to this blather, but one could hear him up and down the street, ordering his servants, shouting at his sons. This is no way for a man of wealth and position to behave. He was a lout. A lout with much wealth, but a lout, Don Alvaro. He got the death he deserved."

"I've seen wealthy louts in Oropa and Al-Andalus," Halvar said. "They are unpleasant, but they don't deserve the kind of death that came to Ochiye."

Samuel raised his head to look down his nose again.

"It is not for us to judge," he stated piously. "Ochiye is facing Heavenly Court, far stricter than the sultan's Grand Divan."

Halvar nodded gravely. "Have you any ideas as to who might have sent Ochiye to that court?"

"Not I," Samuel said quickly. "I disliked Ochiye, but I did not hate him enough to kill him."

"Is there anyone who did?"

Samuel shook his head slowly. "I do not venture to guess what happens in another man's house. However..."

Here it comes, Halvar said to himself. *This is what he wants to tell me.*

"I am not one who eavesdrops on my neighbors, but the windows of our houses are open to the breeze, and one can hear noises from within. Not the words, but the tone of voice. And I heard a very loud quarrel yesterday. Ochiye was shouting at someone, I know not who. As always, Ochiye's voice could be heard above everyone else's."

"That is good to know," Halvar said. "I thank you for your information, Samuel Igbo. If you or any of your people have any more information about Ochiye or his household, you may tell Tenente Flores of the Town Guard, or you may find me either at the Rabat or at the Mermaid Taberna on the waterfront."

"We have no more information for you," Samuel declared. "As for the Town Guard, let them keep order better! We have been forced to hire our own guards for this street, to keep away the Scavengers."

"There are plenty of soldiers without work who would gladly do so," Halvar said. "Some of them will surely make their way here to Manatas. Keep the peace, Samuel Igbo. *Salaam aleikum.*" Halvar headed for the Broad Way, where Selim waited with a donkey cart.

"Things are getting murkier," he told her as they trotted southward to the tip of the island and the massive fort that stood there. "There was a loud dispute in the Ochiye household yesterday, loud enough to be heard by his neighbors."

"A quarrel? Who fought with whom?"

"Hard to say. Ochiye seems to have fought with everyone. He wouldn't pay his tariffs, he insulted his wives, he brought a concubine into the house, and if I read him right, he bullied his sons and his servants."

"What about the man you were talking to? And the other Afri-kans?"

"The neighbor's a self-righteous prig, but he wasn't a business rival and has no reason to lie about Ochiye's household arrange-ments. Thor's Hammer! Flores might be right. This looks more and more like some domestic scandal, nothing to do with the calif at all, except for two things.

"I saw gold nuggets among Ochiye's beads and bracelets, and Noam the 'vizier' didn't want us to take that paper with the scrib-bles on it. Where did that gold come from?"

Selim's heavy eyebrows nearly met over her nose as she frowned over this latest development.

"You mean, has someone found gold here? And doesn't want anyone to know about it?" She considered this, then said, "I still don't understand how Ochiye was killed, let alone why. Did some-one put poison in his basket accidentally, not knowing what it was? Or could he have taken it himself, on purpose?"

"He didn't know what it was when he put it into his mouth," Halvar pointed out. "He just reached into the basket and popped a morsel in."

"And tried to say something," Selim reminded him. "What was he trying to say?"

"I'm not sure," Halvar said. "It just sounded like moaning and groaning, the sounds you'd make if you ate something bad. His mouth was burning, and he spoke like an Afrikan."

"If I was dying, I'd try to name the one I thought did it," Selim said. "But I still don't understand why anyone would want to kill him. He wasn't a very pleasant person—he shouted and blustered, and wouldn't pay his tariffs, and threatened to urge other Afrikans to withhold their money, too, but you don't kill someone just for being unpleasant."

"It depends on how unpleasant he was, and for how long," Hal-var said. "It's like a wound that festers until something breaks the skin and the pus comes out."

"Ugh!" Selim grimaced at the metaphor. "But that leads right back to Ochiye's household. The cook says she never put anything into Ochiye's basket that wasn't the dried fruit we found in her kitchen. All of it bought right here in Manatas, and all of it com-mon to the souk and the roving Local vendors who sell on the streets."

"Not all of it," Halvar reminded her, tapping the crock in his lap. "This persimmon preserve—that's not from around here. The cook said it was brought by Ochiye himself, from the south. And we don't know what the dog ate."

"What about the Maya girl? Could she have added poison to the fruit in the basket? Or the drink in the jug?".

"Could be," Halvar said. "But the Maya girl was terrified when Ochiye died. She's all alone now, without her protector, in a strange land, not even able to speak the language. Why would she kill the only one who kept her safe?"

They had reached the Rabat, the fortress that guarded the tip of Manatas Island from possible invasion. Halvar paid the donkey-driver the required wumpum and added an extra white bead as a gratuity. The donkey-driver salaamed happily and drove off to seek his next customer, leaving Halvar and Selim alone at the gates of the Rabat.

11

THE WALLS OF THE FORTRESS LOOMED OVER THEM, RE-
flecting the afternoon sun.

"Where is everyone?" Selim asked as they entered the courtyard.

The only person in sight was a Local woman who hovered over
a small brazier tending the pot of hot water that would be poured
over ground mokka beans that had been augmented with the buds
from the chicory plant.

"The sultan takes his lady to the feria," the Local woman told
them. "The guards go with them."

"At last, Ayesha's out of her rooms," Selim said. "And my father's out of his tower. Now maybe he'll pay more attention to Manatas and less to that new baby."

Halvar ignored the youngster's jealous sniping and headed for
Dr. Moise's quarters, a long shed built against the inner wall of the
Rabat.

"Never mind the new baby, laddie. I want to know what killed
Ochiye."

"I thought we'd decided it was the mal-chinee."

"Dr. Moise had doubts. I trust his judgment."

Halvar tapped on the door of the shed before letting himself
in. It took a moment for his eyes to adjust to the gloomy interior
after the glare of the afternoon sunlight on the stones of the courtyard. He glanced around the room that served as Dr. Moise's office and consulting room to see if the lanky Afrikan was there.

"*Salaam aleikum*, Dr. Moise," he called. "I've brought you something from Ochiye's kitchen that might answer some of your questions about his death."

"*Aleikum salaam*, Don Alvaro," Dr. Moise responded from the adjoining room, where he stood beside a long table on which lay the body of Ochiye Aboutiye, naked except for a cloth over his male parts. The man's body had already been laid opened, revealing ribs, twisted intestines, and other inner organs Halvar preferred not to see.

"I see you've wasted no time," he observed after one horrified glance at the remains of the Afrikan. "Here's a crock of some kind of preserved fruit Ochiye brought with him from the south. It could be that the mal-chinee poison was added to it. There's not much left, though. And a dog died after eating something from the household garbage basket that had been left for the Scavengers. I told Flores to gather everything he could find and send it and the dog here for you to examine."

Dr. Moise took the crock and carefully set it down on the dissecting-table.

"I will treat this stuff very carefully. When the dog and the garbage get here, I will examine them, as well. However, as regards Ochiye, I have some doubts as to the cause of death."

"Not mal-chinee?" Halvar sounded disappointed.

"Oh, mal-chinee was most certainly involved, but there may have been some complications due to the man's condition. I have requested Eva Hakim join us, since her brother Leon claims she is an expert on local plants."

He led them away from the body, much to Halvar's relief, and into the adjoining room, where he kept his vials of potions. Eva Hakim, the female physician who headed the Sisters of Fatima, greeted them gravely.

She was as tall as her brother, but her features were sharper than his, her eyes dark brown under straight brows. Her hair was covered by her green hijab, and she wore a simple dark-brown robe over a green tunic and trousers. She regarded Selim with raised eyebrows.

"I see you have taken an apprentice, Don Alvaro."

"You might say the apprentice has taken me!" Halvar tugged at his mustache in embarrassment. "What can you tell us about this mal-chinee stuff? Where does it come from? Is it as poisonous as they say?

Eva Hakim's serene countenance tightened in concern.

"Don Alvaro, I am compiling a list of all plants native to Nova Mundum, with particular emphasis on how they are used by the Locals. Some of these plants are poisonous, if improperly prepared. Batatas, for instance, come from the lands far to the south and must be carefully cooked."

Halvar opened his mouth to cut off the lecture, but Eva Hakim continued.

"As for this mal-chinee, I asked some of the Mahak and Algonkin women who work at the House of the Green Crescent what they know of it, but none of them has ever actually seen it."

"Then it's all nonsense," Selim snapped.

Eva Hakim glared at her for interrupting.

"I did not say that the tree does not exist. I recall a servant of one of the Afrikans who came from the southern territories who told us that, when her people arrived in Nova Mundum, they were met by Locals with poisoned arrows."

"Really?" Selim gasped in horrified glee.

"They were warned the arrows had been made from the wood of a certain tree, which was then dubbed *mal-chinee*—that is to say, 'the bad tree.' According to this servant, every part of this tree is poisonous—the leaves, the fruit, even the sap that drifted down from it. Even to stand under the tree meant death."

Selim squealed in mingled horror and delight.

"I suspect that the tale has been exaggerated," Eva Hakim said. "Even so, I touched the piece of the fruit that was left in the basket belonging to the dead man and received a painful sting on my fingers." She showed the blisters on her thumb and forefinger. "Therefore, one is led to the conclusion that some of the tale is true."

"Whoever cut it up and put it into the basket had to have used gloves," Halvar mused.

"Ahem!" Dr. Moise joined the discussion. "I examined the contents of the stomach. Ochiye had eaten a morning meal of maiz mush sweetened with berries."

"And mal-chinee?" Selim asked.

"I did not see any such remains," Dr. Moise said primly. 'There were bits of the fruit in his teeth. I used a small instrument to remove them, after seeing what they did to my esteemed Eva Hakim's fingers."

"But if the mal-chinee wasn't in his stomach, how did it kill him?" Selim persisted.

"It didn't. At least, not today. It may, however, have been introduced into his food or drink in small doses over the last few days."

"*What?*" Halvar exclaimed. "How?"

Dr. Moise assumed a professorial tone.

"I examined his urine and found it smelled oddly sweet. It is my opinion that he suffered from a rare disease, a malfunction of the digestion, whereby sugar is improperly absorbed into the body. I find a reference to it in the works of Galen, where he calls it *diabetes mellitus.*"

"Never heard of it," Halvar sniffed.

"Ochiye's Afrikan wife Tekla is one of the supporters of the Sisters of Fatima. She consulted me about her husband," Eva Hakim put in. "She was worried about his appearance, which had changed since his last visit. He had lost weight, was urinating frequently, had sudden spasms of weakness after meals. I could not diagnose his condition without seeing him, but I recommended that he carry a small amount of fruit—raisins or dried berries—and that he eat some if he felt faint. He should also drink water to replace the urine."

"So, Tekla bought dried fruit from the Local women who sell it at the souk…" Selim said.

"And someone added some of this mal-chinee to it," Halvar finished for her. "But I was there when he put it into his mouth. It burned him unbearably. He could never have eaten the stuff."

"But how did it get here, if it's not the kind of thing you find in the souk?" Selim demanded. "Not if it comes from the southern territories, I mean. And if it's that nasty, and so poisonous to touch, how would someone get it in the first place? Pick it up with gloves on and cut it up and dry it? And then, how to store it? In a crock or jar? And carry it all the way here, to Manatas? For what?"

"To poison Ochiye Aboutiye," Halvar said grimly. "This could be no accidental death. It's deliberate murder."

"And that leads us right back to Ochiye's household," Selim said. "Flores was right—this is a harem intrigue, Don Alvaro. Better leave it to him."

Halvar shook his head.

"I think it's more than that. There's malice in this, something really vicious about poisoning a man slowly, watching him sicken and die. Whoever did this really hated Ochiye. It might be a family feud, it might be something more, but I'm not going to stop looking until I find out who did it…and why."

12

HALVAR DREW A DEEP BREATH AS HE LEFT DR. MOISE'S
quarters and stepped into a whirling maelstrom of humanity. Sultan Petrus and his young wife were back from their excursion, along with the sultan's personal guard, a squad of Town Guards, the servants from the harem, and Lady Ayesha's two female servants.

Sultan Petrus hailed Halvar boisterously. The old soldier had donned his second-best jacket and trousers for his jaunt so he could ride his horse through the streets of Manatas, towering over the rest of the populace and their humble donkeys. Lady Ayesha had been carried in a litter, borne by a quartet of muscular Andalusians. She emerged from the litter and adjusted the thin veil that covered her face, well aware that her trim figure was visible, imperfectly disguised by a billowing sheer cape worn over a silk tunic and trousers. For a woman who had recently given birth, she was remarkably agile as she crossed the courtyard to the stairs that led to the harem.

"Well met, Don Alvaro!" Sultan Petrus greeted Halvar like the soldier he had been. "What's this about some Afrikan dying at the Feria?"

"Nothing to do with you, honored sultan," Halvar assured him. "According to Tenente Flores, this is a private matter, a personal grievance within his household that festered until someone resorted to extreme measures to put a stop to it. At the moment, I'm inclined to agree with him, but there *are* a few questions I want answered before I close the case."

"Tenente Flores!" The sultan looked about him for the newly appointed commander of his guardsman. "You joined us at the Street of Afrikans. What have you to say about this Afrikan?"

Flores leaped to the Sultan's side.

"It's as Don Alvaro says," he stated. "The death occurred in the Feria, but the poison, if such it was, must have been given to the Afrikan in his home, which makes it a matter for the Town Guard. I've got questions to ask that Maya girl, the concubine."

"Where *is* the girl?" Halvar asked.

"She came with the body to Dr. Moise and had to be forcibly taken away to a cell in the Rabat. I've sent word to the souk and the waterfront to find someone who's traveled in Mechican territories and can speak her language, since she doesn't seem to know Arabi, and no one here can understand her Afrikan."

"Indeed." Sultan Petrus dismissed his underling with a wave if his hand. "Carry on, then, get a full confession from the girl, and I'll sentence her at the Grand Divan."

"I'll do that!" Flores promised, with a rough salaam.

"But don't use harsh means!" Halvar warned him. "A forced confession is useless. Probably a lie, to stop the pain."

"I know my business," Flores snapped back. "Tenente Gomez said I was one of the best at getting a confession out of a prisoner."

"And you're sure this Maya girl is the poisoner?" Sultan Petrus put in.

"Who else? She is from the south, she traveled with Ochiye, she gave him the fruit. Only she could have put this mal-chinee into the basket."

"Did you find any at the house?" Halvar persisted.

"Only what you might have in that crock of preserve. I've sent the dog and the stuff he ate over to Dr. Moise. Whatever poison might have been there is probably inside the poor critter. Nasty stuff!"

"One more thing," Halvar said as Flores turned to follow his men to the cells. "Step up your patrols, and keep an eye out for Scavengers. According to Samuel Igbo, they're picking up more than refuse during their rounds. Emir Achmet is getting even with us for cutting off his funds"

"We can always pay him like Gomez did," Flores grumbled.

"Gomez is gone. Get me the evidence of this Maya person's guilt," Sultan Petrus ordered Flores. "If you're sure she's guilty, hold the girl until you can find someone to get her confession.

Well done, Flores." He turned to Halvar. "Don Alvaro, I want a word with you about something else. Help me up the stairs to my rooms."

Selim started to follow her father, but the old soldier stopped her.

"*You* go with Lady Ayesha," he commanded. "What I have to say to Don Alvaro doesn't concern you."

The girl pouted rebelliously.

"Be nice to the baby," Halvar told her. "And make sure Dr. Moise gets that dog and the basket of garbage."

Selim began to protest, then closed her mouth again. Halvar hoped that, just once, this teenaged follower of his would do as she was told!

He braced himself against the older man's bulk as they maneuvered up the winding staircase to the second floor of the central tower of the Rabat, where Petrus could collapse into his Oropan chair and put his ivory leg up on a small footstool. Petrus sighed in relief, then sat up and glared at Halvar over his beard.

"Now, Hireling, you can tell me why you were summoned to the Local council and I was not!"

Halvar recognized the tone of injured pride in the sultan's complaint.

"I was in the Feria," he explained. "I can only suppose the Locals picked on me because I was there and they couldn't find you, because you had taken time to ride through Manatas. I'm sure no insult was intended." He hoped this would soothe the sultan's sense of his own importance.

Sultan Petrus snorted in derision.

Halvar went on, choosing his words carefully.

"Honored Sultan, I told the Locals—the Mahak and the Algonkin—that they should deal with you, but they said I was more likely to know what our calif was like, since I had seen him more recently than you."

"Mff!" Sultan Petrus considered this while his Afrikan attendants brought a pot of mokka and a brass cup and set it down on the small table next to his chair, along with a packet of papers tied with red string. "So, Hireling, what was this great council about, that they should question you?"

"There's a delegation of Locals from the south. They call themselves the Five Nations, and two of them, a Cherokee and a Choctaw, are talking with our Locals about joining them in some kind of jihad against the Afrikans. They must have come right after the big storm, when I was chasing after Franchen assassins, and you were, um, preoccupied with Lady Ayesha and the new baby.

"I don't know why they didn't make themselves known to you. It's some Local thing, not connected with Al-Andalus. They didn't come to trade at the Feria. They came to get the Mahak to join with them in their war."

Petrus frowned and tugged at his beard.

"This is bad news, Don Alvaro." He picked up the packet of papers, untied the string, and leafed through the sheets. "Excuse my inattention, but this may be important."

He peered at the twisted writing, holding the papers up to the light of the fading sun streaming in the narrow windows of the Rabat.

"These are letters from the other sultans of Nova Mundum—Calvero of Powhatan and Penina of Sequannok—with news of important events in their territories," Sultan Petrus explained as he read the first letter. "This is from Sultan Calvero. He has decided to rename his sultanate Terra Mara, for Mother Mara. Being a Roumi Rite Kristo, he credits Mother Mara for his rise to power and wishes to honor her in this way. Hah!" Petrus snorted his opinion of that.

"A Roumi Rite Kristo? Then he's for Lovis?"

Sultan Petrus scanned the letter.

"Not entirely. He's annoyed because Lovis has sent ships to confiscate cargoes of tabac coming from Terra Mara, and the planters can't pay their tariffs to him if they can't sell the tabac in Oropa."

"So he's not going to back Lovis, if it comes to a fight?"

"He owes everything to Don Carolus, may he dwell in Paradise, who looked past his religion to advance him and sent him to Nova Mundum to govern the settlements nearest the Afrikans. He's loyal to Al-Andalus, if not to Don Felipe. Most of the folk in his sultanate are either fishers or tabac growers. He's allowed Kristos, especially the Roumi Rite, to settle in his lands, and keeps the convivencia."

Halvar nodded sagely. "Sounds peaceful enough. No trouble with the Locals?"

"Most of the Locals in his territory have either taken the water or moved west." Sultan Petrus frowned over another document. "I'm more worried about Sultan Penina in Sequannok. He's gone Sufi mystic, writes a lot of blather about the Great Soul and the Universal Peace. I wouldn't be surprised if he started twirling about and chanting, going into a trance."

"Who's running the sultanate while he's off communing with spirits?"

"He's set up some kind of council, and asked the people in all the villages in his sultanate to send someone to speak for them. That's what he's written to me about. Seems he's got some mad ideas from too much reading of the Old Greco philosophers.

"What's more, he's letting almost anyone settle into his territory. He writes about a pack of Danes who have decided that neither Erse Rite nor Roumi Rite is what the Redeemer had in mind and have gone back to the Yehudit Holy Book for their instruction. He's allowed them to settle in Local territories, where they are clearing land and growing wheat.

"He's also allowed a party of Bretains to explore the mountainous part of his territory. The Locals there burn rocks, what the Bretains call *coal*; and if these Bretains are right, there's money to be made if they can get this coal out of the ground. It makes a hotter flame than wood, good for forging iron and making steel."

"And making steel means making weapons, which is something the Bretains are especially good at," Halvar said, slowly following Petrus's thinking processes. "But they haven't made them yet."

"Penina doesn't think of things like that," Petrus said. "He's off in his dream world. But if there is coal in Sequannok, and if there is iron across the river..."

"Is there?"

Sultan Petrus picked up one more paper.

"This is a report from one of the halflings who bring goods to and from Mahak territory, someone who went to madrassa and learned about minerals from the alchemists. He's convinced there is iron on the other side of the Great River. The problem is, how to get it out of the rocks."

"And this coal can do it?"

"I'm no expert on these things, but the Bretains are. They've been making iron and steel tools and weapons for the Franchen and the Danes—whoever can pay for them—since well before my grandfather's time. Once they get a foothold across the river, they'll surround the Andalusian territories, and that will be the end of Al-Andalus in Nova Mundum as well as in Oropa."

"And Sultan Penina and Sultan Calvero won't stop them. For different reasons, but they won't." Halvar considered the situation. "And Don Felipe is still gone, no one knows where."

Sultan Petrus shrugged helplessly.

69

"I will hold Manatas for as long as I can, Don Alvaro, but I only rule this small outpost. It's the Mahak and their allies who really rule here, and that's why I want to know what went on at this council."

Halvar frowned and tugged at his mustache.

"The Choctaw and Cherokee have a legitimate grievance against the Afrikans. The Afrikans have been doing what they always do— raiding each other's villages and taking slaves to work on their kutton farms—and now they've taken to hiring Oropan mercenaries to do their dirty work, raiding Local villages for more slaves. The Cherokee want the Mahak and the Algonkin to join with the other Locals in the south in a general jihad against all intruders—Afrikan, Andalusian, and Oropan."

"And what do our Locals have to say about that?"

"They're holding back judgment until after the Grand Divan," Halvar said. "Sachem Mahmoud doesn't want war. He's no coward, but he's not a fighter, either. All he thinks about is his crops, and his people dying for a cause they don't believe in. He's not going to back a jihad of any kind unless his own lands are threatened. He'll fight against the Huron, but he won't send any of his people south to join the Cherokee. Gray Goose-feather will back Al-Andalus, if only because we stand with him against the Huron to the north."

Sultan Petrus scratched at his beard again.

"There is going to be a war," he decided. "But I don't know if it will be a war of Local against Afrikan, or Lovis against Al-Andalus. Maybe both."

"Whichever it is, it won't be good," was Halvar's opinion. "Still, Honored Sultan, we have to keep living as if the war will stay on the other side of the Storm Sea."

"And the Afrikans?"

"They brought their slaves here. Let them take care of them themselves," Halvar said. "If the Five Nations of the South declare their jihad, all we can do is pray to whatever gods will listen that the Five Nations of the North do not join them, for if they do, there will be greater bloodshed than across all of Oropa."

"What can we do about it?" Sultan Petrus asked the universe. The universe did not reply.

Halvar squared his shoulders, settled his cap on his head, and said, "We go on. Once the Feria is over, and all accounts have been settled, I will get Leon and the silver and get both of them back to

Don Felipe.Meanwhile, I will find out who killed the Afrikan, and why, and whether it has anything to do with this refusal to pay the tariffs due to Don Felipe. And then I will find out exactly what is going on here in Manatas that no one wants me to find out!"

13

SELIM WAS WAITING IMPATIENTLY AT THE FOOT OF THE
stairs when Halvar emerged into the courtyard.

"The garbage and the dog got here. I sent them to Dr. Moise.
What do we do next?"

"We? *You* go write up the notes on all the people we talked to.
And here's that paper we took from the office in Ochiye's house.
See what you can make of that." He handed the mysterious draw-
ing to Selim, who tucked it into her notebook.

The muezzin's cry signaled the end of the day, and Selim obediently bowed and knelt to recite the evening prayer. Halvar clutched
his amulet and repeated his usual plea to Mother Mara, the Redeemer, and the god Thor for a peaceful night.

He stretched his shoulder under his constricting coat and heeded
the pangs in his middle.

"As for me," he continued as if never interrupted, "I'm going
to have a meal at the Mermaid Taberna, and then I am going to try
out that grand bed of Leon's. I've had a few slats put in to firm it
up, and it will have to be better than that plank Gomez assigned
me to in the Rabat."

"It's getting dark," Selim pointed out. "I'll come with you, to
hold the lantern. And you should take one of the Town Guard with
you, too."

Halvar turned on the girl.

"Look here, Salomey, if I need a nursemaid, I'll find one for myself. You don't have to hover over me. I have taken care of myself for longer than you've been alive."

"But this is Nova Mundum," Selim insisted. "And the Scavengers are out at night. They haven't been paid, and they're taking advantage."

"Then Flores better get his men on the job," Halvar said. "I'm not here to clear the streets, I have other work to do. As for you, you go do what you're supposed to do. Write those notes for your father to look at, copy these markings, front and back, get something to eat, and give some attention to your baby sister. And get a decent night's sleep. I'll be back in the morning, and we can deal with Ochiye's household then."

"You mean I have to be a girl." Selim's pout became a full-blown scowl.

"You *are* a girl," Halvar reminded her. "And I have things to do that have nothing to do with you or the dead Afrikan. There's enough light for me to see my way to the waterfront. Stop fussing!"

He strode out the gate, leaving Selim looking like a puppy who's just been kicked by its master.

He hated to do it, but he had to stop this hero-worship now, before the girl fancied herself in love with him. He'd had his share of female companionship during his years with the Danish Free Company, mostly tavern wenches and farm girls who were glad to enjoy a romp without further consequences. When his itch needed scratching in Corduva, there was a discreet house where he could find relief for a silver dinar. If there had been any issue from these encounters, he didn't want know about it.

The only girl he couldn't quite forget was Dani Glick, who had sent him off on his adventures with a smile, a stolen kiss, and an interrupted rendezvous a lifetime ago in the Dane-March.

Halvar mused on the implications of Selim's crush, if so it was, as he padded across the road Way towards the alley that led to the waterfront. The sun was already dipping below the horizon, sending shadows across the narrow path between the warehouses that led to the noisome alley separating the public latrine and the wall of the Mermaid Taberna. The proprietors of the shops and eating-places were supposed to set lanterns in front of their establishments to light the way along the streets of Manatas, but some neglected to follow the following the sultan's orders.

Halvar heard a step behind him. His hand found the hilt of his dagger; and he turned, blade ready, to feel the whoosh of something long and thin brushing past his ear.

Not again! was his only thought as he slashed out. Another blow landed, this time on his wounded shoulder, and once again he slashed out, this time catching something with his blade.

Two of them? he thought. One more blow caught him between the shoulder blades. *Three!*

He fell heavily into the muck that leaked out of the latrine. Before he could rise, someone grabbed him by the throat, pulling his head back. A knee in the middle of his back held him down as hands thrust into his coat and breeches pockets. He struggled to get up, smelled something oddly musky that was not the reek of the latrine slime.

More hands shoved his head down into the puddle of muck in the path He struggled, twisting his head to avoid the odorous fluid that threatened to drown him.

What an end! he thought. *Drowned in a pool of piss!*

"Hoy!"

A shout from the near end of the alley interrupted the assault, and a gleam of light from the other end sent the attackers flying. His three assailants detached themselves from Halvar's prone body and ran down the alley, leaving him gasping for breath in the muck.

"I told you to take a lantern!" Selim scolded as she helped him to his feet. Behind her, two guardsmen and Flores stood by, barely concealing smug grins.

Hannes Zilberstam, the tavern keeper at the Mermaid, stumped forward from a door under the stairs that led to the pantry and kitchens of the taberna.

"*Verdammetter* Scavengers! They're getting bolder every day. They don't usually get this close to the waterfront."

"They weren't Scavengers," Halvar said. "They wore macassin, not brogues or boots; had leather leggings, not cloth breeches; and they stank of some kind of grease. They were Locals."

"Locals? Mahak? Why would Mahak attack you?" Selim asked as she and Hannes propped Halvar against the wall of the taberna.

"I don't know. I'm not sure they were Mahak. All I know is, somewhere there's a Local with a gash in his belly. There's blood on my knife, and it's not mine."

74

"What were they after?" Selim asked. "Who have you angered this time?"

"They were looking for something," Halvar said. "But they didn't find it. Get me up those stairs, Selim, Flores. Hannes, send one of your lads up with a bowl of your fine soup. I need to think this out."

14

BETWEEN THEM, SELIM AND FLORES HAULED HALVAR UP the outside stairs, where they discovered the door latch destroyed, and into the sitting room of his suite. The Scavengers had stripped it of anything movable, but Hannes provided a table and chair and a small oil lamp to light the dark space.

Halvar dropped into the one chair while Selim stood, hands on hips, tutting at his disheveled appearance. Flores looked for somewhere to sit, but there were only bare floorboards. Leon's fine furnishings were gone with the Scavengers, the swath of brocade curtain that had separated the public from the private area also taken, so that the huge bed that filled the inner chamber was partially in view. Presumably, not even the Scavengers could remove that.

"Another coat ruined," Halvar muttered as he scrubbed at the latrine muck on the front of his newest garment.

"You nearly had your *head* ruined," Selim scolded. "Maybe next time you'll listen to me and take a guard and a lantern-bearer. Manatas isn't Corduva, Don Alvaro, and there are plenty of footpads on the loose."

Halvar moved his injured shoulder and winced.

"They weren't footpads," he said. "They left my wumpum alone. They were after something else."

"What?" Flores asked.

Halvar tried to clear the fuzz that threatened to overtake his aching head.

"Something they thought I had that was small enough to fit in a pocket. Selim, where's that paper I gave you? The one with the scrawl on it."

Selim produced her ever-present notebook from inside her loose jacket.

"I put it here for safekeeping." She handed him the folded sheet of coarse paper.

"Well done." Halvar unfolded it and held it closer to the lamp.

Flores peered over his shoulder.

"What's that supposed to be?"

"I don't know," Halvar admitted.

There was a bang at the inside door. Selim opened it to allow one of Hannes's halfling serving-boys to enter, followed by the Dane himself, puffing with the exertion of negotiating the steep inner staircase with only one flesh-and-blood leg and too much history of sampling his own food. The wooden peg protruded from under his seaman's trousers as he hobbled over to the table, carrying a lantern

"I thought I'd take a look, see what you're renting," Hannes explained as his server set a bowl of thick stew and a large spoon in front of Halvar. "I haven't managed to get up those stairs before." He looked around the room, taking in the meager furnishings and stark walls. " There's not much."

"I'll get some more furnishings in the souk," Halvar said, attacking the stew.

He realized that Flores and Selim were still standing, probably hungry, and had a pang of guilt. Surely, he should offer hospitality? But there was only one table and one chair, and Hannes had only brought up one bowl and one spoon.

He looked up at Selim and Flores for a long moment then turned to Hannes.

"You'll provide for Tenente Flores and my assistant, landsman? When we've finished our business here."

Hannes forced a smile. Free meals for the local constabulary were part of the price of running a taberna.

"Of course, landsman. As you desire." His eye was caught by the odd diagram. "What's this?" He picked up the paper and turned it around, this way and that.

"What do you make of it" Halvar asked. Hannes Zilberstam had been a sailor, a trader, a cook—and perhaps something more sinister as well.

77

"If there was a key to show north from south, I'd say it was some kind of chart or map," Hannes said. "Of course, it could just be someone trying out his pen. But these lines here—this zigzag? Could be mountains. And the wiggling line through them, that could be a river or stream. And that's the Giant in the Sky—see his belt?"

"And the numbers?" Flores was intrigued by this explanation.

"Could be anything. On sea charts, that's how many days from one port to the next." Hannes laid the paper back on the table.

"A chart," Halvar mused. "A map. Of what? Leading to what?"

"No idea." Hannes shrugged. "There's nothing to say where it is. A chart's no use unless you know where you are to begin with, and where it's telling you to go."

"Well, it's not Manatas," Flores stated firmly. "There are some hills on this island, but there are no rivers or streams running through them. The only mountains near here are across the river. There are some mountains in the Bretain territory, though. And we call that square in the sky Orion, after an Old Roumi tale, but it doesn't hang over the mountains or hills anywhere near here."

"Wherever this map leads, it was important enough for some-one to attack you to get it back," Selim pointed out. "It has to mean something more than just squiggles, or trying out a pen." She turned the paper over. "But I don't understand *these* squiggles. Looks like some kind of writing, but it's nothing I've ever seen before. Not Arabi, not Rune, not Ogham. Some kind of coded message?"

"It may be why Ochiye was killed," Halvar said, slurping up the last of his stew. "And then again, this map or chart, if that's what it is, may have nothing to do with Ochiye's death." He sighed and winced again. "Ach! My head hurts." He moved his shoulder and groaned. "Why do they always have to whack me on the shoulder?"

"Maybe the ones who attacked knew you'd been wounded there," Selim suggested. "The Scavengers would know that for certain."

"The ones who attacked me weren't Scavengers," Halvar insisted. "They didn't take my dagger or my wumpum, and those are the only things I carry that would be of any value in the souk. No, I'm sure these were Locals."

"Mahak don't come into Manatas Town," Flores stated. "They stay on their own side of the wall."

"What about those folks in the souk? The women who sell grilled fish and maiz cakes, and the men who herd geese?" Halvar objected.

"Algonkin," Flores sniffed. "They don't attack anyone. They run away."

Halvar tried to visualize his attackers.

"There were three of them. They hit me with some kind of long stick. The third one got me down while I was busy with the other two, and had a knee in my back. I don't know why they didn't slice me right away."

"They saw the lantern and heard us coming," Hannes said. "I saw those sticks in the glow of the lantern, long things with a circle at one end. Not war-clubs—too long and thin for that."

"Good thing you were wearing two caps," Selim said sagely. "Or we'd be picking your brains out of the latrine muck."

Halvar took off the araghoun cap to reveal his own soft Danic headgear with its boiled-leather lining. The long stick had left a mark across the fur crown.

"They weren't Algonkin. Algonkin wear trousers—they've become Andalusian in all but name. The ones who attacked me wore leather leggings," he repeated firmly. "And they smelled different from the Mahak."

"How different?" Selim asked.

"I can't say. But they weren't Algonkin, and they weren't Mahak."

"Who else is there?" Flores shrugged.

"Cherokee...Choctaw," Halvar said slowly. "Those visitors from the south."

"But what has this chart or map or whatever it is got to do with them?" Selim wondered.

"I'll have to ask them when I see them again. Meanwhile, you'd better get back to the Rabat." He turned to Flores. "See to it that Selim goes to the sultan's quarters. And have you found anyone who can speak to the Maya girl?"

"Not yet, but we're still looking. Maybe one of the sailors on the waterfront has been that far south." Flores shrugged again. "I don't see why you bother. She's guilty, and she'll hang."

"You won't know anything until you hear her story," Halvar said. "And I hope you haven't mistreated her. She's had food and water? And a chance at the necessary?"

"She's in a cell," Flores said. "She was given maiz-cakes and a jug of water, but she didn't eat any of it. There's a pot in the cell, should she need it. What do you want us to do, bring her to the Sultan's harem and let the girls bathe and perfume her? She's a concubine, she's a Local, and she's going to hang. What else is there to say?"

Halvar frowned and winced again at the pain in head and shoulder.

"Thor's Hammer, Flores! She may be guilty of nothing more than putting something into a basket, not knowing what it was, under orders from someone else. We won't know until we can question her, and we can't do that until morning."

"Assuming we can make any sense of what she has to say." Flores shrugged. Those shrugs were beginning to irritate Halvar. "Maybe someone in Ochiye's household can get through to her."

A thought occurred to Halvar.

"Hannes, downstairs among those sailor, there must be someone who's been to the Mechican Sea. Ask if any of them has a few words of the language." He turned to Selim. "As for you, you get back to the Rabat where you belong."

"I should stay here," Selim insisted.

"No!" Halvar yelped.

A series of horrifying visions flew through his brain—the sultan accusing him of molesting his child and carrying out the sentence demanded by Sharia. Worse, the sultan deciding that perhaps the best way of getting rid of an unwanted girl was to marry her off, posthaste, to someone with ties to the calif and the court!

"I can do well enough now, and as you can see, there's no place for you to sleep here." He gestured to indicate the bare walls and floor. He was fairly sure Selim had never occupied that vast bed in the inner room. Leon may have taken lovers into that bed, but Selim hadn't been one of them.

"Come on, boy." Flores headed for the inside stairs. "Innkeeper, we'll have a bowl of that stew of yours, just to keep our spirits up. And we'll ask some of those sailors if they can speak Mechican."

"Get Selim back to the Rabat!" Halvar ordered. He didn't know how perceptive Flores was, but Hannes winked as he stumped back to the inner staircase.

"I'll see the...lad...comes to no harm," the old pirate promised.

So much for secrecy! Halvar thought as he made his way to the inner room. He just managed to shuck his ruined coat and boots before he collapsed on the well-sprung bed.

His last thought before oblivion was *I'm missing something.*

15

HE WOKE WITH AN ACHING HEAD, A STIFF ARM, AND A sense of impending doom. At first he wasn't too sure where he was—the inner room was dark, only a square of light on the floor beyond the open doorway where the rays of the rising sun filtered through the glass-paned window of the outer room.

Halvar groaned as he rolled off the huge bed. Thor's Hammer! He'd missed the morning prayers! He didn't know whether any of his patron deities would mind, but he didn't want any of them to forget that Halvar Danske was there, usually in trouble and in need of help. So far, he'd kept on their good side; he didn't like thinking about what might happen if they withdrew their favor.

He quickly muttered his morning rubric as he inspected his soiled coat. Maybe, if he brushed it, the dried muck wouldn't be so noticeable. He heard the voice of Old Sergeant Olaf in the back of his mind: *Folks respect a man who takes care of his gear.* Halvar was no jack-a-dandy, but he hated to appear in public unkempt, in a soiled coat. It would reflect badly on the calif.

He ran a hand through his hair then over his chin. He'd been shaved the day before; maybe he could put off the next one for another day.

The delicious aroma of boiling mokka drew him down to the dining hall, where Hannes Zilberstam was preparing a pot of porridge, doling it out to men seated at tables lined up in neat rows.

"You're up!" Hannes greeted him. "Tenente Flores sent a runner with a message. He's waiting for you at the Rabat."

81

Halvar sat in one of the seats and accepted a bowl of porridge. He took a tentative taste.

"Not maiz?"

"Oats," Hannes told him. "Brought over by the Bretains. They grow oats and rye on those mountains in West Caster. Can't grow anything else, I suppose."

Halvar tasted his porridge again.

"Sweet. You have sugar?"

"Sugar? Here? Not likely! That stuff's expensive!" Hannes said with a snort. "But there was a crock of something in the pantry left over from the Kibbick folks. One of the halfling lads told me it was a kind of syrup the Locals make from tree sap. Not bad, either."

Halvar agreed.

Porridge and mokka definitely improved his mood. He looked around the room, assessing the customers. Most wore the blue kutton loose trousers and jacket preferred by sailors, although he spotted a few in the tight trousers, well-fitting coats, and broad-brimmed hats favored by Franchen merchants, and one dark-skinned man in colorful kaftan and tall tarboosh who might have come from the Berber ports just across from Al-Andalus. There were no women present, and no Locals.

"Tell me, Hannes," Halvar said as he finished his mug of mokka. "Have you found anyone who can speak to the Mechican girl?"

Hannes looked around the room and sighed.

"There's a fellow just in from the south." He nodded towards the man in the kaftan. "But he claims he never goes past the islands and doesn't want anything to do with the Mechicans."

"Introduce me," Halvar ordered, strolling to the man's table. "*Salaam aleikum*," he greeted him.

The seaman looked up from his mokka.

"*Aleikum salaam*," he grunted, and went back to staring into his mug.

Hannes cleared his throat.

"Hem! Captain, this is Halvar Danske, the Calif's Hireling. He wishes to ask you some questions."

"Don't know why. I just got here, and I'm leaving as soon as I load up with the next lot going south."

"I have heard some rumors about conflicts between Afrikans and Locals in the southern territories," Halvar explained, sitting on the stool across from the seaman. "I wanted to hear the truth from someone who'd actually been there."

"I am Zafar ibn Rafi, ship's master sailing out of Savana Port, and I haven't heard anything about any fighting between Afrikans and Locals near the sea. What happens in the mountains, that I don't know. Not that it should be any concern of the calif or his hireling. The southern territories are not part of Al-Andalus. They are Afrikan, ruled by Afrikans. I only deal with Afrikans, not Andalusians."

"In that case, I regret to tell you of the death of an Afrikan, one Ochiye Aboutiye, yesterday." Halvar watched Zafar's face, but the Afrikan did not change expression except for a slight tightening of the muscles around his mouth.

"I never met this Ochiye, so it's nothing to me." Zafar took another sip of his mokka, apparently dismissing Halvar.

Halvar would not be dismissed.

"I am told that you travel far to the south, to the Mechican Sea. The calif is interested in knowing what, if anything, the Mechicans are up to."

"I don't go past the islands," Zafar insisted. "And I don't deal with Mechicans. I leave that to fools who are willing to risk their necks for a few baubles, stones or gold. I carry kutton and indigo and a few passengers, nothing more."

"Passengers like Ochiye?"

"Not him. Others, maybe. Back in the spring, he sent a servant, an old man, to the portside to do his dickering for him. This old man was in Savanna Port looking for a ship to take this Ochiye and his people north to Manatas.

"I showed him my ship, the *Sword of the Prophet*, and he turned up his nose at it, said it was too small. Ochiye traveled in style, with a whole tribe—wife, concubine, son, servants, and special cargo. The geezer said my dhow wasn't big enough for the cargo and wanted cabins for the passengers. In the end, he took Franchen Girard's *Belle Fleur* instead. One of those new Danic-built ships. It wallows like a swine in a pen."

The insult to his ship rankled Captain Zafar more than the loss of a lucrative passenger fare.

"Is the captain of that ship still in port?" Halvar asked, scanning the room.

"Haven't seen him this trip. I expect Captain Gerard is with the rest of the Franchen, lying in wait to seize any ship that tries to cross the Storm Sea with cargo. I'm sticking close to shore these days. No

83

point taking chances, not with those new guns mounted on the round ships."

Halvar decided there was no more to be got from Zafar.

"I thank you for your company, Captain."

He headed for the door, nodding to Hannes as he left. He closed his eyes against the sudden glare of sunlight as he went from the comfortable gloom of the Mermaid Taberna to the bustling plaza of the waterfront.

Clouds were scudding across the morning sky, threatening rain. The wind ruffled the surface of the bay and set the narrow canoes of the Locals bobbing. Even the heavy barges made little headway against the rising current as the rowers tried to get their burdens to the ships waiting to carry the goods paid for at the Feria to their final destinations.

The plaza was crowded with people shouting in Arabi, Erse, Franchen, Danic, and Munsi hauling boxes, bales and bundles to be loaded onto the barges that took the goods and passengers out of the harbor to the bay, where the dhows and round ships bobbed at anchor. The whole town was emptying, now that the Feria was breaking up. The deals had been struck; now the goods had to be delivered.

Adding to the confusion were the people disembarking from the incoming ships. Whole families seemed to be fleeing the devastation of war—men in garb that ranged from Andalusian woolen jackets to Berber kaftans to Danic breeches and coats; women in a variety of long skirts, some veiled, some in neat caps; children ranging in age from babies still at the breast to nearly grown adolescents. All of them carried bundles, boxes, bags of whatever belongings they could salvage from the wreckage of their former lives. They argued with the outgoing vendors in Erse, Arabi, and Danic. Babies wailed, children shouted.

Bringing the noise level to the point where normal speech could not be heard, livestock was hauled across the bay—goats, sheep, chickens, even a cow with a calf, added their moos, squawks, brays and bleats to the general din. Halvar wondered whether all these people would find living space in the already crowded settlement then shrugged. It was Sultan Petrus's problem, not his.

He winced as the noise penetrated his skull, still aching from the previous night's attack. The sight of the exodus reminded him he still had a mission to accomplish. It would take another week for the tally men to finish their accounts and come to an agreement

84

as to how much silver and goods should be sent back to Al-Andalus. Then Halvar could get on the ship that would take him, the tribute, and Leon di Vicenza to Don Felipe.

He turned away from the colorful scene and stepped carefully through the alley where he'd been attacked. The marks of macassins were faint, but he could make out three sets of footprints besides his own boots and those of his rescuers. He stooped to pick up a tiny object half-buried in the muck. It looked like a small section of hollow quill, dyed with indigo to a deep blue. He fished the wumpum string out of his coat pocket and added the blue object to it. Then he headed off toward the center of the island and the Rabat.

For a moment, he thought he heard someone calling his name. He turned, and looked toward the crowded plaza, but could not make out anyone he knew in that multitude. The wind whistled through the alley between the latrine and the taberna, sending the dust of the street whirling, wafting the pungent odor of the latrine into his nostrils.

Halvar shrugged, settled the Local fur cap more firmly over the soft Danic one, and trudged up the hill to the Rabat. Whoever wanted him could wait. He had more urgent business to attend to.

16

OCHIYE'S HALFLING SON ISAI WAS WAITING FOR HIM AT the gate of the Rabat.

"Don Alvaro! *Salaam aleikum.* I am so glad to see you!" Isai greeted him frantically.

"You must get this fool to open up! I must speak to Tenente Flores right away! What have they done with Maya? Where is she?"

"She's safe," Halvar assured him. "We've been trying to find someone who speaks her language, to find out what she knows about your father's death."

"I taught her a few words of Hausa—that's the Yoruba language we speak at home," Isai said. "And she taught me some of her tongue."

"I see." Halvar assessed the situation. Young fellow, young girl, together on a long trip, and the lure of forbidden fruit with that. "Well, come on in, and let's see what you get out of her." He banged at the gate. "It's me, the Calif's Hireling. Open up!"

The gate creaked open, and a bleary-eyed guardsman poked his head out.

"Tenente Flores is waiting for you," the guardsman said ungraciously. "In the cells. Eva Hakim is there, too. The girl tried to harm herself."

"Oh, no!" Isai shoved the man aside and dashed into the courtyard, looking wildly around not sure which of the three towers held the prisoners' cells.

"Follow me."

Halvar stalked across the cobbles, seething. If Flores had followed the example of his former commander Gomez and tried brutal tactics on the girl, he would pay dearly for it. There was something about Flores's delight in using his strength on those weaker than himself Halvar did not like. Could he have recommended the wrong man for the job again?

They found Flores at the gate to the corridor on the ground floor of the eastern tower of the Rabat.

"I didn't know she was that desperate!" he blustered. "I left her with a jug of water and a dish of maiz-cakes. She broke the jug, got a shard of pottery, tried to cut her wrist. Eva Hakim was visiting Lady Ayesha, came down to check on the girl, and found her like this!"

He stepped aside, to reveal a horrific scene. Eva Hakim knelt over the recumbent form of Maya, The girl was covered in blood. Selim hung back near the door to the cell, horrified.

"She's still breathing," she told Halvar as he joined her. "I see her chest moving. Why would she do such a thing?"

"Will she live?" he asked.

"She has lost much blood," Eva Hakim said, her tone angry. "How did this happen? What did this child do that you should lock her up, all alone, with no other woman to help her?" She rose to her full height, eye-to-eye with Flores, who had also joined them.

"She's a murderess," Flores quavered. "She killed Ochiye."

"We think," Selim amended.

"You don't know?" Eva Hakim's voice could have shaken the walls of the fortress in her wrath.

"We were coming to question her. Isai ibn Ochiye says he can speak some of her language."

Halvar looked around to the youth, but Isai was in no condition to speak to anyone. He clung to the doorway, his face twisted in anguish, tears running down his face

"Can she be questioned?" Halvar tried to see past the enraged woman, but Eva Hakim blocked his view.

"The cuts were shallow," she pronounced. "The earthenware jug could not produce a sharp enough edge to make more than superficial cuts. She has lost blood, but she may yet live. I should take her to the House of the Green Crescent, but it would be difficult. She cannot stay in this cell. She needs warmth, and healing broth."

"Can you move her at all?" Halvar asked.

"Carefully, very carefully," Eva Hakim said.

"There's the room I had. It's got a decent bed, a little window, light and air," Halvar said. "Take her there. Get one of Lady Ayesha's women to sit with her until you can call one of your Sisters of Fatima to tend her. I want this girl alive at the Grand Divan!"

Eva Hakim nodded. "I will send for Nokomis. She is very wise in the ways of Locals, knows healing herbs. She might also be able to communicate with the girl."

"Not likely," Isai said. "The Mechican language is nothing like Munsi. It's not like anything I've ever heard before."

"Then let us hope that this girl will live long enough to learn to speak Arabi," Flores said. He motioned for two of the guardsmen to carry the limp girl to the room assigned to her.

"And while Eva Hakim tends to her, young man, you and I will have a little chat." Halvar turned to Selim, who was visibly shaken by the gory scene. "Come along, laddie. I want you to take notes. And don't lose your breakfast!" he added in an undertone.

17

THE SORRY PROCESSION CROSSED THE COURTYARD. HAL-
var, Selim and Isai headed for the barracks, where the late Tenente
Ruiz had appropriated a small room for his office. During his brief
time as Tenente, Ruiz had furnished the room in the Andalusian
style with a low table, and had added cushions to make for a more
decorative environment.

Halvar cautiously lowered himself onto one of the cushions
and motioned for Selim to take her place in a corner, where she
could write down what was said while remaining in the shadows.

"And now," Halvar said when Isai was arranged on another cushion opposite him, "what brings you to the Rabat, Isai ibn Ochiye?
Aside from the Maya girl?"

"I–I don't know where to begin," Isai stammered. "When I heard
that Maya had been taken prisoner, I didn't believe it. She would
never harm my father. Never!"

"Why not?" Halvar asked.

A guardsman poked his head into the room.

"Tenente Flores told me to tell you that the girl is in your old
cell. Lady Ayesha's servant Hanna is sitting with her. Eva Hakim
has sent a messenger to the House of the Green Crescent. She will
speak with you when you finish with this one." He jerked his head
toward Isai.

"Good to hear." Halvar said. "Tell Tenente Flores I'll see him as
soon as this young sprout tells me what's eating at him."

The guardsman disappeared. Isai gaped at Halvar.

"How did you know…?"

"You couldn't speak freely in front of your mother, could you? You're smitten with the Maya girl, and she's your father's concubine. Not a good thing."

Isai's reddish-copper skin darkened.

"I can't help it."

Halvar leaned forward to rest his arms on the table and take some of the pressure off his aching shoulder.

"Tell me, laddie. When did this start?"

Isai passed his tongue over his dry lips.

"It was on the trading trip to the south," he began. "It is how our life is arranged. Ochiye would spend the winter months in Savana Port with my mother and sisters and me. He would come from Manatas after the fall Feria, stay a few weeks, then go on a selling journey through Yoruba territory, through the mountains where the Choctaw and Chickasaw rule all the way to the Mechican borderlands. He'd come back with goods for sale and sail back to Manatas for the spring Feria. He'd stay in Andalusian territory in the summer while my mother took us to the mountains where her people live to get away from the fevers of Savana Port."

He stopped for breath, choking.

Halvar beckoned to Selim.

"Get us something to drink—cider or mokka, even water, if you can find any fit to drink." He waited until Selim was out of the room to ask, "Where did this Maya girl come from?"

Isai took a deep breath to steady himself.

"I'm getting to that. During the time Ochiye was away on his selling and buying journeys, I attended the madrassa in Savana Port. Ochiye wanted me to study the law, to become a cadi or an advocate, so that he could use the law to become richer. I prefer to study philosophy and literature, especially languages. I'm good at languages. I've learned Erse and Franchen, as well as Munsi and Arabi.

"My mother persuaded Ochiye to take me with him on his selling journey this winter, to act as translator. We traveled with a caravan, buying and selling."

"This is when you picked up those lizard hides? And the sugar?"

"And, most unfortunately, rhum. And when I noticed that my father was eating much sugar in his food, and drinking the rhum, and becoming intoxicated."

90

"Where does the Maya girl come into this saga?"

"She traveled with one of the other vendors. He said he got her from the Seminole, who live in the place they call The Pizzle, because it sticks into the Mechican Sea like a man's part. It's a terrible place, full of wild beasts and fevers. No one but the Seminole can survive there for long.

"They raid the settlements on their borders but don't go past a certain river. They must have captured this girl when she was a child. I never learned how she came to be with the Seminole, but they were willing to sell her to the vendor, and he was willing to give her to my father for a lump of gold."

"A lump? Not a coin?" Halvar tugged at his mustache. "Where'd that come from?"

Isai shrugged. "I don't know. My father had a pouch of these lumps, these 'nuggets,' that he would use when he wanted to buy something in bulk, or something very rare, that he could not match with the goods he brought from Manatas."

Halvar thought this over.

"So, you traveled with this Maya girl," he summed it up. "And she was, um, familiar with your father."

"She was not!" Isai burst out. "It was not that way at all! He *could* not! I could hear them, in the tent next to mine, and he would try and fail, and try and fail. And he would beat her, and she would cry! I wanted to help her, I tried to teach her Hausa. I love her!"

Selim arrived with a jug of cider and three birchbark cups. Isai grabbed the jug, poured a drink, and gulped it thirstily.

"What's the matter with him?" she asked Halva, as she filled and then handed him a cup of the cool fruit juice.

"Unrequited love," Halvar muttered. In a louder tone, he said, "So, you traveled with your father, you came back to Savanna Port, and then what?"

"I asked to be allowed to accompany him to Manatas," Isai said. "I wanted to attend the madrassa here."

"What was wrong with the one in Savanna Port?"

"It's provincial!" Isai sneered. "All they teach is the Holy Book and the Hadith that goes with it. I want more! If I can't get to Corduva, at least I can learn from those who did. Mathematics, philosophy, rhetoric, languages! Especially languages. Why are there so many? And how is it that some resemble each other, while some are so different?

"There are Afrikan sounds that are not heard in the Local languages, and neither Afrikan nor Local are anything like Arabi, and that's not like Erse or Franchen. The teachers at the madrassa in Savana Port taught Arabi, because that is the language of the Holy Book, and I picked up a little Erse from the sailors in Savana Port. And I learned Cherokee from my mother's people, who use Munsi when they trade with those Mahak who come south to trade for tabac."

"Sounds like you want to know a lot," Halvar observed when Isai stopped to take another drink. "What did Ochiye have to say about this thirst for knowledge?"

"After consulting with my mother, my father decided that perhaps it would not be a bad thing if one of his sons became an expert in languages. It would help him in his trading. So, he agreed that I should come north with him this year."

"And your mother insisted on coming along?" *To protect her son*, he thought, thinking of the soft-spoken Local woman with the underlying steel who was forced to stay in the same house as her Afrikan rival. "That must be annoying, to have your mother looking after you when you are studying at the madrassa."

"She told me she was worried about my father. He was losing weight, drinking rhum, getting weak during the day, running to the privy during the night. There was something wrong, but he would not allow her to call a physician. He must not appear weak, lest one of his rivals take advantage of him!" Isai ended bitterly. "Besides, I have my room at the Afrikan lodgings, behind the madrassa. I only came home for the Rest Day sermon at the muskat, and to eat the meal with the family afterwards."

"Did you see anything that would lead you to also worry about your father's health?"

Isai shrugged again. "I am not a physician, and it is not for a son to criticize his father. I knew that his efforts with Maya were fruitless, but he kept her with him, like Daoud of the Holy Book of the Yehudit, to warm him at night. And to serve him, to flaunt her in front of Lady Tekla. I do not think my father cared very much for Lady Tekla, but he needed her to run his business here in Manatas while he was in the south, or away on trading journeys in West Caster."

Halvar's eyebrows raised. "He traveled in West Caster?"

"Buying and selling," Isai said. "Between the spring and fall Ferias, he would go to West Caster. He'd take sugar and beaded jewelry, small things that he would trade for the candy they make from tree sap, and dried apples and cider, and barrels of salted fish, which will keep for the winter. Whatever was not sold at the spring Feria he'd take to West Caster, to sell to the Bretains who did not come to Manatas. Then he'd come back to Manatas for the fall Feria, and do it all over again, selling what he had found and buying more to bring back to Savana Port."

Selim, who had returned to her corner, had an idea.

"What about other things? Books, letters, the *Gazetta*. Did Ochiye carry *them* to West Caster?"

"Not books, but yes, Ochiye sometimes carried letters from settlement to settlement when we traded in the in the south," Isai admitted. "And he took some of the news-sheets, the gazettas, with him when he went to West Caster this summer."

"And did you go with him?"

"I was busy with my studies," Isai said. "Noam went, and my father insisted on having Maya with him," he added bitterly. "He took his Afrikan servants, too, but let my mother keep her Cherokee guards."

"While you amused yourself with the stick-and-stone game," Selim said, drawing closer to the table. "Not exactly what your father had in mind when he brought you all the way to Manatas for your education."

Isai said, "I could not stay indoors on the long summer days. The Peace Game is a good way to keep one's mind sharp. Did not the Old Roumi say, 'A sound mind in a sound body'?"

Halvar ignored the byplay.

"So, you and your father went a-Viking through the south, trading. A trader makes a good spy, but spies don't get poisoned. Knifed, garroted, maybe even hanged, but not poisoned."

"And with this mal-chinee stuff," Selim added.

"Yes, let's get to that. What do you know about mal-chinee?" Halvar looked sternly at the young halfling, who quailed under his gaze.

"The bad tree? It's what the Seminole use to poison their arrows," Isai said.

"So I've heard. How is it that you know about this tree?"

"It was one of the traders in the caravan, the Yehudit Levi Hillerman, who told us of it. We were telling tales to pass the time. You know how it is."

Halvar smiled under his mustache, recalling nights spent around a campfire, listening to the older soldiers telling of battles fought, brave deeds done by mighty heroes of olden times, stories of gods and goddesses, of miracles performed by Kristo holy men and women, of talking animals and weird creatures that had never been seen by human eyes.

"The other traders were talking about the Mechicans, each tale more gruesome than the next. So, Levi Hillerman told about this mal-chinee. According to him, it grows along the shore, in sandy low places like beaches. The Seminole harvest the fruit, which looks like an apple, by piercing it with a stick. They hold the fruit on the stick over a jar or pot and let the juice drip into the pot. Then they dip their arrows into the pot to cover the arrowhead with the poisonous juice."

"What happens to the fruit?" Selim wanted to know.

"I suppose some animal eats it and dies," Isai said. "And then the plant takes root, using the body of the dead animal as nourishment."

"Ugh!" Selim shuddered.

Halvar tugged at his mustache in thought.

"So, someone could get a jar of this mal-chinee poison from the Seminole," he reasoned. "And maybe some of the dried fruit of the tree, using the same method. Then, this someone could chop it up, if they wore gloves, and put it in with Ochiye's fruit mixture."

"Someone who was on that trading journey?" Selim suggested.

"Like you," Halvar said, grimly eying Isai.

"Or Maya," Selim added.

"Of course, if someone told him this mal-chinee would increase his, um, powers, Ochiye might have believed it," Halvar mused. "He could have poisoned himself by mistake."

"Not a chance of it," Isai scoffed. "The traders told some spicy stories, too, about all the things that are supposed to increase a man's powers, but that wasn't among them!"

"Who were these traders you traveled with?" An idea was creeping into Halvar's mind, something to do with the mysterious paper he had found in Ochiye's study. "You say there was a Yehudit?"

"Levi Hillerman, the Yehudit, was the leader of the caravan. He'd been in that country for many years. He knew the Seminole, could talk their language. He had a way of telling wild yarns—you didn't know if what he said was true or not.

"There were two Igbo, they were from Savanna Port. They often traveled with my father. He didn't like Igbo, but no merchant travels alone in Local territory, so they joined with us. And there was one Bretain. He was called Rufus because his face burned red in the heat. He was the one who bought the rhum. I learned some Erse from him, but by the way the other students looked at me when I spoke, perhaps it was not the most refined Erse."

"You said this Yehudit had the Maya girl?"

"They were together. I'm not sure what their relationship was, but when Ochiye wanted her, Levi sold her to him."

"For gold," Halvar mused. "Where did Ochiye get it?"

"You would have to ask Noam—he's the one who stocked our wagons, and he provided my father with coins to offer those who did not wish to trade goods for goods."

"Noam? That vizier fellow?" Halvar frowned. "He acted as if he was there to run the household, even when Lady Tekla told him not to. What was he doing on a trading journey?"

"Oh, he's been my father's servant since they were boys in Afrika," Isai said. "He's always looked after him. They travel together, north to south and south to north. It's Noam who arranges things, hires the servants, stocks the wagons, hires the drivers, does the bargaining with Locals. He wasn't too pleased when Maya joined the caravan. He hadn't planned for a third servant, only Gavril—he's my servant—and himself for my father. And then along came Maya, and Noam was very put out by it."

"According to your mother, it was you who located the lizard hides and sugar," Halvar said.

Isai smiled sadly. "My mother is my mother. I have three sisters and a younger brother, but I am her oldest son, and she cares for me too much, I think. She insisted on coming north this year instead of going west to Cherokee country as she usually does in the summer because she said she wanted to make sure I would come to no harm at the madrassa in Manatas. She left my sisters and younger brother in Savanna Port with my aunts. She doesn't like Manatas, too many people and too smelly. Lady Tekla resents her being here, but both of them cared for Ochiye, each in her own way."

Halvar thought this over while Isai finished the jug of cider.

"So, Isai ibn Ochiye, who do you think put the mal-chinee into your father's basket?"

Isai's eyes filled with tears.

"I don't know!" he cried. "It has to be someone in the household, but who hated my father so much? It was not Maya, that I know. It could not be."

"Because she's pretty, and scared, and you want to protect her?" Selim's voice dripped scorn.

"Because she is never allowed anywhere near the kitchens," Isai snapped back. "She stayed in my father's rooms, ate with him, was always with him."

"That must have pleased your mother," Selim sniped.

"My mother did not care for Maya, but she would not offend Ochiye, either."

Halvar considered this odd domestic arrangement for a moment, then said, "You may go, Isai. I will return your father to you for proper burial as soon as Dr. Moise has finished his report. I suppose your brother Yakub has made arrangements?"

"Yakub takes much on himself," Isai said resentfully. "He is the eldest son by Afrikan law, and he claims the whole of my father's estate. I am to be given a small share, my sisters get nothing, my mother gets only what Yakub and Lady Tekla decide to give her. It is grossly unfair!"

"Take your petition to the sultan at the Grand Divan," Halvar advised him.

Isai got up from his cushion.

"One more thing," Halvar said. "What do you make of this?" He handed Isai the paper he had taken from Ochiye's study.

Isai stared at it blankly, then turned it over.

"How did you get this?" he gasped. "I thought I'd put it back with my father's papers. Noam was making such a fuss about it, blaming the servants for interfering with Ochiye's business papers."

"This is your writing?" Halvar pointed to the odd picture.

Isai turned the paper over again.

"Oh, that. I don't know what that is. I just needed something to write on, and this piece of paper was on top of the pile when I had my idea."

"Your idea?" Halvar echoed.

Isai's face brightened. "It was after Rav Nachum's lecture on the different languages of the world. He mentioned Arabi, Erse, languages used in Manatas, and said there are many, many more, such as Old Roumi and Old Greco, and Danic, and that each of the great languages was inscribed in writing. All the languages of the great peoples are put into writing. Even the Mechicans have writing, and Maya said that her people had a kind of writing, known to the priests and rulers. I thought, *I will devise a kind of writing that the Cherokee people could use. I will write a treatise on the Cherokee language for Rav Nachum."*

"A treatise on languages. Very scholarly. And what did Rav Nachum think of this idea?"

"Rav Nachum praised my effort on behalf of the Cherokee, although he doesn't think it will do much good if no one else can read my symbols."

"What about this other stuff?" Halvar turned the paper over to reveal the odd markings.

"That? I don't know what that means. I was so excited about my idea, I had to write it down as soon as I could. It was after the imam's sermon last week, when I made my visit to the villa. I was telling my mother about it, and she thought I should make some symbols, like the Old Greco alpha-beta. Only that doesn't quite work for Cherokee."

"And what did your father think of this grand idea ?"

"He thought it was interesting but not practical, unless I found a way to teach every Cherokee how to read my letters. He looked at what I'd done, said it was clever, told me to copy it properly, on good paper. So I did, and put the first paper back on his table with the rest of the receipts. Noam was making a terrible fuss about my taking things without asking first."

"He takes a good deal on himself, this Noam," Halvar said, tugging his mustache. "You may go, Isai. Thank you for being so open with me."

"I want my father's killer brought to justice," Isai. "He was not always the best of men, but he was my father, and I loved him."

Selim watched him as he left the room, then said, "What do you make of that tale? How much do you think is true?"

Halvar frowned and tugged at his mustache again.

"He's told us more than we knew before. Have you made that copy? Both sides, mind!"

"Yes, but I didn't know which way was up, so I don't know what good it will do."

Halvar's frown deepened.

"We'd better get Flores and his men," he said finally. "The answer to this riddle lies in Ochiye's villa. I want another word with that vizier, Noam. He knows more than he's telling us."

"He won't talk," Selim warned,

Halvar smiled nastily. "This time I think I'll let Flores do what he will. One way or another, that old nut is going to get cracked."

18

HALVAR STRODE PURPOSEFULLY THROUGH THE COURT-
yard of the Rabat, Selim trotting behind him. Before he could
reach the gate, Eva Hakim accosted him; Isai was at her side.

"Don Alvaro! The girl is awake and wants to talk to you."

Halvar stopped in mid-stride. Selim nearly bumped into him.

"Have you found someone who speaks her language?"

"I can do it," Isai insisted.

"Not good enough. You're in love with her, laddie. If she says
anything that might count against her, you won't want to tell us."

"I swear by the Prophet and all the Orishas of the Yoruba, I will
hold nothing back." Isai said fervently. "Please, let me do this!"

Halvar wavered, then said, "How is the girl? Will she live?"

"If you mean, will she live long enough to bear witness at the
Grand Divan, that is in the hands of Ilha," Eva Hakim said. "But
she insists on speaking to you now, and I would advise you to hear
her while she still has breath to do it."

While Halvar was thinking it over, Flores came through the gate
dragging a shaggy-bearded man in seamans' slops behind him.

"This fellow says he was sent by Hannes Zilberstam from the
Mermaid Taberna."

The sailor raised his hand to his forehead in the Bretain manner of greeting, indicating that he had no weapon and his face was
not covered by a helmet. He introduced himself.

"God be with all within. I'm Shamus MacManus, seaman, just in
from Lagos. I've sailed into Mechican waters, aye, and survived it.
I could tell you tales—"

"Not now," Halvar cut him off. "Can you speak any of the languages of the Seminole or the Mechicans?"

Shamus shrugged. "Enough to get a meal and get me out of a fight."

"Maya has learned Hausa," Isai reminded the group. "I can tell you what she says."

"Whatever you decide, do it quickly," Eva Hakim warned.

Halvar sighed. "All right, Isai, you can come. Shamus, if he's not saying what the girl says, you tell me. Flores, take a squad and get back to the Ochiye villa. Make sure no one leaves. I want to have another word with those wives of his, and that steward or vizier or whatever he calls himself."

"No one leaves that house without my say-so," Flores promised. He swaggered across the courtyard, gathering four guardsman as he did.

"Let's hear what the Maya girl has to say," Halvar said.

Eva Hakim led the way to the cell where Halvar had spent the previous two weeks. It had not become any warmer or more cheerful since he'd decamped for the Mermaid Taberna.

Maya lay on the plank bed, covered with the thin wool blanket that had protected Halvar during his bout of fever. A plump Andalusian woman in the kutton shirt and loose trousers favored by Lady Ayesha's servants sat on a small stool at the head of the bed; a Local woman in the dark brown tunic and trousers and green hijab of the Sisters of Fatima stood at the other end. Between them, Maya seemed very fragile, her usually dark skin pale. She scanned the room for a friendly face, and found only one.

"Isai!" she called out, reaching for him.

The young man leaped forward to kneel at her bedside, his hands enfolding hers. The two lovers murmured to each other.

"What's she saying?" Halvar broke into their reunion.

"She's sorry she tried to take her own life," Isai said. "She was frightened. She thought she might be raped again."

"Again?" Halvar scowled. "If Flores let his men at her…"

"I think she means the Seminole," Isai said hastily.

Halvar motioned for Shamus to come forward.

"All right, Sailor Shamus, let's see what you can do."

Shamus squatted next to the bed and said a few words in a language no one else understood. Maya's eyes widened, and she clutched Isai's hand tighter as she responded to Shamus's questions.

The sailor stood to face Halvar.

"I asked her who she was, where she came from. She said she is Maya, that her people were taken by the Mechicans, and she was left by herself. Then the Seminole came and took whatever the Mechicans had left, which was mainly her and two other children. The other two died; she's the only one left."

"That explains who she is and how she came to be with the Seminole," Halvar said. "Now, ask her about something called mal-chi-nee."

"That stuff? That's the poison the Seminole use on their arrows!" Shamus stared down at the girl. "Is that what this is about? I heard the news-criers say that some Afrikan had died in the Feria, anyone with knowledge should come to the Rabat, but...poison? And mal-chinee?" He spat his contempt of anyone who would use such an unsporting method of murder.

"What do you know about it?" Halvar asked.

"Only that it's the nastiest stuff on this earth," Shamus snapped. "Me and my mates, we were wrecked on the shore down south. There was this tree with good-looking fruit. One of my mates picked it, bit into it, and howled until he died of it. I learned the stuff was called mal-chinee—bad tree—and for good reason!" He looked down at Maya. "Did this girl use it to poison her master?"

"That's what we want you to find out," Halvar said.

"No...I...did not!" Maya cried out in halting Arabi.

Everyone stared at her.

"I...I have words. Hausa...Arabi?" Maya tried to lift herself up against Isai's arm. "I have fear! I tell...I die!"

"Someone threatened to kill you?" Halvar knelt beside the bed.

Maya said something to Isai in Hausa.

"She says she did not put the mal-chinee into the basket, but she knows who did. He traded with the Seminole, got a jar of the stuff from them. She didn't know what it was then, but now she does."

"Why didn't she tell us sooner?"

"She couldn't!" Isai said, his face twisted in sorrow.

"Because he was standing there," Halvar said slowly. "It was Noam, wasn't it?"

"Noam," Maya nodded.

"The steward? Why would he poison his master?" Selim wondered.

"We'll have to ask him," Halvar said. "Eva Hakim, keep this girl alive so she can bear witness at the Grand Divan. This is one murderer I want caught alive."

Eva Hakim nodded. "There is only one place for her. I will ask Lady Ayesha to take this child into the harem, to protect her from danger."

"Good idea," Halvar told her. He started to leave the cell. "Selim, come on. I want to hear what Noam has to say for himself."

Shamus stepped in front of him.

"I have a message from Heer Zilberstam. He told me to tell you that your friends are well-suited, and that they said you will not mind if they use your rooms while you are at the Rabat."

"My friends?" Halvar's eyebrows rose. Then he shrugged. Plenty of former mercenaries were making their way to Nova Mundum these days, according to Sultan Petrus's reports. Were these mysterious friends the ones he thought he'd heard call his name on the waterfront?

Whoever they were, he had no time to deal with them now. He'd catch up with them when he'd finished the job at hand.

19

A WAITING DONKEY CART TOOK HALVAR, SELIM AND TWO
guardsmen back to Afrika Street, where Flores stood at the door to
Ochiye's villa.

"What are you doing out in the street?" Halvar demanded.

"That Shaitan-led Vizier has bolted the doors," Flores said with
a curse. "There's a servant inside, won't open up. Short of firing a
cannon, there's no getting past him."

"There's that back door in the alley behind the villa where the
Scavengers pick up the household garbage," Halvar said. "Go back
to the Broad Way and try that door. Ochiye had at least two Afrikan bodyguards, and I saw a couple of Cherokee, but they don't
have an army in there. Do what you have to do, but try not to kill
anyone."

Flores motioned for two of his halberdiers to follow him.

"And what are you going to do while we're playing hide-and-
find?"

"I'll try to keep the doorkeeper's interest here," Halvar said.
"And watch for that vizier Noam. He's the one we're after."

"Noam? That skinny little geezer?"

"It's those skinny geezers who survive when the world falls
down around the rest of our ears," Halvar said. "He's the key to
this mess. We've got to get him."

Flores and his men headed for the alley while Halvar remained
at the door, trying to ignore the crowd that seemed to form when-

ever something interesting was happening in Manatas. Market-women, Scavengers, servants from the adjoining houses, even the imam from the muskat at the end of the street all ranged themselves in small groups along the street, muttering to each other. He had the sense they could easily become a mob. He would have to speak carefully, or he'd be the target of street filth or worse.

The peephole opened to reveal one suspicious eye.

"This is a house of mourning." The doorkeeper's voice was muffled but clear. "Go away!"

"I hold the calif's seal!" Halvar announced loudly, as much to the waiting crowd as to the doorman. "I can go anywhere, do anything, under the calif's seal."

"You can't come in here!" Another voice, this one female, took the place of the doorkeeper's.

"Is that you, Lady Tekla? I have information about the death of your husband, Ochiye Aboutiye. Do you want the entire street to hear it?"

"Ochiye is dead. That is all anyone has to know."

"Aren't you worried about how he died?"

"You said it was mal-chinee poison. That is enough for me."

"Don't you care who put it into his food?"

"It was the Maya girl." Lady Tekla sounded very certain.

"She says not."

"She would! That girl is trouble. She is a liar. She can speak Hausa well enough to talk to our servants and has already learned some Arabi. She has ensnared the Cherokee woman's son, but she won't snare mine!"

"Lady Tekla, we can't talk like this, through this door. Let me in, please, and I will tell you what I know of Ochiye's death."

"There is nothing to be said. Ochiye called himself *Aboutiye*, but he was an empty barrel, blowing wind. It was Yakub and I who kept his trade going, sending silver and goods to Savanna Port to keep him and his Local brats in luxury while we froze here in Manatas. Now that is over! Isai will have to give up his foolish games and useless maundering and do some honest work. Cherokee Yona will go back to her Local people."

"You seem to have everything planned nicely," Halvar said. He heard a scuffle inside.

"What is happening?" Lady Tekla shouted. "Help! Bandits!"

"Your back door is not guarded as well as this one," Halvar said. "Now, open this one, or I will break it open!"

There was the scrape of a bar being moved, and the door opened to reveal Flores and his guards, halberds lowered to herd a crowd of Afrikan servants, led by the cook, into the atrium of the house. Halvar ducked into the villa and shut the door in the faces of the interested bystanders.

"Nice work," he complimented Flores. "Any trouble?"

Flores dabbed at a cut on his cheek.

"They had one of those big Afrikan bodyguards by the kitchen door. My men were quicker, but one of those slicers got me. And that cook is a handful!" He leered at the stout Afrikan woman, who glared back in disdain.

"Get that cut seen to as soon as we finish here," Halvar ordered.

He turned to Lady Tekla, who had changed from her gaudy wrappings to the dark tunic, skirt, and head-shawl of widowhood.

"Where can we sit?"

He looked around for a suitable room and found only the bare foyer where they had interviewed her the day before. He considered the open courtyard, but a chilly breeze reminded him that summer was definitely gone, and winter was only a few weeks away.

Tekla noted his discomfort.

"There is the banqueting hall," she admitted. "Come."

She led the group through the inner door to a wide room furnished with low tables and carved stools. Halvar eased himself onto one stool and indicated Lady Tekla should take the one opposite. Selim found a table and stool for herself and prepared to take notes.

"Now, Lady, you and I will talk, without informing every Afrikan in Manatas of our business. And I want a word with Lady Yona, too. And where is that vizier, Noam?"

"He is gone," Tekla said triumphantly.

"Where?"

"I don't know or care. He was Ochiye's man, not mine." She pulled the shawl around to cover her lower face. "He was with us when we came from Afrika. He insisted on doing everything for Ochiye—picking out his clothes, arranging his household, even ordering his food."

"Even here? In this house?"

"This is my house. I live here all the year, from the spring Feria to the Fall Feria. He only comes when Ochiye comes. I told him to stop his meddling."

Halvar tugged at his mustache.

"Samuel Igbo next door says that he heard a loud argument the day before Ochiye died. What was that about?"

Tekla grimaced. "That Igbo! He puts his long nose into everyone's affairs! What he heard was a discussion. Regarding money."

Halvar persisted.

"Money for what?"

Tekla hesitated.

"For the madrassa." Lady Yona had entered the banqueting hall unnoticed in her maccasin-clad feet. "This Afrikan woman would deny my son the small payment for decent lodgings. She wanted him to remain here, in this house, where he would have to travel back and forth to attend the classes and could not listen to the other students in the mokka-shops."

"Why should Isai live in a separate lodging when he has a room here?" Tekla turned on the Cherokee. "He spends wumpum and silver on frivolities, books and gambling, money that Yakub and I work hard to earn."

"Isai is gaining honor for the clan of Ochiye," Yona said. "He is learning many languages that will be useful in trading. He is making friends, meeting important people who will help him rise in the future. He gains honor in the Peace Game."

"Honor chasing a ball around a field?" Tekla scoffed. "Is that why he spends so much time running back and forth with a stick, trying to get a ball across a line? And placing wagers on how many times he can do it?"

"What's this about?" Halvar murmured to Selim. "Some kind of sport or game?"

"It's a Locals' game," Selim told him. "We call it stick-and-stone in Arabi. The Franchen call it la-crux, because the sticks they use to catch the stone look like the Kristo crux. The Mahak call it the Peace Game."

"A waste of time!" Tekla complained. "Isai did not come all this way to play a game. Ochiye's silver should not be spent so that Isai can run about waving a stick."

"It is the Cherokee way," Yona stated firmly. "We play the Peace Game, we meet other warriors, we learn who they are, how they think."

Flores ended the inter-spousal sniping.

"None of this matters," he barked. "Where is Noam?"

"He left the house this morning with Yakub. First they went to the muskat, to arrange for Ochiye's funeral. Then they went to finish the trading at the Feria and take down the pavilion." Yona said.

105

"Ochiye will be buried here, in Manatas!" Tekla decreed. "As soon as the doctor releases the body, it must be put into the ground before nightfall. So says the Prophet, and so it shall be done."

"He should be taken to Savana Port. He has other children. They must mourn their father." Yona's voice was soft, but firm.

"I suppose you would have him taken into the forest and left for the wolves, like your savage people do," Tekla snarled.

"Thor's Hammer!" Halvar swore. "Ladies, what happens to your husband now is of little matter given his murderer still runs free!"

Tekla's well-rounded bosom heaved with pent-up emotion.

"You have his murderer locked in your Rabat. It was Maya."

Yona nodded. It was the first time both women agreed on anything.

"She says she did it on orders from Noam," Halvar said. "When did he leave?" He turned to Flores. "Get your men to the Feria, track him down."

"You cannot arrest him," Yona said. "The Feria is in Mahak territory. He is out of your reach, Hireling." She smirked with triumph.

"Thor's Hammer! This is getting out of hand. Every time someone breaks the laws of Al-Andalus, they flee to Green Village or Local territory. There has to be an end to this!"

"That's for Sultan Petrus to worry about," Flores said. "Right now, we have to find this Noam and get him to the Rabat. And then, Dane, I'll show you how to get information out of a reluctant witness!".

"You'll have to wait until we get him back to Manatas Town," Halvar reminded him. "You and your men will have to stay at the wall while the lad and I go to the Feria. I only hope the Mahak watchmen are ready to give chase. They seem to be more interested in this stick-and-stone game than in keeping folk safe from thieves and murderers."

Flores snorted disdainfully.

"You'd do better facing the old geezer alone. That lot won't be as gentle as me, you can take a wager on it."

"And we'd better do it quickly," Selim added as they headed for the street. "There's another storm brewing. I can hear the wind from here."

"Manatas weather changes too fast," Halvar complained.

"If you don't like it, wait till the next prayers," Flores said philosophically as he followed Halvar and Selim out the door. "You'll get something different."

The wind picked up as they headed for the Broad Way, tugging at the ends of Selim's turban, raising clouds of dust in the street. Halvar looked up, and sent a quick message to Thor: *Hold off the rain until we finish our business at the Feria.*

20

THE VOICE OF THE MUEZZIN RANG OUT FROM THE AFRI-
kan muskat as Halvar and his party emerged from the Ochiye villa.
Flores and Selim prostrated themselves, along with most of the onlookers in the street, while Halvar clutched his amulet and murmured his midday formula.

Religious duty done, the crowd dispersed, robbed of the oppor-
tunity to see action. Halvar looked around for his transport, the donkey driver attached to the Rabat.

"What do we do now?" Selim asked.

Halvar settled the fur cap firmly on his head.

"We go to the Feria, we find Noam, and we take him back to
the Rabat, and we ask him what he knows about mal-chinee."

"Suppose we don't find him?"

"We'll find him," Halvar said confidently. "There aren't too many
places he can go. Green Village isn't too friendly to Afrikans. Mahak aren't friendly to Afrikans, either, so he won't go to them,"

"There's the Algonkin village," Selim reminded him. "Noam ordered food for the household from the women at the small market, so he must know some of them. And Algonkin women attach
themselves to Afrikan households. I thought I saw one in the kitchen
at the villa."

Halvar tugged as his mustache.

"Maybe, maybe not. Let's see what's happening at Ochiye's
pavilion."

108

He strode to the Broad Way and stopped, gazing over a scene that rivaled the one on the waterfront for confusion.

A line of donkey carts loaded with the goods from the Feria filled the street. Drivers cursed their animals and each other in Arabi, Erse, and Munsi; the donkeys brayed and kicked in response. Among the donkey-powered wagons, men and women hauled handcarts or guided large dogs hitched to three-pole carriers around the larger animals. Whole families straggled between the merchants, the women and children carrying purchases while the man of the house chivvied them along. Everyone was intent on hauling merchandise, and themselves, away from the Feria grounds before the looming storm broke.

"We'd do better walking," Selim groused.

Halvar had to agree with her. He turned back to signal the donkey cart, giving the driver instructions to follow them as best he could. Then he slogged onward towards the Manatas Town wall and the Feria beyond, pushing through the line to head in the opposite direction. Selim and Flores struggled to keep up with him.

The guards at the gate greeted their commander with a spate of excuses about the chaos. Flores took charge, posting his two men just inside the wall and ordering them to assist.

"I know who we're looking for," Flores assured him. "Besides, most the vendors in this mob have stalls at the souk, so you've seen them before. Keep your eyes open for a skinny old Afrikan man. Last time I saw him, he was wearing a striped kaftan and an embroidered cap." To the waiting crowd, he yelled, "One line, and keep moving!"

Halvar shrugged and left Flores struggling to create order. The wind was picking up, and neither the vendors nor the customers wanted to be in the open when the darkening clouds burst and deposited their burden on Manatas. It didn't look as bad as the storm that had leveled the Feria ten days before, but it would be nasty, just the same.

Past the wall, things were even more chaotic. Even the vendors who had stayed for the bitter end of the Feria were dismantling their tents, folding the rough hempen covers into bundles, stacking the posts neatly, then packing the lot onto waiting donkey carts, dog-poles, or the backs of slaves. The temporary wooden sheds that had served as warehouses for kutton, tabac and indigo were taken down to be stored in the permanent warehouses at the waterfront against the coming winter storms. Late-coming customers threaded through the chaos, haggling over whatever merchandise the vendors didn't want to haul back with them to their Afrikan or Bretain or Franchen bases.

The voice of Daoud the News-crier cut through the hubbub of Arabi, Erse, and Munsi.

"To all who listen, hear me! All vendors must clear the Feria grounds by sundown today! Tomorrow this field will be reserved for sports and games and contests of strength and skill! The day after, our most excellent Sultan will give judgment at the Grand Divan!"

"Sports and games?" Halvar turned to Selim. "What kind of sports and games?"

"Oh, footraces, and the Locals' playing their stick-and-stone Peace Game," Selim explained. "And men trying to lift an iron bar, or tossing a log. Malik the Smith usually wins the lifting contest, and last year Padraig MacCormack won the tossing."

"Isai thinks he can get into this stick-and-stone game?" Halvar peered at the two groups of Locals in the distance, brandishing long sticks with some kind of netting tied to one end. One group ran at the other, both chased something on the ground, there was a whoop, and they all stopped for a brief respite then did it again. It was mystifying, but harmless as far as he could see.

"If they let him play. It's a Local thing, they do it to please their forest spirits." Selim scanned the crowd.

"How do they get all this stuff off Manatas Island?" Halvar wondered aloud, looking at the laden donkeys, handcarts and porters, all hauling boxes and bales of goods out of the grounds.

"It all goes to the waterfront," Selim told him. "The bargemen row it out to the big ships. Some of the coasters take passengers to the Long Island. The Locals take their canoes up the Great River when the tide is running right. Oh, yes, Don Alvaro, everyone leaves Manatas before winter sets in, even the Locals. Everyone except us Andalusians, who are mad enough to stay here. It's only at the Feria times that Manatas can boast a great population, almost as big as Corduba."

They walked on, pushing through the exiting vendors until they reached the center of the field.

"*Salaam*, Firebrand!" Halvar shouted as he recognized the Mahak, who was carrying one of the long playing-sticks. "What are you doing? I thought you were supposed to be in charge of overseeing the Feria?"

"No thieving today," Firebrand assured him. "And it is important for my team to win, for the honor of the Mahak. The Cherokee and Choctaw are joining the game this year. I have never played against them." He shook his stick for emphasis.

"I hear there will be a team from the madrassa," Selim said, with the air of a connoisseur. "One of the Afrikan students, Isai ibn Ochiye, is supposed to be their leader."

"Pah!" Firebrand snorted. "Halflings! Afrikans and Franchen and Bretain fathers with Algonkin mothers. They don't understand anything about the game except to run around and shout."

"But you'll let them play?"

He shrugged. "They won't last long. The wagers are already set. No one is wagering more than a white wumpum on the madrassa team." He turned, heading for the shouting group of Locals at the north end of the field.

"You can't just drop everything for a game," Halvar protested. "I need you now!"

Firebrand stopped.

"What is so important that you take me away from the game?"

"The Afrikan, Noam, who served as Ochiye's chief servant. We have to talk to him, but he's hiding here somewhere." He stretched to his full height to see over the mass of people.

"Ochiye's pavilion is over there." Selim pointed to the spot where Yakub was directing brawny bodyguards in packing the remaining goods. Halvar marched through the shouting, cursing, stumbling crowd.

"*Salaam*, Yakub ibn Ochiye. I was told I'd find you here. Dr. Moise is finished with his examination; you may claim your father's body for burial when you will."

"I'll send Noam," Yakub said. "If I can find him, that is. He's supposed to be helping me with the packing, but he's gone off on some errand. He's impossible! Thinks he's the master of the house now that my father is gone."

Isai pushed through the crowd to join his brother. Yakub turned on him angrily.

"Where have you been? Chasing stones? Waving your foolish stick?"

Isai looked at the long stick with the small woven net attached to the end that had been bent into a half-circle.

"You don't understand," he protested. "This is for the honor of Ochiye! I am no less Cherokee because my father came from Afrika."

"Our father will be buried tomorrow," Yakub snapped. "It is no time for you to be running around with your arse bare, pretending to be what you are not. If you can't do anything else, you can go to the muskat and arrange for Imam Talib to bury our father properly."

"I'll do that as soon as I can find Owen," Isai promised. "He told me after our morning practice that he had to go to Green Village to say goodbye to his father, but he promised he'd meet us after midday prayers for the second practice. He hasn't shown up yet."

"Who is Owen?" Halvar asked.

"He's from West Caster, a fresh student just entered since the beginning of the fall Feria," Isai said. "His father lodges in Green Village, so Owen spends part of his time there. He's very keen on the Peace Game, says he learned from the Locals in West Caster. I need him to make up the ten for the team."

"Your game is not important," Yakub scoffed. "We have to get this merchandise under cover before it is ruined by rain. We have to bury our father. We do not have time to run around waving a stick, chasing a stone!"

"You don't understand!" Isai wailed.

Halvar stopped the argument.

"You two can settle this later. Right now, what's really important is to find Noam."

"There he is!" Selim yelped, pointing at the crowd.

Halvar strained to make out one person in the shifting kaleidoscope of colorful tunics, long and short shirts, jackets and coats. He spotted Noam, in his striped tunic and white embroidered cap, making his way along the path that led to the nearly dismantled tent.

"Over there!" Selim shoved her way into the crowd.

Halvar turned to Firebrand, but the Mahak was already ahead of him.

"Stop that man!" Firebrand gestured with the stick he was still holding.

The watchmen started toward Noam, who looked up, realized that someone was after him, and showed he was sprier than his years would indicate. He slid through the crowd, pushing vendors and donkeys out of his way.

Firebrand let out a whoop that was echoed by his watchmen. The chase was on!

112

21

THE MAHAK WATCHMEN DODGED THROUGH THE CROWD, unhampered by clinging clothing. Halvar panted in the rear, furious that he could not keep up with the agile Locals.

Noam's white-capped head bobbed here and there as he slithered through the mass of vendors, who muttered and cursed at the pursuers. Donkeys brayed their annoyance at being unceremoniously kicked out of the path of the pursuers. Dogs yelped as they were shoved aside. Porters cursed in three languages.

"Stop that man!" Halvar shouted, first in Arabi and then in Erse. "I want him alive!"

Muttering and murmuring, men and women edged aside, making a path for the watchmen as they went after their prey. Whooping in glee, the Mahak pursued their quarry as he headed north past the boundary of the Feria into Local territory.

Halvar's long legs shortened the distance between him and Noam, but the agile Afrikan eluded his grasp, dodging in and out of the tents and sheds, pushing piles of baskets and jars into the path. Loud curses followed him as the owners of the baskets and jars tried to salvage their belongings as Halvar and the Mahaks pounded by.

Noam stopped briefly to catch his breath. Halvar lunged forward, only to lose sight of the older man as he knocked a tent-pole out from under the roof of a pavilion. The owner of the tent screamed in wrath as Halvar thrashed his way out of the enveloping canvas.

"Where'd he go?" Halvar panted, looking around for that bobbing white cap.

"Over there!" Firebrand had avoided the tent but had run afoul of a line of donkeys being loaded with packs instead of hitched to carts.

They had reached the line of trees that marked the edge of the Feria. The Mahak was barely breathing fast; Halvar gasped for air. Selim trotted behind him.

"He's gone into the woods. We'll have to track him."

Halvar tugged at his mustache.

"He's not running away, he's running *to* something or someone who he thinks will protect him."

"Not in Green Village." Selim looked across the Feria to where the bulk of the Gardens of Paradise loomed above the trees. "Afrikans don't stay there. Too many Oropans for their taste."

"Who does this Afrikan know in Manatas?" Firebrand scowled. "He comes with Ochiye from the south. He doesn't stay here long, just for the Feria."

"He's traveled in the south," Halvar said. "He knows the Cherokee." He turned to Firebrand. "Where are your Cherokee and Choctaw visitors staying? Are they in your village, or do they have their own camps?"

"They have their own camp, just past our village. They have set up tents, like the Huron."

"Not huts, like the Algonkin?" Halvar asked.

"When they travel, they use tents. They call them tipi."

Halvar thought aloud. "If Noam knows the Cherokee, it could be he's going to the Cherokee camp. He thinks the Cherokee will protect him."

"Not if we catch him first!" Firebrand shouted something in Munsi to his watchmen. The squad gathered at the path that led north from the Feria to the Local's villages.

"He may know the Cherokee, but he does not know Manatas," Firebrand said confidently.

"I think he does," Halvar said grimly. "He travels with Ochiye, so he's been here often. It strikes me now we may be looking at something more than a family quarrel."

The path wound around the beaver pond then forked one way going west to Green Village, the other east to the Local villages. A faint trail was visible on the broken twigs and fallen leaves, signs of the coming winter, that carpeted the forest floor. Firebrand squatted to examine the signs. Halvar joined him. He patted the leaves, frowning at some red dust that came off on his fingers.

"He's headed east," he stated, "but not on the path to the Mahak village. He'd take the beaten path if he was going there."

"Cherokee or Choctaw?" Firebrand asked.

"Most likely Cherokee. Yona is Cherokee." Halvar pointed to scuff-marks. "He's wearing leather shoes. Not maccasin. Here are his footprints. He's running but losing speed. He's not a young man, no matter how fit he is."

"You are a good tracker," Firebrand observed.

"That' s what I was trained to do. Like Old Sergeant Olaf said, 'Notice everything, even what isn't there."

"A wise man, your Sergeant."

"The best I ever knew."

Halvar turned back to the scuff-marks. Ahead of them, someone yipped,"He's here!" Halvar and Firebrand loped through the trees, following the footsteps.

A large Local in the Cherokee costume of deerskin hunting shirt and leggings, his hair bound with a simple leather band, stood guard at the entrance to the circle of tents that made up the Cherokee camp. Noam ducked behind him as the guard stepped forward, tomahawk in hand, to face the oncoming pursuers.

"This place is Cherokee! You will not pass!" he announced in halting Arabi.

Firebrand moved forward.

"That man is wanted for questioning," he said in Munsi.

"He says he is Cherokee. He says he has a Cherokee woman. He says he will not go to the stone place." The guard punctuated his determination by slapping the blade of his drawn tomahawk on his open palm.

"We don't want a fight," Halvar said in Arabi. "But that man, Noam, knows who killed an Afrikan named Ochiye. We do not want to harm him, we only want to talk to him."

"I do not have to talk to you!" Noam sneered from behind his guardian.

"It would be better if you did," Halvar said. "Tenente Flores might not be allowed to do his worst here, but there's a good reason this Mahak has been named Firebrand. He doesn't like poisoners, Noam Vizier, and you poisoned your master Ochiye."

"Master? Hah!" Noam spat out. "We were brothers, of the same father! Only *his* mother was the chief wife, and mine was a servant."

"A slave," Halvar said, with a knowing nod.

"Ochiye could not have survived a day without me!" Noam said. "I learned the Cherokee language, I found the goods to sell. I even found him the Cherokee woman."

"But not the Afrikan," Halvar said.

"Lady Tekla was chosen for him in Afrika," Noam admitted. "He did not want her the way he wanted the Cherokee."

"So you suggested that he leave her here in Manatas," Halvar guessed.

"Oh, she agreed with me," Noam said snidely. "She and Ochiye did not like each other. He only gave her the one son. No more children from her! Not like Yona. Not like Yona's servant, my woman. She gave me Gavril."

"And you ran the business in the south," Halvar said.

"Yes! It was I who found the big lizard hides, it was I who found the planters who were growing sugar." His voice swelled louder with each statement. "Ochiye would be nothing without me!"

"It was also you who found the Maya girl. How did it make you feel when Ochiye took her for himself?"

Halvar had edged over to the right of the Cherokee guard during the exchange, his hand on the hilt of his dagger. Firebrand stepped to the left, the bent stick with the netting at the end still in his hand. Halvar slid his dagger out of its sheath, never taking his eyes off the guard.

"Ochiye took her, but he could not use her!" Noam jeered. "And the boy, Isai, he wanted her, but he would not go where his father had lain. It is *haram*, forbidden."

"So, you decided you'd had enough of Ochiye and his bullying," Halvar said. "You got the mal-chinee. You made Maya put the poisoned fruit into the basket."

"You have no proof!" Noam's voice quavered. "I will not say yes or no. You will have no confession from me."

"We have the jar with poisoned preserves. A dog ate something that was left for the Scavengers and died. Dr. Moise has the dog right now. He will find proof the dog died of your poison." Halvar stepped closer to the Cherokee guard's right, while Firebrand moved to the left.

Noam looked uneasily right and left. He suddenly darted out from behind his guardian, dodging Firebrand, who slashed out with his game-stick. The Cherokee parried the blow with is tomahawk while Noam scurried closer to the Cherokee camp.

116

Halvar stretched one long arm to catch Noam while the guard was distracted. Noam skipped back, shouting something in Cherokee that brought the Locals boiling out of their tents. Halvar found himself facing not one but four enraged Locals, each carrying some kind of weapon.

He backed away, hands raised. There was a time to fight and a time to give in, and he had no wish to end his days sliced to pieces on this island in the middle of Nova Mundum.

Firebrand, however, was not about to give in to a mere Cherokee. He and the guard circled each other, one with a tomahawk, the other armed only with his playing-stick, each looking for an opening.

The guard raised his arm for a killing blow. Halvar 's booted foot slid on a stone, sending him crashing into the Cherokee guard. Firebrand leaped out of their path, leaving Halvar to wrestle with the guard, using all his strength to keep the blade of the tomahawk from his face.

Slowly, inch by inch, Halvar levered the tomahawk away. One final effort, and he rolled over, pinning the Cherokee underneath, Now it was Halvar's blade that threatened his opponent.

"What is this!"

The voice above them stopped the fight. Se-Kwa-Ya and Te-Kum-Se had emerged from their camp to see who was fighting whom. Halvar scrambled to his feet and made a hasty salaam.

"Honored sachems, we ask your pardon, but the man Noam is accused of killing the Afrikan trader Ochiye Aboutiye. We must take him back to Manatas Town to question him further. He refuses to go with us."

"I claim protection from the Cherokee!" Noam quavered, appealing to the Cherokee sachem.

Halvar brushed dead leaves and dirt from his coat. At least he had retained his cap! Once again he salaamed, and hoped the Cherokee would recognize the gesture as one of conciliation.

"According to our law, which is called Sharia, one who is accused must stand trial. We must bring this man back to face his accusers. Sultan Petrus will judge him at the Grand Divan."

Se-Kwa-Ya turned to Noam.

"This man Ochiye. I know him. He is married to a woman of my second wife's clan. Why do these people say you killed him?"

"They have no proof," Noam said, his eyes glittering with malice. "Only suppositions. There was poison used that comes from the south, and I come from the south."

Se-Kwa-Ya eyed Halvar warily and continued to speak in stilted Arabi, with a strong Munsi accent.

"I know this man. He comes to the Cherokee territory with trade goods. He had a Cherokee woman. If he wants the protection of the Cherokee, he has it."

Noam grinned at Halvar and turned to follow the Cherokee to the safety of their camp.

"What if I can prove, beyond a doubt, that it was this man Noam and no other who put poison into Ochiye's food?" Halvar shouted at Se-Kwa-Ya's retreating back.

The Cherokee turned to speak just as Selim and the watchmen came panting up the path.

"In two day's time there will be a Grand Divan." Selim stepped forward, speaking Munsi between gasps for breath. "My father, Sultan Petrus, will sit as judge. Halvar Danske will prove that this man, Noam, is a murderer."

"If that is so," Se-Kwa-Ya said slowly, "then we will not protect him. But if you speak lies, we will treat you badly."

"I do not speak lies," Halvar said. "And I will prove that Noam, and no other, poisoned Ochiye."

I only hope I can do it, he added to himself as Noam marched to the Cherokee camp in triumph.

Halvar plodded back in a thickening drizzle that turned into a torrent just as he reached the safety of the town walls. He had to report to the sultan, and he wanted to find out what Dr. Moise had learned from his study of the dead dog.

Should I go back to the taberna tonight? Better not. It's dark, it's raining, and my new coat is messed up as it is. Better to stay at the Rabat barracks.

For a moment, he wondered about the mysterious friends who had appropriated his rooms at the Mermaid Taberna His chest, shoved under the bed, contained nothing of value except his best jacket, the black velvet with silver braid trim, he had been saving for his appearance at the Grand Divan. His small fortune in gold reales was hidden in the false bottom of that chest.

He would deal with all that in the morning. Meanwhile, he had to finish his business at the Rabat.

Some time later, as he headed across the courtyard, splashing in the puddles, he was joined by Dr. Moise.

"I do not thank you for sending that dog to me," the tall Afri-kan complained. "It was badly infested with fleas. I shall be all day in the *hammam* getting rid of them."

"Never mind the fleas. What killed the dog?" Halvar wiped rain-drops off his mustache.

"Most interesting. There was no sign of fruit in its mouth. How-ever, its tongue was blistered, as if it had been lapping some caus-tic substance," Dr. Moise reported. "I checked the basket of refuse from the villa and found a small jug with a crack in the bottom. I surmise that whatever was in the jug must have leaked out into the street, perhaps into a puddle that would attract a thirsty dog."

"That lapped it up and died," Halvar finished. "That makes a difference. It's possible we're looking for two different poisoners."

"With the same victim?" Moise sounded skeptical.

"It happens," Halvar said. He sniffed the aromas emanating from the barracks kitchen. "Something hot would be a good idea, Doctor. Join me for a meal?"

"As long as I don't have to listen to Flores's boasting about the cleverness of Tenente Gomez," Dr. Moise said.

They found places at one of the long tables in the barracks re-fectory, where they got their share of stringy roasted fowl, a bowl of vegetable mush, and a cup of mokka. Dr. Moise left the moment he could. Halvar remained.

Even if half of Flores's yarns were exaggerations, it was be-coming increasingly clear that Manatas was a world apart. He had to know more about it, if only to impart what he learned to the calif…when he found him again.

PART 2
The Grim Peace Game

22

"AND THERE THE MATTER STANDS," HALVAR TOLD SULTAN
Petrus the following day in sultan's quarters in the central tower
at the Rabat.

He had spent the previous evening in the guards' barracks listening to Flores boast of his predecessor Gomez's schemes and
stratagems in dealing with the Locals and the Scavengers. When
he'd had enough of it, he headed for his old room in the Rabat
tower, and the hard plank bed he had hoped he would never use
again. At dawn he had availed himself of the hammam and the
barber attached to the barracks. He handed the soiled coat to the
sultan's servants to be cleaned.

He then sent one of the sultan's servants to the Mermaid Taberna for his second shirt and braes. Another went to fetch Yussuf
the Tailor, who hurried to the Rabat to offer his newest creation, a
natty coat in Bretain-made woolen cloth; it covered Halvar's
thighs but allowed him to exercise more freedom of movement
than the long coats favored by the Andalusians.

His underclothes were delivered with a cryptic message: *Baas
Zilberstam told me to tell you that your friends had soup and mokka and
will find you later.*

Halvar frowned slightly. He would have to confront these mysterious friends—as soon as he finished this business with Noam.
He put the possibility of thievery out of his thoughts and tried to

get his mind back on the business at hand while the tailor fussed about him and Sultan Petrus frowned over his cup of mokka.

Halvar continued his report.

"Noam has the Cherokees' protection. The Maya girl is in the Rabat—I have ordered Flores to make sure his men do not molest her. Dr. Moise examined the dog, which he concludes drank something that leaked from the garbage basket outside Ochiye's villa and died of it. What we have to do is connect Noam with whatever killed the dog."

"I have placed a pocket inside the lining," Yussuf interjected. "And you will note the braid on the hem, which will not hinder your stride, Don Alvaro, but will draw attention to the length of your limbs. The collar will protect against a blade, and I have left room for you to draw your dagger. The cloth is the best of the Bretain woolen, the lining is fine kutton. A good coat, Don Alvaro! And I must thank you for your custom. Three coats in three weeks! At this rate, I will have to hire an assistant, maybe two. You are setting a fashion, Don Alvaro!"

"I didn't mean to," Halvar mumbled. "How much?"

Yussuf waved a hand.

"This is a gift, Don Alvaro. When you are seen wearing it, others will want the same. I will profit from them."

"I don't take favors," Halvar protested. "I'll send silver to your shop."

"But not today," Yussuf said. "Today is a festival day for Yehudit. We mark the end of the Harvest Festival and celebrate our Law. We Yehudit don't handle money on festivals."

Halvar recalled seeing processions in the Yehudit quarter of Corduva, with chanting Yehudit holding the scrolls of their Law in their elaborately decorated boxes.

"Enjoy yourself, Yussuf Tailor," he said. "Thank you for taking the time to bring me this coat."

Once the tailor had bowed himself out, Halvar turned to the sultan.

"I'll speak with the Maya girl again."

"The girl is quite safe," Petrus reminded him. "Eva Hakim sent her up to Lady Ayesha's rooms."

"And what does Lady Ayesha think of that?"

"Ayesha gets bored sitting up in the tower with no one but the same girls who came with her from Al-Andalus. Once she heard about Maya, she readily agreed to take the girl into her care, just to have someone different to talk to. No one will get to her there, I can assure you of that. My own guards are stationed at the stairs, and no one can get in or out without going past them."

Halvar considered the occasions at the Calif's House in Corduva when guards had been bribed to look the other way while nefarious persons got into places they should not be. Then he dismissed the unworthy thoughts. The Sultan's Guards, unlike the Manatas Town Guards, were pure Andalusian. They knew only Arabi, and treated the Locals and Afrikans with lordly disdain. Maya would be safe in the sultan's harem.

"The problem is, Excellent Sultan, that there are too many places here on Manatas for a criminal to escape punishment. The Scavengers, Green Village, the Local villages—each is a law unto itself. There should be one law on this island. It's not that big a place, after all. The laws of Al-Andalus are just. Why can't they rule this whole island instead of just this one bit of it?"

"I've been talking with the Sachems on this very matter," Petrus said. "Their shaman Sees-in-the-clouds has advised Gray Goose-feather that it's time to retreat to the Mahak home territory. Mahmoud wants to go to his village on the Long Island. I've offered to make their two villages part of Manatas Town, extending the rule of Al-Andalus to cover all of this island. They've agreed, since they don't use the sites during the winter, as long as we leave a space between our houses where they can construct their villages when they return in the spring."

"What do they want in exchange?"

"Trade goods, of course. Steel tools, knives, hatchets, cloth, and glass beads for decorations. And guns. They want guns." Petrus's scowl deepened. "Guns I don't have, and don't want to have."

"But the Bretains and Franchen have them," Halvar pointed out. "Lovis has enough of them to arm whole regiments. He's got the small cannons, too. Word on the waterfront is that he's mounted them on ships. If Al-Andalus is going to keep Manatas, we'll *need* guns."

"I hate guns!" The sultan gazed down at the ivory peg that had replaced the part of his left leg shot away by Lovis's artillery.

"The calif needs them if he's ever going to take back his lands," Halvar stated flatly. "That means he needs the money and goods from the Feria to pay for them. How long before the tally men finish their accounting? These storms aren't going to get any easier, and I have to get back to Al-Andalus."

"You don't have Leon," Sultan Petrus pointed out. "How are you going to get him out of the Fratery?"

"Place Green Village under Al-Andalus rule, and I'll get him out!" Halvar said firmly.

"Green Village has always been under Mahak rule," Petrus said.

"If the Mahak cede their village to Al-Andalus and go upriver to their own territory, that means Green Village is no longer Mahak," Halvar reasoned. "And once Green Village is under Andalusian rule, Sharia law applies, and Leon di Vicenza must answer to it, along with everyone else on Manatas Island. I'll have him on that ship before winter!"

"Unless something else comes along to distract you," Sultan Petrus murmured.

The Afrikan servant put his head into the room to announce, "A messenger, Excellent Sultan. From Green Village."

"What does Green Village want with me?"

"Not you, excellent Sultan—the Calif's Hireling. They've just found another body."

23

THE MESSENGER FROM GREEN VILLAGE WAS PADRAIG MAC-
Cormack, the oversize Bretain youth who had been one of Leon di
Vicenza's Seekers of Truth and who had apparently taken on a new
profession. He wore an ink-stained apron over his red smock and
gaudy red-and-blue-checked trews, and a folded paper cap covered
his curly red hair instead of the floppy flat cloth cap sported by most
Bretains.

He bowed awkwardly to the sultan and approached Halvar
diffidently.

"It's Owen MacAllan," he said. "A Local found him this morning. Fru Glick said that we should send for you, because you are
the best one to find out who murdered him."

"Oh, she did? Kind of her to think of me," Halvar muttered. "Who
is this Owen, and what makes you think he was murdered?" Owen
was a common enough name among the Bretains,

"He was new to Manatas," Padraig explained. "He'd just come
from West Caster to study at the madrassa. He had no enemies that
anyone knows of."

"What about his family?" Halvar mentally ran down the common motives for murder. "Was he rich?" This might be nothing but
a common robbery, after all.

"His father, Allan MacAndrew, owns a manufactory in West
Caster," Padraig said. "He belongs to one of those Erse Rite sects
that keep to themselves and declare that everyone else is misread-

ing the Holy Book. He's lodging with a pack of them, in a place near the Fratery, well away from the Gardens of Paradises."

"Afraid they might be tainted with sin?"

Padraig's grin grew broader. "They spend what time they're not at the Feria arguing what the Redeemer said or didn't say, and what the Holy Book really means. They're loud about it, too."

"I've met a few such in my travels," Halvar said, with a twist of his lips under his mustache. "What led this fellow to Manatas?"

"No idea. I suppose Owen had a mind to attend the madrassa here, and he persuaded his father to let him stay in student lodgings to be nearer the classes." Padraig sighed. "I wanted to do the same, but you've heard my father. He wants me to learn a useful trade."

"Like printing?" Halvar guessed. "I already know about the printing press. I think Dani Glick keeps it in her attics at the Garden of Paradise. What else can you tell me about this Owen MacAllan?"

"Not much. Like I said, he stayed in lodgings near the madrassa with the other foreign students. The Bretains and Franchen have a house next to the Afrikans, where they have a cook who makes the food they like. Andalusian food doesn't agree with Bretain stomachs. They say it's too spicy; they like things with onions, not peppers."

Halvar thought for a moment, then said, "I've been told over and over that Green Village is not a part of Manatas, that you take care of your own people. Why send for me?"

Padraig's freckles nearly disappeared into his mortified blush.

"Yes, Don Alvaro, that's true. And most of the time we do take care of our own. Donal, at the Gardens of Paradise, acts as our constable if there is a dispute, or a robbery. But this time, there are other considerations. Owen's body was found just outside the boundary between Green Village and the Feria. And there are indications that the one who did it might be connected to the stick-and-stone game. Please come, Don Alvaro."

"If this body was found on the Feria grounds, I suppose I *should* be the one to investigate," Halvar said grudgingly.

"Go, go," Sultan Petrus urged. "Don't worry about Maya. She will still be here when you return."

Halvar settled into his new coat and adjusted his old leather-lined cap. He added the new fur cap to his ensemble.

128

"I've brought the pony cart," Padraig said, leading the way through the courtyard. He stopped as they were accosted by Selim. The teenager wore a crimson jacket of quilted silk that closed over the chest with braided loops, and blue kutton trousers. Her hair was tucked under a small blue turban.

"I'm coming with you," she stated. "I'm Don Alvaro's trusted assistant. He needs me to take notes. I was of great help yesterday. He said so." She looked to Halvar for approval.

He nodded. He couldn't get rid of Selim without revealing her secret, and he did need someone to take notes as he proceeded with his investigations.

"Get into the cart, and be quiet," he ordered.

Padraig muttered something in Erse Halvar hoped Selim didn't understand.

The mare, Mollie, was stamping impatiently outside the Rabat gate. She clearly did not like the donkeys who were the preferred mode of transport in Manatas.

"Hoy! *Salaam aleikum!* Wait for me!" They were interrupted again, this time by a stout young Yehudit in a black coat and broad-brimmed hat, his side-curls bouncing as he trotted along the path to the Rabat from the Broad Way.

"Benyamin? What are you doing here?" Padraig asked.

`Benyamin ibn Mendel gasped for breath.

"I just heard about Owen MacAllan."

"How?" Halvar frowned. News didn't travel that fast in Al-Andalus, not even gossip.

Benyamin held out one of the increasingly ubiquitous news-sheets.

"It's right here, in the *Gazetta*," he said.

Padraig's blush deepened under Halvar's disapproving frown.

"It's news," he argued. "When the body was discovered, we... that is, Simon Singer, the printer...had me set the type in Arabi and Ogham, and run off a few copies to distribute around the Feria and the Madrassa. Fru Glick said that it was the best way to let folk know what had happened, so that if anyone knew anything more, they would come forward. See?"

He pointed out a line of curling Arabi writing, which Halvar could not read, and a matching line of round Ogham letters, which he couldn't read either. His learning had not gotten beyond the ability to make out the Patri Nostri and his own name in Rune.

Selim scanned the news-sheet.

"It says here that the body of Owen MacAllan, a student at the madrassa, was discovered on the playing-grounds of the Local Peace Game, and that anyone with knowledge of the cause of death should report the same to Halvar Danske, the Calif's Hireling. That's you, Don Alvaro,"

"Indeed. What's your interest in this, Benyamin?" Halvar asked.

"I knew Owen," Benyamin explained. "I'm one of the senior students charged with introducing the fresh ones to the rules and customs of the madrassa. I helped him settle into the Bretain lodgings, next to the Afrikans. He wasn't very fluent in Arabi, only knew a few things like *'salaam aleikum'* and words for *yes, no,* that sort of thing, so I explained some of the notices and showed him where the best eating-houses were. "

"Kind of you," Halvar remarked.

Benyamin shrugged.

"I receive a small stipend for lecturing to the fresh students, giving them the rudiments of both Sharia and Oropan Law, before they go on to the more complicated classes.

"Owen arrived at the beginning of the Feria, a month ago. He attended some of the lectures, but I think he spent more time chasing the stone than chasing the Law. And then, to see this!" He took the news-sheet from Selim and waved it under Padraig's nose."This is going too far, Padraig. It is outrageous, to find out that someone one knows has been killed, and in such a...an impersonal way!"

Padraig wiped his inky hands on his inkier apron.

"Simon Singer says it's new tidings, and we have to keep people informed. Besides, at a white wumpum a sheet, we can sell a lot of them. Folk want to know what's happening."

Halvar made a quick decision.

"Benyamin, did you meet with the lad's father when he started his term at the madrassa?"

"I did. Not a good meeting—he's one of those Bretains who scorns anyone not Bretain, especially Andalusians and Yehudit. I had to talk fast to convince him we would not try to divert his son from the path to Godliness."

Halvar sighed, knowing his chances of dissuading the youth were nil.

"Come with us, then, and keep your eyes and ears open. You three call yourselves Seekers of Truth, so help me find it."

24

THE BROAD WAY, WHICH HAD BEEN CROWDED WITH DON-
key carts, strollers, vendors and buyers the day before, seemed nearly
deserted by comparison.

"It's not Frigg's Day already, is it?" Halvar wondered. "Is everyone at the muskat for Mullah Abadul's sermon?"

"It's a Festival for the Yehudit," Benyamin said, and Halvar recalled Yussuf's having told him that earlier. "With the Feria almost
over, a lot of the merchants are at the waterfront, waiting for their
ships to take them back south, like the birds who pass the winter
in warmer climates. Of course, there are still people who have cases
pending at the Grand Divan. They're staying until their legal prob-
lems are resolved. Then, there are the ones who want to wager on
the stick-and-stone game."

"And the students stay at the madrassa all through the winter." Halvar tried to understand the workings of this odd settlement. "And the Andalusians who serve them."

"And some of the Locals," Selim put in.

"And the folk at Green Village, they stay all winter, too. Leon
held his debates at the Mermaid Taberna all last winter. It must
have heated the place up!" Padraig chuckled. "I wanted to stay
last year, but my father insisted we go back to our place in West
Caster to forge more knives. This year, I can stay, because I'm
learning the printing trade." He glared defiantly at Halvar.

They passed the street of Afrikan villas, where a crowd had
gathered to send Ochiye Aboutiye on his final journey. Halvar gripped

131

his amulet and murmured a brief prayer, asking the Redeemer and his Mother Mara to allow the Afrikan to go wherever he belonged. Valhalla seemed an unlikely place for a trader, but surely he didn't deserve the torments of the fiery Kristo Hell, or the freezing cold of Niflheim, no matter how unpleasant he had been to his wives, children and servants.

Once past the wall, Halvar barely recognized the swath of ground before him. The tents and sheds of the Feria had been removed, leaving an expanse of beaten earth with only occasional tufts of grass and shrubs that had not been cut away to make more room for the vendors. Scavengers picked through the grounds for anything that might have been lost or discarded, and geese followed the Scavengers, pecking at the ground and daring anyone to stop them.

At the entrance to the Feria grounds, a gang of carpenters were busy constructing a wooden scaffold where Sultan Petrus and the other civic leaders could sit and observe the Local game, which would be played once the decisions arrived at the Grand Divan had been made public. Across from them, several groups of Locals had gathered, their sticks in hand. Halvar hoped their game would not result in too much bloodshed. He recalled the melees of his youth in the Dane-March, chasing an inflated pig's bladder through the streets of Koben Haven, and the brawls that had ensured after similar bouts when one Free Company had challenged another during the lulls between battles.

"How seriously do the Locals take this game?" he asked as they approached the lane that led out of the Feria to the fence that surrounded the Gardens of Paradise.

"Very seriously," Benyamin said. "The Mahak and the Algonkin used to be bitter enemies, until the Andalusians came and started regulating trade on Manatas. Even now, Mahak don't marry Algonkin.

"The sachems made peace before my father and I came here, and now they restrict their battles to the Local game. Their shamans chant and invoke the spirits of their ancestors before the game, and whoever scores the most goals is declared the winner."

"And they use those sticks with the nets on the end to catch the stone." Halvar nodded. He might not know the fine points, but he felt he had a basic grasp of what this game was about.

"There's the body," Padraig interrupted, pointing to a knot of people gathered at a line of shrubbery. He stopped the pony, and held the cart while the passengers got down.

A narrow dirt path had been trampled between the iron fence that surrounded the Gardens of Paradise and the field of the Feria just beyond it. More shrubbery discreetly veiled what Halvar recognized by sight and smell as the privies used by the patrons and staff of Green Village's premiere center of entertainment.

Firebrand was waiting for him with a squad of his Mahak watchmen. Next to Firebrand stood Dani Glick and her hulking doorman, Donal. Beside them was another Bretain, a well-fed man of middle years dressed in the Bretain woolen smock and trews who stood out from the rest like a crow in a flowerbed. Unlike the other Bretains, his smock was a grubby brown with no other color in it at all, and his head was covered with a broad-brimmed high-crowned hat instead of a flat cap in the checked and striped clan patterns favored by the Green Villagers.

Frater Iosip, Green Village's principal medical expert, stood over the corpse, scanning it without touching it.

"What cheer?" Halvar greeted the Mahak.

"No cheer," Firebrand said grimly. "I tell you, Hireling, as I told this Bretain. I did not kill this lad."

"Who says you did?" Halvar looked at the Green Villagers.

"Him. Allan MacAndrew. The father of the dead boy," Padraig murmured to Halvar, nodding towards the severely dressed Bretain.

"He's a Red One, a savage! They kill any who get in their way," the stout Bretain snarled at Firebrand. "They are ungodly, worshiping forest demons!"

"Why does he think you did this?" Halvar turned to Firebrand.

"Because I found him," Firebrand explained. "I was walking the field, as I always do before the game, and I saw him lying in the bushes, just as he is now."

"You haven't moved him?" Halvar stepped closer to the body. It lay halfway into a shrub—not burnweed, he thanked the Redeemer and Thor for that!—stiff and cold.

"I turned him over when I saw the body to see who it was."

"He was lying on his face, then?"

"He was. I knew he was dead when I saw the back of his head." Firebrand gingerly put out one foot to point to the gray matter that had seeped out of the cracked skull.

"When was this?" Halvar swallowed hard, grateful that he'd had a light breakfast of maiz cakes and mokka at the Rabat instead of the porridge he would have had at the Mermaid Taberna.

"Just after daybreak, when the bells in Green Village ring for prayers and the shouters in Manatas do the same. It was light enough to see."

"What did you do when you found him?" Halvar edged gingerly around the body, scanning the ground for footprints or other signs left by the murderer.

"He called out to me," Donal put in. "I was using the necessary in the back of the house. I came to the fence, looked over, and saw the body. I got Fru Glick."

"And when I saw the body, I sent for Frater Iosip," Dani added.

"A dreadful thing, for one so young to be brutally taken from this world," the Kristo said. "May the Redeemer and his Mother Mara accept him into Paradise."

"Then you ran to your printer and had him put out a *Gazetta*," Halvar complained to Dani Glick. "Only when you had done all that did you send for me. Why not leave it to your tame Bretain?" He jerked his head at Donal, who growled something in Erse under his breath.

"But you're so good at finding murderers, Halvar," Dani said sweetly. "Donal is good at breaking up fights, but murder is something that needs a professional."

"What are you doing, standing around talking? Why haven't you taken this Local and hanged him?" the burly Bretain roared. "Who are you, anyway?"

Halvar turned to the infuriated man.

"I am Halvar Danske, the Hireling of the Calif of Al-Andalus. I have dealt with other murders, here in Manatas and in Corduva, which is why Fru Glick has called on me to find out who killed your son."

"*He* did!" Allan waved at Firebrand, who stood, tall and impassive. "I saw him standing over my son's body! He's even holding the very weapon that killed him!"

Halvar eyed the arched stick with the net that Firebrand carried, then peered at the wound in the young man's head.

"Unless he had time and means to wipe this thing clean of all blood and brains, this is not what that killed your son," he pronounced. "The body is stiff. There are leaves over it. He has to have been here overnight, maybe since as long ago as yesterday afternoon. You may ask your own medical man, Frater Iosip, if you don't believe me."

"Quite true," Frater Iosip confirmed. "The limbs have already stiffened. The insects have had time to lay their eggs, but no beasts have come to feast upon him. I would say the time of his passing was just after sunset last night, perhaps a little later, but certainly not this morning."

"What was he doing out after sunset?" Selim spoke for them all.

"Meeting his murderer," Halvar said grimly. "Frater Iosip, this lad was Bretain, so there should be no difficulty in taking him to your deadhouse. Will you look at him well and see if you can find out what killed him?"

"That is easy enough to see," Allan sneered. "It was one of those Devil-damned Local game sticks. I told him not to get into their games. I told him it was not seemly for a Bretain to mix with Locals. They are not of the Elect, they pray to their forest demons. I told him and told him!"

"But he did anyway," Halvar said. "Then he came here, to Manatas, in the country ruled by Islim and the Prophet. Isn't there a collegium in West Caster?"

"Not as good as the madrassa in Manatas," Allan admitted with reluctance. "One must learn Sharia in Nova Mundum if one is to do business in Manatas."

"Owen was far more interested in the stick-and-stone game than in my lectures on Sharia Law," Benyamin said with a rueful smile.

"Why would a Bretain play this game?" Halvar wondered aloud. "Not to say anything against you, Allan."

Allan's face reddened, whether with shame or rage Halvar could not tell.

"My good wife's father was Bretain, come with mine to Nova Mundum when the Erse Rite became corrupted by evil, sinful men who refused to do the Lord's Will!" he sputtered. "The Wampanoag are our neighbors, and they play the game all summer. They let Owen join them as a jest last year, and he got so good at it they allowed him to play on their team when they went against the Narragansett. He scored the winning goal, and after that, he could do no wrong. He played with them again this summer. It was for this reason that I brought him to Manatas, to get him away from that ungodly savage game."

"In short, he found kindred souls here," Halvar said. "Like Old Sergeant Olaf always said, 'Folk find some things, some things find folk.' I suppose it was kismet. The Three Old Women wanted your son to play this game, no matter what you did to stop him."

Firebrand frowned. "It is not fitting for the halflings at the madrassa to ask to join us," he said. "But Isai the Afrikan said he was part Cherokee, and others of his group had Cherokee or Powhatan or Algonkin or Lenape mothers, and Sachem Mahmoud was willing to allow them to play the first round. I do not think they would have lasted past that." He sniffed his scorn at the ineptitude of non-Mahak athletes.

Halvar squatted to feel the ground around the body.

"It rained early last night," he observed, "but the leaves over the body are dry." He squinted at a faint mark near the body, tracked another like it from the shrubbery to the path. He looked at the lad's sturdy brogues, then at the scuff marks on the path.

"Someone's been clever," he stated. "The footprints were brushed out. Even so, there's something here. Firebrand, I've seen beads on your macassin, but nothing like this." He picked up a small blue-dyed object from the path. It looked familiar

"That's made from a porcupine's quill." Firebrand joined Halvar on the path. "Someone running tripped on something, maybe slick mud from the rain?" He pointed to a dent in the gravel of the path. "This came off a macassin."

"We can't go looking at every pair of macassin on Manatas Island," Halvar said. "But quills? Do the Mahak use quills for beads?"

"Some do," Firebrand admitted. "Most prefer to use the beads we buy from Andalusians. This is dyed blue, not a color Mahak use. It is more common among the Huron, who still prefer the old ways."

Halvar checked Firebrand's feet. His macassin were plain, tied at the ankles with sinew.

"You don't decorate your macassins at all."

"Even if I did, I still did not kill this Owen boy."

"I believe you." Halvar took his string of wumpum from his pocket to add the blue quill bead to it and frowned. It matched the one he'd picked up in the mud behind the Mermaid Taberna. Whoever wore those macassins must have been one of those attackers.

"I had no quarrel with him," Firebrand went on. "I did not want him to play our game, but I would not kill him for trying to do it."

"Someone killed him," Halvar said slowly, "but I don't think the game had anything to do with it."

"Then, why is he dead?"

"I'm beginning to think it's not because of anything he did but because of something he saw or heard." Halvar shivered in the growing wind. "Dani Glick, you called for me, you've got me. But I do the job my way, as I see fit. And the first thing to do is find out as much as I can about this poor lad, and the place to start is in Green Village."

Padraig held the pony while Donal and Frater Iosip put the body of Owen MacAllan into the cart. Halvar drew Firebrand aside.

"I'll take care of things in Green Village. Can you get into the Cherokee camp?"

"What for? The Cherokee have nothing to do with the Bretains. Their lands are closer to the Afrikans. They speak Munsi with an odd accent, and some of the sachems and shamans know some Arabi because they trade with Afrikans, but they don't speak Erse."

"At least one Bretain has traveled near Cherokee territory that I know of. They have a habit of popping up where you don't expect them. And there's that Afrikan, Noam, who also traveled in Cherokee territory and claims protection from them. Find out if he's still there, and what he's up to."

"Why do you suspect him of wrongdoing? Have you any proof?"

"You heard what I told the Cherokee sachem. The poison that killed Ochiye came from the south; Noam could have got it when he went there with Ochiye. He said he hated Ochiye, and I'm sure he is lying when he says he did not know Ochiye had a strange illness that made him weak and dizzy."

"The Afrikan's voice was loud enough," Firebrand observed. "I will go to the Cherokee and see what they have to say about this Noam. The Peace Game is to begin at noon. I will meet you at the playing field then."

Halvar watched the Mahak amble up the path and disappear into the trees. Then, he followed the procession to Green Village. There was something tickling the back of his mind, something that had been said when no one knew he'd been listening, something that stuck like a burr under his pack. He'd get to it in time.

First, though, he had to solve this puzzle before the outraged father started a war against the Locals that could only end in tragedy for both sides.

25

GREEN VILLAGE WAS HUMMING WITH THE NEWS OF OWEN
MacAllan's gruesome death. The entire population had come out
to view the body of the boy who had been among them so briefly.

Workmen in colorfully patterned trews or plain breeches, their
smocks covered with leather or canvas aprons, waited at the common
ground in the middle of the settlement in a row, arms folded.
Behind them were the Green Village women—sturdy laundresses,
spinners and weavers in checked and striped skirts and close-laced
bodices, their hair covered with white caps or colorful scarves.
Even the boys had been released from their lessons at the Fratery
school, and the young girls stood beside their mothers. They had
seen much bloodshed, but this time the corpse was one of their
own.

It was Cormack MacCormack, Padraig's father, who spoke for
the townspeople.

"What happened? Who did this?"

"Someone struck this lad down," Halvar informed the group.
"Frater Iosip thinks it must have been some time last night. He's
been dead about twelve hours, from the look of him. Did anyone
see him last night?"

Cormack made a quick calculation in his head.

"Just after the last prayer bell rang at the Fratery? All good folk
should be indoors by then, and in their beds soon after that."

"Some aren't," Halvar reminded him. "Fru Glick's establishment
is open until nearly dawn."

"True. The lights burn at the Gardens of Paradise until the stars go to bed," Dani agreed with a sly smile. "However, I can assure you this lad was not among my customers. I have no idea what he was doing lurking behind the necessaries, on the path to the Feria after sundown."

Halvar surveyed the crowd over.

"If anyone can tell me anything about this lad, Owen MacAllan, come forward and meet me in the main hall of the Gardens of Paradise." Before Dani could protest, he told her, "I need somewhere to conduct interviews, and yours is the largest place in Green Village, except for the Fratery. I don't think Abbas Mikhael will let these good ladies into his compound, even if they have important information. So, the Gardens of Paradise it will have to be. And I will keep my trousers on," he murmured for her ears alone as Dani reluctantly opened the iron gate to allow him into her domain.

He turned to Selim.

"Stay here," he ordered.

"You need me to take notes!" Selim protested.

"Not in here," Halvar told her. "I want you to find out all you can about Owen from these young folk. They won't tell me, but they'll tell you. It's important!" he added to stop further discussion. "Someone must have seen or heard something. Remember what Old Sergeant Olaf said: 'Everything is important, even what isn't there.'"

With that, he left Selim to question the Green Village youngsters as he followed Dani into her pleasure palace.

The central room of the Gardens of Paradise looked considerably less tempting in the cold light of morning than when filled with hazy smoke and flickering lamplight. The paintings of nymphs and satyrs with which Leon di Vicenza had decorated the walls seemed garish instead of glorious. There was a stale smell of tabac and hemp, reinforced by residues on the bits of clay pipes that littered the floor.

Dani looked almost apologetic as she regarded the mess.

"All this bother about Owen has distracted my help," she explained. She called out sharply, "Where are you, you lazy sluts? Get this mess cleaned up!"

Halvar regarded the detritus of the previous night's revelry with disdain.

"Is there another room we can use? Not your office. That's too small, and I wouldn't want to put you out." He headed towards the stairs that led to the second story.

"Those rooms are not suitable," Dani said quickly. "You can use the private dining room."

She steered him to the corner farthest from the stairs, where a door opened into another room furnished with a large table, Oropan-style chairs, a sideboard laden with crockery, and an iron apparatus that emitted pleasant warmth. It was something like a brazier, but one that enclosed the fire so that it could be placed in the center of the room, and had a long pipe leading from the fire to a window, where it discharged the smoke outside. Halvar regarded this with approval. The morning chill had been penetrating after the rain.

"One of Leon's ideas," Dani explained. "It warms the room better than the open fireplace."

"Made by Malik the Smith, I suppose," Halvar said. "So, Dani Glick, what can you tell me about Owen MacAllan and his father. When did they arrive? Where did they stay? Did the father patronize your fine taberna?"

"What makes you think I know anything about this boy?" she countered.

"You make it your business to know everyone who comes in and out of Green Village," Halvar said. "You're the queen of this place, no matter what the men think. So, Queen Dani Glick, who is this Allan the Bretain, and why would someone want to kill his son?"

Dani sank into the nearest chair.

"They came for the Feria. Allan MacAndrew has never been to Manatas before, and from the way he took on about how sinful Green Village is, I don't think he's coming back. One visit to the Gardens of Paradise had him ranting in the street about Scarlet Women and wagering and the sins of gluttony and avarice."

"So, a prude and a prig, the father," Halvar said. "With a hate against the Locals, too."

"Some of the Bretains and Danes are like that," Dani said. "They can't wrap their heads around the idea that someone with a skin darker than theirs is anything more than an animal. Fools!"

Halvar shrugged.

"Small-minded," he agreed with her. "That makes them dangerous enemies. Did this MacAndrew manage to spur any of the Locals to murderous rage by his actions?"

"Not that I know of," Dani said. "Of course, none of the Mahak come to the Gardens of Paradise, and most of my halfling girls are the result of Oropan or Andalusian men taking Algonkin women, either by force or by consent.

"I think that's mainly what put him off—seeing how well people get on here in Manatas. He was loud about how dreadful it was that Afrikan and Local women were allowed to serve Oropan men."

"What did he expect, Danic beauties?" Halvar scoffed. "One of your halfling girls might take that as an insult, but I don't see any of *them* taking their wrath out on the lad."

"They keep their mouths shut, or they're out in the cold," Dani snapped. "And it gets very cold on Manatas Island in the winter. Whatever happened to that boy, Halvar, didn't happen because of anything his father said in here."

Halvar pulled at his mustache.

"Then, why?"

"That's for you to find out," Dani said with another sly smile.

Halvar sat for a moment, tugging at his mustache. That something was still lurking in the back of his mind, something important that he'd missed.

His attempt to track it down was were interrupted by a tap at the door. A young frater, his scalp newly scraped for tonsure front to back, poked his head into the room.

"With your permission, Fru Glick. Don Alvaro, Frater Iosip sent me to tell you that he has made an examination of the young man Owen MacAllan and wishes to speak with you."

"Go, hear what he has to say," Dani said.

"Not coming with me?" Halvar asked.

Dani shuddered.

"I leave such details to you. I have to make my Gardens of Paradise clean again."

26

HALVAR FOLLOWED THE YOUNG FRATER ACROSS GREEN VIL-
lage to the palisade that separated the fratery from the rest of the settlement. Selim shadowed him, determined to regain the position she
had somehow lost overnight.

"You don't want to see this," Halvar warned her.

"You need me to take notes. You told me so." She stood at the
gate as the surly porter eyed them suspiciously.

"You know why you can't go into the fratery," Halvar hissed.

"If I stay outside, people will ask why." She pouted.

"Come along, if you must, but no fainting or losing your lunch."

"There wasn't much blood," Selim protested as she tagged along
behind Halvar and the young frater.

"Indeed, there wasn't." Halvar considered that as he stepped into
Frater Iosip's domain.

Like Dr. Moise's shack at the Rabat, it reeked of herbs and dead
flesh. A cabinet held vials and jars of potions and salves. A rack
against one wall held an assortment of fearsome-looking imple-
ments. The primary difference between these rooms and those of
Dr. Moise was the Crux over the door where Dr. Moise had a quo-
tation from the Prophet's writings invoking the blessings of Ilha
on the sick.

"What have you learned, Frater?" Halvar asked as he regarded
the body stretched out on the table in the center of the room.

"That this young man received a very nasty blow to the back of his head, what we call the occiput. It cracked the bone, and the brain leaked out."

Halvar's frown deepened. "What kind of weapon made those marks? There's almost no blood."

"A rather odd anomaly, for which anatomists have no answer. The brain consists of spongy gray matter, enclosed by the bones of the skull. Under most circumstances, that is enough to protect the brain from blows. Whoever did this was either very strong or possessed of a fury that lent strength to his arm."

"What did it?" Halvar peered at the wound.

"I cannot say with certainty what the weapon was," Frater Iosip said. "The marks indicate something long and slender—a stick, or a branch. Observe, the wound is aligned with the spine vertically, not across the neck horizontally."

"Like a cane, or one of those game sticks," Halvar reasoned.

Selim had drawn closer to the table and was making a careful drawing of the bruises.

"That's odd. It looks just like the mark on the back of *your* head, Don Alvaro."

"What's that? Have you been wounded again?"

Frater Iosip peered through his lenses at Halvar's neck, which still showed signs of bruises inflicted the night before.

Halvar shrugged. "Just some robbers, nothing serious. They didn't get what they were after."

"Sit down and let me examine you!" Frater Iosip insisted. "A blow to the head can be deadly."

"As we see here," Halvar agreed, indicating the late Owen Mac-Allan. "But I had my cap on. It's lined with boiled leather, and I had a fur cap over that. That softened the blow."

"Which appears to have been made with the same sort of instrument as put an end to this lad's life. The Redeemer and his Mother Mara must have you in their keeping, Halvar Danske."

Or the god Thor and the Three Old Women, Halvar added silently.

Selim distracted the medical man from further examination.

"What's this?" She pointed to a tiny fragment lodged in the hair that curled down Owen's neck.

"Interesting." Frater Iosip carefully removed the bit of fiber. "It looks like a hemp strand."

"How did it get there?" Halvar asked.

"It's not part of his clothing," Selim observed. "That's all Bretain wool. Smock, trews—all wool. They raise sheep in West Caster. Padraig told me so."

"So, not something this lad owned," Halvar concluded. "Something from the weapon, perhaps?" He turned to Selim. "Can you spare a scrap from that notebook of yours, laddie?'

Selim tore a page in half, and Halvar slid the paper under the bit of hemp. He then eased the two quill beads from his wumpum string, folded the evidence into the paper, and handed it to Selim.

"Take care of this, laddie" he said. "This piece of hemp and these two beads may be enough to hang a man." He turned back to Frater Iosip as Selim secured the precious paper in her notebook.

"What else can you tell me about the one who did this? Did the killer strike from the right or the left? He was a good-sized lad. Was the killer taller than he?"

Frater Iosip studied the body again.

"As to whether the killer favored the right or left hand, that is difficult to say. The blow came directly from the back. Height? Again, difficult to say. Not much shorter, but not taller. Perhaps a little shorter. If the weapon was one of those Local game sticks…"

"If?" Halvar's eyebrows rose.

"I do not want to accuse one of our Mahak protectors of such a vicious attack," Frater Iosip said, "but I must admit there is a strong possibility the weapon used *was* a game stick. Look for one covered in gray matter and red hair.

"On further reflection, I would say the killer was at least as tall as his victim. Not shorter, or the blow would not have been deadly, although it might well have left this poor soul senseless, or paralyzed. I once saw a sailor caught by a swinging spar knocked down and left without feeling in his entire body. He died soon after when his poor lungs could no longer take in air. If this lad died immediately, it is because the Redeemer would not, in his mercy, leave him in such a state."

Halvar walked around the table.

"So, this lad goes out after sundown to meet someone at the edge of the Gardens of Paradise. Why?"

"To join a friend?" Selim's eyebrows nearly met over her snub nose as she concentrated. "Who? The boys told me he spent most of his time at the madrassa in Manatas Town. When he came to Green Village, it was to the Sabbath Service with the Pure Sect, who won't go to the Fratery. They didn't think much of his obsession with the stick-and-stone game, either. The lads in Green Village play kick-the-bladder, not stick-and-stone."

"According to Benyamin, the only friends he'd made in Manatas were the students at the madrassa. Mostly the ones who had joined Isai ibn Ochiye's stick-and-stone team," Halvar said. "They wouldn't be here in Green Village.

"Isai said that someone called Owen was supposed to join his team, but he didn't turn up. If this is the same Owen, then we have to conclude that none of the others on that team saw him after their practice or would have reason to seek him out.

"So, whoever he met, it likely wasn't someone from either Manatas Town or Green Village. Selim, come with me. I think we have to have a word with Benyamin's students."

"You won't have to go far," Selim said. "They're all gathered at the playing field to watch Isai and his Manatas team play stick-and-stone against the Mahak and Cherokee."

Halvar grimaced. In Corduva, it had been foot-racing and wrestling that drew the young men away from their studies. In the Dane-March, as here in Green village, it had been kick-the-bladder. As Old Sergeant Olaf said, "Young bucks have to test their horns."

They left the deadhouse. Halvar gratefully drew in a breath, savoring the scent of wood smoke, fallen leaves, and cooking. Someone was preparing a hearty soup for their midday meal.

"Let's get to the playing field," Selim urged. "They'll be setting the boundaries for the game soon. My father will be there—he enjoys watching them practice."

"And I can talk with those madrassa lads," Halvar said.

Dani Glick joined them as they passed the Gardens of Paradise, Donal at her heels.

"Shall we go together?" She smiled gave him her practiced innocent smile.

"What's your interest in this game?" Halvar asked.

"My people are collecting the wagers," Dani said. "Last year, it was the Mahak who prevailed over the Algonkin, but these Cherokee are something new. The odds may be different."

"And the madrassa boys?"

"No odds at all," she said with a dismissive shrug. "Amateurs. They can't possibly last beyond the first round."

"Still, they'll give it all they have," Selim said loyally as they followed the path around the Gardens of Paradise back to the playing field.

27

THE FERIA GROUNDS, WHICH HAD BEEN NEARLY DESERTED
a few hours before, was now filled with people. What looked like the
entire population of Manatas Town had come out to witness the
opening shots of the epic battle between the Locals of Manatas and
the visiting Cherokee and Choctaw.

The sachems of all tribes were present in their ceremonial rega-
lia, with necklaces of beads and cloth turbans decorated with feathers. Their women wore beaded dresses, some of deerskin, some of
Bretain cloth, their braided hair decorated with more beads, feathers and brightly colored ribbons. Sultan Petrus had emerged from
the Rabat decked out in his most impressive military gear, topped
with a large turban decorated with an ostrich plume that bobbed
in the freshening breeze.

He was accompanied by Flores and a squad of Town Guards in
their best green coats, and a squad of his personal guards resplen-
dent in red coats decorated with gold braid. A curtained litter had
been placed near the reviewing stand so that Lady Ayesha could witness the stirring scene in relative privacy, attended by two of her
personal servants. Even a few black-clad Yehudit had forsaken their
ceremonies to witness the great event.

Around the perimeter of the crowd, the inevitable vendors had
set up temporary shops. Several Local women grilled small fish and
maiz-cakes over small braziers. A stout Bretain man had a brazier
from which came the delectable aroma of sausages, forbidden in

Manatas Town but allowed outside its walls. Another Bretain was filling small bark cups from a barrel, the odor of its contents definitely alcoholic. Afrikan women wove through the crowd with baskets of nguba beans, and Local women followed them with baskets of maiz kernels that had burst when heated.

The crowd around the barrel was the target of wrathful imprecations from the bearded imam, who had set up his stand opposite the line of refreshment-servers, punctuating his diatribe with quotations from the Prophet. His counterpart, a Bretain in drab trews and tall hat, echoed his predictions of horrific consequences in the afterlife for those who drank alcoholic beverages to excess and placed wagers on sporting events such as these, citing the Kristo Holy Book and the Redeemer's pleas against worldly vices. Their diatribes drew some spectators, but most of the crowd huddled over copies of the *Gazetta*.

A young man with a sparse red beard read aloud in Arabi to the Andalusians, while a contingent of Danes and Franchen listened to a Bretain's halting translation into Erse. A knot of men surrounded a fellow in a patched kaftan, shabby trousers, and red fez, arguing loudly in various languages and dialects about the calif's tariffs and their possible disposition. A gang of Oropans in well-worn leather coats and jackets, heads topped with broad-brimmed hats trimmed with gobbler feathers, scanned the prancing Locals, shouting encouragement to the nearly naked players, loudly announcing their favorites in salacious terms, convinced the Locals could not understand their language.

Willem of Cos, the entertainer from the Gardens of Paradise, had set up his stand and was declaiming some of his verses; Halvar hoped he had written something to replace "The Stranger and the Sekonk." Would he ever live that disgraceful encounter down?

He caught a fragment of song: "Under the stinking beast..." He gritted his teeth, realizing his battle for that stolen book would never be forgotten. He was now a part of Manatas lore.

The sun had risen to its zenith. The bells of the Fratery rang for midday prayer just as the muezzin's call echoed over the walls of Manatas Town. Everyone stopped to perform their religious duties, whether they bowed, knelt, or simply recited a brief plea to whatever gods or spirits they thought would assist them through their daily toil. Those Locals who had adopted either Kristo or Islim beliefs joined in the prayers, while the rest waited for their friends to finish. Even the Mahak shaman, Sees-in-the-Clouds, recited what

148

Halvar assumed was an invocation to the forest spirits and ancestors revered by his people.

Two large groups of Locals had gathered at the eastern end of
the field. Halvar noted Firebrand at the head of the Mahak team;
the other was led by a muscular Local. Halvar recognized the Cherokee he had fought the day before. The man looked just as formi-
dable carrying a playing stick as he had wielding a tomahawk.

Apart from them, defiantly holding a playing stick, Isai stood
at the head of his small but determined band of madrassa students.

Halvar pushed through the crowd to where Sultan Petrus sat
on a folding camp-chair, his ivory leg propped up before him on a
small cushion.

"What's going on?"

"The madrassa students are demanding the right to play," the
sultan explained.

Halvar looked the opposing teams over. The madrassa team consisted of nine youngsters not yet grown to full manhood; their opponents were taller, broader, and more experienced.

"Why?"

"Honor," Petrus said. "They're halflings, most of them. They say
they are Local through their mothers. They play this game instead
of going to war. It's a test of manhood. Youngsters have to be allowed to show their skills somehow. Better this way than by split-
ting skulls."

Halvar had to agree. Students had plenty of ways of getting
into trouble. High spirits had often led to rough horseplay in Corduva. This game sounded like another version of the same thing.

The sachems of both North and South approached Sultan Petrus with the leaders of all three teams trailing behind them. Behind
them came Benyamin and Sees-in-the-Clouds in their roles as advocates for their two groups.

"Now what?" Halvar wondered.

"Excellent Sultan," Gray Goose-feather said. "We call upon you
as a fair mediator, as you have been in the past, to judge our dispute."

Sultan Petrus sat straight in his chair.

"I act for Al-Andalus, as an *independent* judge," he reminded
them. "I do not favor one party over another. What is your dispute?"

"These halflings want to desecrate the Peace Game!" the Cherokee shouted.

149

"We are children of Local mothers," Isai countered. "We may not be of full blood, but we are as much of our mothers' people as our fathers', whether they be Afrikan, Bretain, Franchen or Andalusian. We play for the honor of Manatas, and our madrassa."

"The Game is a celebration of the spirits of our ancestors," Sees-in-the-Clouds intoned. "It is not a mere pastime. It is not for wagers or for wumpum that we fight, but to please our ancestors."

"It's a test of strength and will," Benyamin argued. "Gods or spirits or whatever are not involved."

Firebrand looked the madrassa team over.

"You cannot play," he stated. "You have only nine. It has been decided that there will be ten warriors from each side on the field."

"We are waiting for Owen MacAllan," Isai said, with a worried glance towards Green Village. "He has not been seen since yesterday."

"He will not join you," Firebrand said bluntly. "He was killed some time last night."

Isai's dark face paled.

"One of you!" He pointed to the Cherokee. "You knew he was our best catcher. You killed him to win this game!"

The Cherokee responded in their own language. Halvar couldn't understand the words, but the meaning was unmistakable, punctuated with waving sticks and fierce scowls.

"That's foolish talk!" He stepped into what he saw was about to become a brawl. "Why would one of these people, who are new to Manatas, kill someone they barely knew?"

Dani Glick had edged closer to the dispute. Now she spoke up.

"Perhaps you can get someone to replace your missing player."

Isai looked baffled.

"Who? We've got all our players from the madrassa right here. Owen made the tenth man, the one we needed to complete our team."

"Does your tenth person have to be a student at the madrassa?" Dani's eyes gleamed as she looked around, sizing up prospective players.

"We *are* the madrassa team," Isai said proudly.

"I have heard that Don Alvaro attended Madrassa in Corduva," Dani hinted, glancing at Halvar from the corner of her eye.

"I didn't attend. I followed Don Felipe to classes," Halvar demurred.

150

"Yet you must have learned *something* when you sat in the room with him."

"I learned Arabi," Halvar admitted. "And some of their philosophy, and Sharia law."

"Then you can be considered a student." Benyamin saw where this discussion was headed. "Isai, will you accept Don Alvaro as your goal tender?"

"What! Me? I don't know anything about this game!" Halvar sputtered.

Benyamin grabbed him by the arm.

"If you don't do this, I'll have to, and I'm not up to it," he hissed into Halvar's ear.

Isai grabbed Halvar by the other arm.

"Don Alvaro! You *must* join us!"

"Why?"

"We need ten to play. We must take the field, if only to prove that we are the equals of these Cherokee from the south."

"Benyamin knows this game. Let him be your goal tender. Leave me out of it!" Halvar shook off his captor and settled his cap firmly on his head.

"Benyamin is too slow and fat," Isai said with brutal candor. "And sometimes he doesn't see the ball when it comes towards him. It's not that hard. We'll do most of the running. We will score the goals on the Mahak side of the field. All you have to do is stand there and not let anyone past you. You can do that much, can't you?" He glanced at Firebrand and the Cherokee. "I know Red Knife, the leader of the Cherokee team. He's a war leader; they've brought him here to take the measure of the Andalusians as fighters. I can tell you a lot about the Cherokee—after the game. Please!"

Halvar looked around for help and didn't find any. Dani Glick had a speculative gleam in her eye. Sultan Petrus was conferring with the Local sachems and shamans. Benyamin, Padraig and Selim stood next to Isai and his eight stalwarts, all of them regarding him with *please please please* looks.

The sultan and the sachems finished their discussion.

"It is agreed," Sultan Petrus announced. "It will be thus. There will be a testing game, not to be counted as part of the true contest. The madrassa team, with the addition of Don Alvaro Danico, the Calif's Hireling, will play a combined team—five from the North, five from the South. There will be ten goals. If the madrassa team can match the Local team in goals, they may continue to play the

Peace Game against the Mahak, the Cherokee, the Choctaw, or who-ever else may wish to join them."

Red Knife, the leader of the Cherokee, advanced on Isai.

"You, Yona's son. You are halfling, Afrikan. You think you are as good as we who are of the full Nation the Cherokee?"

Isai stood his ground.

"I know you, Red Knife. You are a bully. You take meat from small boys and eat it yourself! You force yourself on girls who will not have you!"

Halvar interposed his bulk between the two. *This is personal,* he thought. *Isai has something to prove, and this game is his way of doing it.*

Aloud he said, "What are the rules of this game? I've seen how you run at the ball, or stone, or whatever it is. Do you throw it, or kick it, or what?"

The Cherokee handed him one of his sticks. Halvar gripped and hefted it, testing its weight in his hands. Two slender poles had been bound together with animal sinews to form a heavy club. The wil-low circle at the end was jammed into a gap between the poles, tied down with a hemp cord, smeared with sticky resin to hold the cir-cle in place. It was much heavier than the object preferred by the Mahak, which was willow, bent into a wide arc that held a loosely woven net of hemp cords.

"The ball must be thrown using the net at the end of the stick," Benyamin explained. "You may not touch it with your hands. You may do whatever it takes to keep the other players from picking up the ball with their nets, but you may not hit them with your closed fist."

Halvar nodded. "No hands. I'll remember that. What's this line I'm supposed to defend?"

Selim and Padraig followed Benyamin and Halvar to the west-ern end of the field, where two posts had been set up with a deep scratch in the ground between them.

"That's the goal. The Locals are going to try to get the ball over it. You have to stop them with the stick. You can shove or trip someone, but you can't use your hands, and you can't let go of the stick. That's all you have to know. The rest is up to Isai and his men."

"You should be doing this, not me," Halvar muttered.

"Isai is right, I'm too slow and fat," Benyamin said with a wry smile. "Selim's too small, and Padraig is too clumsy."

"I'm not good at this," Padraig said. "I'm a lummox, can't run to save my soul from the Deceiver. But you're bigger than most of us. They won't get past you!"

"Better take off your new coat," Selim said. "You don't want to get it mucked up."

"And your knife," Benyamin added. "No blades on the field."

Halvar reluctantly slid his dagger out of its sheath and handed it to Selim, along with his new coat.

"Do you really want to keep that cap on your head?" Selim asked, wrinkling her nose. "It looks awful and still stinks of sekonk."

"It reminds me of who I am. And it's lined with leather. I may need it," Halvar said. "I'll put the araghoun cap on over it, just to be on the safe side."

He settled both caps firmly on his head and stood squarely between the two posts, tossing the game stick back and forth in his hands. *Just like my old halberd,* he thought. *Except a bit shorter, and it's got a circle on the end instead of a blade.*

He might not know the fine points of this game, but he knew how to stand his ground. This was no different than his old battle orders: *Stand firm, don't let them get past you!* Only, then, he'd had Old Sergeant Olaf and the rest of the company beside him. Now he was alone, with a horde of howling Locals across the field.

He gripped the stick and stood proudly, ready to face the foe. At least, this time, it wasn't a sekonk!

28

HALVAR STOOD ASTRIDE, HIS HEELS TOUCHING THE LINE between the two posts, gripping the playing stick with both hands. He heard shouts of encouragement in Arabi and Erse from onlookers. Someone was calling out, "Odds on the Hireling, ten to one!"

One way or another, Dani Glick will make me pay for refusing her tempting offer, he thought.

He forced his mind to concentrate on what was happening across the field. The madrassa team had removed coats and shirts but retained their lower garments, whether breeches, trousers or trews. The Locals, on the other hand, had stripped down to breechclouts and paint, even removing their headdresses, feathers, and turbans. The Mahak were conspicuous for their scalp locks, which they stiffened with grease so they stood upright on their heads; the Cherokee had long braids down their backs, wrapped with beaded leather thongs.

Sees-in-the-Clouds and the Cherokee shaman, a woman called Walks-in-the-Mist, followed the action from the sidelines, while Benyamin called out the plays first in Munsi, then in Arabi, finally in Erse. The sachems and the sultan watched from their places on either side of the field, while the rest of the onlookers were kept back by Mahak watchmen and the Town Guards, the first armed with war-clubs, the second with halberds.

As far as Halvar could tell, the game consisted of both sides running back and forth shouting at each other, waving their sticks, and occasionally hitting one another in their pursuit of the "stone,"

154

a wooden orb covered in deer hide. The previous night's rain had left puddles and slippery spots where the grass was still damp; one of the madrassa lads skidded on the heels of his boots, and the Locals pounded on him with glee. While they were pounding their victim, however, Isai managed to find the ball and maneuver it across the Local goal.

"One for madrassa!" Benyamin announced, to the dismay of some and the glee of others. Apparently, Dani Glick's motive for putting Halvar on the field wasn't entirely altruistic. She'd make a tidy sum if these underdogs actually won their match!

Sees-in-the-Clouds hefted the ball again, and the scrum continued. The madrassa team flipped the ball back and forth while the Locals chased them, raising clouds of dust from the drying ground.

Once again, Benyamin shouted, "Goal, for madrassa!"

There was a brief break while the two teams regrouped. Halvar located Firebrand in the huddle, instructing his teammates. Apparently, the Cherokee didn't agree with his strategy, which led to his making a mistake. The Cherokee went after one or another of the madrassa lads, only to find that the ball had been taken from them and was at the goal. Two more for madrassa, and the Locals hadn't even gotten near the madrassa goal. Easy work for Halvar.

He grinned under his mustache. Someone had given young Isai a good lesson in tactics. He wondered which of the old soldiers in Manatas or Green Village had instructed the young halfling, then squinted across the field to see what was happening.

Firebrand gathered his forces and glared at Halvar. This time, when the ball went up, it was a Local who netted it. The whole team headed for the madrassa team's goal.

Halvar gripped the stick, determined that, if he went down, he'd do it fighting. He swung his stick at the first Mahak who reached him, catching his opponent in the midriff. Another Local, a Cherokee, attacked, but Halvar was ready with a backhanded swing. He had no idea where the ball was, but he brandished the stick back and forth, daring the Mahak and Cherokee to close in. He squinted through the dust, trying to make out where Firebrand was. If anyone had that ball, it would be him.

Something came at him over his head. He stuck the stick up to deflect it. The ball bounced off the leather circlet and flew back towards the Locals. The madrassa team had caught up with them, and the fighting began in earnest, shoving and kicking, sticks flailing and thumping on bare flesh.

155

The two shamans and Benyamin tried to break up the fight. Halvar stood back, then noticed the small ball sitting just over the line. Should he tell them?

For a moment, he hesitated. If he nudged the ball back over the line, it would be back in play. The madrassa team could get it back to the opposite side of the field…

His sense of right and wrong took over. He would not cheat a foe of a rightful victory.

"Hoy! Over here!" He waved his arms to get the attention of the players.

The fighting stopped. The two shamans and Benyamin peered at the ball and came to a decision.

"Goal, Mahak!"

"Sorry, lads," Halvar said, with a shrug that told the madrassa team more than words. He was a Dane; the Danes did not cheat.

"We can still win," Isai said. "Five more goals. You did well, Don Alvaro."

"We've already shown what we can do," one of the other halflings said, flipping his long braids back.

"Can we win?" Another of the madrassa players, whose scraggly beard and blue eyes indicated he had some Oropan in his lineage, sounded dubious.

"Even if we lose, we've shown them that halflings are at least as good as they are." Isai squared his shoulders. "We carry on!"

Indeed, they did. Two more goals for the madrassa, one for the Mahak. Groans of dismay from the sidelines indicated that gamblers had lost wagers. The Cherokee attacks grew more vicious. The Madrassa lads were bruised and bleeding by the time they scored the next goal, and Halvar had taken a few blows himself in a vain effort to keep the ball off his line.

The sultan and sachems had a hasty conference. Benyamin, in his role of announcer, called for attention in Arabi, Erse and Munsi.

"Noble sachems, excellent sultan, honored players! The day grows late, and the Grand Divan must hear many cases tomorrow. It has been decided. This will be the final goal. Whoever wins this is the declared winner of the First Heat. Tomorrow, Sultan Petrus will decide those cases which merit his full attention. On the day following, the Peace Game will be played in earnest, by all who participated today."

"All!" Red Knife burst out, full of indignation. "Even these…these halflings? They have not won their game!"

156

Sees-in-the-Clouds strode onto the field.

"They have won half the goals. They have covered themselves with honor. They have earned the right to take part in the game."

Red Knife turned on his own shaman.

"Do you agree, Walks-in-the-Mist? You would let these halflings, these mongrels, these white-and-black skins, defame our sacred rituals?"

Walks-in-the-Mist nodded.

"The color of their skins is not important. They have shown that their hearts are Mahak, Algonkin, Cherokee."

Red Knife's eyes narrowed. "We will see what color their blood is," he muttered as he marched back to his team.

At his end of the field, Halvar braced himself. This was going to get ugly.

The ball went up. Sticks waved and clashed. The shoving match turned into an all-out fight, with the Cherokee using the rounded ends of their sticks to whack the unprotected heads of their hated halfling opponents.

Meanwhile, the Mahak had netted the ball and were pounding down the field towards Halvar. He met the first player as he had done before, with a downward slash of the Cherokee stick. A light willow Mahak stick cracked against his head, but the stout leather lining of his cap absorbed some of the force of the blow, and the stick broke. The netting flapped into Halvar's face, distracting him from the next attacker. Before he could retaliate, three more Mahak were upon him.

He fought them off as best he could, gripping the stick with both hands. Blows rained on his ribcage and back, as thorough a drubbing as he'd ever gotten, but he still stood. Only after someone yelled "Goal!" did the beating stop.

"Goal to madrassa!"

While the Mahak had been concentrating on Halvar, Isai and his team had abstracted the ball and sent it over the Local goal line.

"Good for them!" Halvar said and collapsed onto the ground.

In front of him was one of the Mahak playing-sticks, its net torn away from the arch of the willow branch. Where had he seen something shaped like that? Very recently, too?

He surrendered to his pain. He was aware of being led off the field, put onto a cart, and hauled away, to the sounds of cheering. He recalled another incident, many years before, when the same thing had happened to him. Then, he had come to consciousness in a strange bed, in a place he did not know, with attendants whose language he could not understand.

Was he to repeat the experience?

29

THE NEXT FEW HOURS WERE A BLUR. SOMEONE SHOUTED
that he was a hero, someone else helped him walk up some stairs.
Someone scolded him for being a fool, someone else took off his
shirt and breeches. Two voices, one shrill, one more melodious, argued over his head. He closed his eyes.

When he opened them again, he was lying on a feather-filled
quilt laid over a hard plank bed, in a small chamber lit by the rays
of a setting sun coming through a small window. He could hear
voices somewhere below him, and smelled the aromas of cooking
meats. He was certain he had never been in this room before.

He groaned as he tried to move; there was something wound
tight around his middle, and his shoulder ached, He reached up
and touched the thin hair that straggled over his head.

"My cap! Where's my cap?"

"It's right here." Selim was sitting beside his bed on a small stool.
"It's horrid. It stinks of sekonk, it looks silly, but if it's so important to you, I thought you'd better have it."

"It reminds me of the Dane-March. It reminds me who I am."
Halvar fell back on the bed. "Where am I?"

"In the Gardens of Paradise, in one of their upstairs rooms." Selim sniffed, whether in scorn or at the scent of incense Halvar could
not tell.

"What are you doing here? You should be at the Rabat with your
father."

"I couldn't leave you, not even when that Yehudit woman insisted on bringing you here. I sent for Frater Iosip to tend to you, and I told my father that I had to stay with you because I am your apprentice, and it's my duty to be with my master." She tried to look dutiful and succeeded in looking stubborn.

"And Dani Glick let you stay?"

"She wasn't happy, but she said I was right to send for the frater. She said that she had other things to attend to, and that I was welcome to you, whatever that means."

Halvar closed his eyes, partly because of the pain of the light hitting them, partly to wince at the mental vision of the young woman and the experienced one fighting over his prostrate body.

"How long have I been out?"

"Quite a while. They're already ringing bells for the fraters to do whatever they do at sundown, and the muezzins are calling for evening prayer."

"All afternoon! Thor's Hammer!" Halvar swore. "Noam could have got off Manatas by now!"

"Not likely," Selim said confidently. "Flores has his men watching the waterfront, checking everyone who tries to get off the island."

"There are those light boats the Locals use."

"Canoes? The Cherokee came in their own canoes, and they aren't leaving until after the Peace Game. And the Mahak aren't friendly with the Cherokee, especially now that they think the Cherokee are trying to beat them at stick-and-stone. So, Noam can't use the Mahak canoes to get away, either."

"There's another way off Manatas," Halvar muttered. "I know there is. It's what Dani Glick didn't want me to find. It's why Leon had to leave the Rabat. It's why Sultan Petrus kept the money from last year's Feria. It's what this whole mess is really about."

"How is our patient?" Frater Iosip bustled in, with Leon di Vicenza behind him.

"As good as can be expected, Frater." Once again Halvar tried to sit up. Frater Iosip pushed him back onto the bed. "Practicing your apothecary skills, Leon? Or making sure I'm not dead yet?"

"You're too stubborn to kill," Leon retorted. "Frater Iosip is using my skills, as well he should. I am now his assistant. I've made you a willow bark potion that should ease some of the pain in your head." He handed Selim a small pottery jar. "See that he takes a sip of this if you can get him to admit that he hurts."

160

"You may have cracked ribs, and if it wasn't for that ridiculous cap, you'd have likely had a cracked crown as well," the tubby cleric scolded him. "You've been well battered and bruised. I've bound up the ribs, but you have to be still or they'll move and puncture a lung, and you wouldn't want that, would you?"

"You're quite safe here," Leon assured him. "No nasty Locals to beat you with their sticks or jab you with knives. A beautiful woman to serve your every need." He cocked an eyebrow at Selim, who scowled back at her erstwhile tutor.

"I can't stay here," Halvar protested. "I have work to do!" He shifted uneasily on the bed.

"If you mean me, I am not leaving the Fratery," Leon said. "And as you know, Manatas is an island. The only way off is by boat."

"Is it?" Halvar asked with a quizzical tilt of his head.

Leon said nothing, only smirked knowingly.

"But that's not what I meant. Where are those madrassa lads, the ones who played stick-and-stone?"

"Celebrating their victory downstairs," Selim sniffed. Again. Probably not the incense, then. "They're drinking cider and telling the girls how brave and strong they are."

"I want to see them. Right now."

"Why?"

"Because they can tell me something about Owen that will lead me to his killer."

"What?"

"I won't know until I ask them." Halvar tried to push himself into a sitting position.

"Stay put!" Selim scolded him. "Why can't you just lie there?"

"Because he's a stubborn Dane who never gives up," Leon said. "Here, let me help you."

Together, Selim and Leon got Halvar propped up against the board at the head of the bed.

"Just why *are* you here, Leon? Making sure I'm not able to chase you?"

"If I wanted to leave Manatas, you wouldn't be able to catch me," Leon said confidently. "But for now, I'm on your side. That Bretain lad was harmless. He didn't have to be killed."

"You know who did it? But you're not going to tell me." Halvar hissed in pain as he tried to make himself more comfortable and failed. "You know, if someone's that desperate, you may be his next target."

161

"Not as long as I stay at the fratery," Leon said with a smile. "And that is where I am going right now. My bodyguards await me. I wish you well, Halvar. Don't try to call me to the Grand Divan, because I won't go."

"Not even to see if I get the killer?"

"Perhaps then. Out of curiosity." Leon patted Selim on the shoulder. "Take care of our tame Dane, Selim. He's not so cloddish as he likes to appear."

"Send the madrassa lads up!" Halvar called as Leon swept out of the room, Frater Iosip at his heels.

30

ISAI AND HIS FRIENDS FILLED THE SMALL ROOM, CROWD-
ing around the bed, while Benyamin and Padraig lurked behind
them. The game-players ranged in age and color from early ado-
lescence to nearly adult and from the dark brown of Afrikan to the
paler gold of Oropan-Local parentage.

"I wanted to thank you for your efforts on our behalf," Isai said
in formal Arabi. In a more colloquial tone, he added, "You saved our
skins, drawing the Mahak away from us!"

"Not my idea—theirs," Halvar said. "But better the Mahak than
the Cherokee. The Mahak sticks are willow. They bend."

"Cherokee sticks are of hickory, much harder and stronger," a-
greed a tall lad whose braids curled tightly around his dark face.

"But the net is smaller, harder to catch the ball," observed a second player, smaller and lighter in complexion. "The Mahak net is
wider, but softer. And the mesh is wider, so the stone can slip out
if you're not careful."

Halvar stopped the discussion before it got too technical.

"I called you here because of Owen MacAllan. I want you to tell
me everything you know about him."

Isai looked at the team.

"We Afrikans did not know him well," he explained. "He was
not easy with us. I think it was the first time he had ever seen Afrikans. He would not have been friendly with us were it not for stick-
and-stone. We played, and he wanted to play. He saw us practicing,

163

saw our sticks, and asked if he could join us. That was all we knew about him. You must ask the ones who lived with him for more."

Halvar turned to the players whose garb marked them as Oropan with Local somewhere in their backgrounds.

"Very well, lads, tell me what you can. How did he come to the madrassa? Did he want to be there?"

"If he didn't, he wouldn't be," stated a player in a combination of Bretain trews and Afrikan daishiki.

"State your name, so that Selim can record it," Halvar ordered.

"I'm Bartos, from Sequannok, and this is my friend Shulach. I'm studying natural philosophy, he's studying medicine."

"Also mathematics," Shulach added.

"We lived with Owen in Bretain House," Bartos explained in Arabi. "He was of the Pure Sect, from the mountains of West Caster. It was his first time away from their settlements."

"He spoke Erse. Didn't have much Arabi." That was a third player, in Franchen tight breeches and with fussy lace on the collar of his shirt. His Arabi had the nasal twang of Kibbick. "I am Stephane Mercier, my people are from Kibbick but came south to West Caster when I was little. They are Erse Rite, don't like Roumi Rite, can't stay where the Questioners chase them."

"Do you study natural philosophy, too?" Halvar asked casually.

"Law," Stephane said. "It's important to know both Sharia and Bretain law in Nova Mundum."

"That, and languages," Isai stated. "Thanks to Imperator Lovis, there are more and more Oropans coming to Nova Mundum, and not all of them speak Arabi."

Halvar left the linguistics to the scholars.

"What else can you tell me about Owen?" he asked the Franchen lad.

"He was supposed to be studying law with us," Stephane said, nodding at another Franchen-dressed student. "That's Albert Pescier. We were to attend the lectures with Benyamin ibn Mendel, who could translate the parts we didn't understand when the instructor's Arabi was too hard. Owen was not attentive."

"He wanted to get out, to play the Peace Game," Albert said in halting Arabi.

"How did you fellows learn this game?" Halvar was fascinated by the persistence of the Local sport.

164

"The Huron know it. My mother's people, not my father's." Stephane's lips tightened in a grimace that could have been disgust or dismay.

"We play in Narragansett territory," Albert added.

Bartos added. "In Sequannok, my Lenape cousins, they play, so I do, too."

Halvar looked the assemblage over.

"Did any of you know each other before you came here?"

Bartos and Shulach exchanged looks. Bartos spoke for both of them.

"Shulach and I knew each other. We are from Sequannok Sultanate. We studied at the collegium in the new town that Sultan Penina is building. He calls it Salaamabad—Peaceful City."

"If I know city life, it won't be peaceful for long," Halvar observed. "I do hear the Locals there mix well with the Oropans and Andalusian who come to farm."

"My mother's people are Lenape," Barton admitted. "Shulach's people came to Salaamabad when Oropans burnt their village. He is all Lenape, but we are sworn brothers."

"What about you two, Stephane and Albert? You're both Franchen. How do you come to be in Manatas"

"My father owns a manufactory, a mill with many spinners," Stephane said proudly. "Albert's father is a fisherman."

"But he still goes to madrassa," Halvar pointed out.

"I serve at mokka-shop to earn fees and rent," Albert said, facing the others defiantly.

"On the playing-field, we are all equal," Isai put in. "It doesn't matter whose father is rich and whose is poor. My father is a trader. Gavril is my servant. Stephane's father is a mill owner. No one knows who Hasan's father is—his mother works on Maiden Lane—but in the madrassa, he is a student like the rest of us."

"And all of you have some Local connection," Halvar mused.

Isai shrugged. "It matters only to the Cherokee. Not to us."

Halvar thought this over.

"Convivencia," he said, finally. "Islim and Kristo and Yehudit, living together. Afrikan, Oropan, Andalusian, Local." He let that thought hang in the air for a moment then said, "What can you tell me about Owen himself? What was he like? Did he pick quarrels, did he study hard?"

"He was amiable," Stephane said. "He did not pick quarrels because he did not know enough Arabi to understand if someone

165

insulted him. I don't think it mattered to him if someone did insult him. He went to the Pure Erse Rite meetings in Green Village, but he did not argue about religion. He came with us to the class that Benyamin taught for us freshers, who had to learn Arabi before we could attend the advanced lectures. "

"He knew Munsi," Albert said. "I heard him talking with some of the Mahak on the playing field when we went to practice. He was friendly with them, because of the Peace Game."

"He didn't know any of you fellows, but he knew someone else?" Halvar turned this over in his mind.

"He must have, because I heard him talk to someone as we were leaving the practice," Bartos spoke up.

"When was this?" Halvar was instantly alert.

"The day before he was found dead," Bartos said slowly. "Is this important?"

"Everything he did is important. What did he say?"

Bartso frowned. "He said, 'Why are you here?'"

"That's not right," Isai corrected him. "Owen spoke Erse, not Arabi, and Erse is one of the languages where the stress and the tone are as important as the order of the words. I heard him, too. We were leaving the field with some of the Locals, and he suddenly turned around and said, 'What are you doing here?' In Erse. And the way he said it, was with the stress on *you*. As if to say, *Why is this person, who I address, in this place.*" Isai stopped for breath.

"He did know someone," Selim surmised. "Not one of you fellows, because you all come from different places, and none of you knew *him*. He recognized someone *else*, someone on the Local team."

"Someone who killed him?" Isai gasped in horror. "But...why?"

"Because someone isn't who he says he is," Halvar said slowly. "And for some reason, it's a matter of life and death that this person stay hidden."

"But you're going to find him," Selim said.

"As soon as I can get out of this *verdammitte* bed!" He swung his legs over the side of the bed then realized he was missing his breeches. He hastily covered his bare legs with the coverlet.

"Get out, lads, and let me dress," he ordered. "I'll meet you downstairs."

"You will not!" Dani Glick stood in the doorway, two large females behind her. One held a crock with something hot, the other a small lantern that cut some of the darkness that had come while

Halvar interviewed the students. "Out of here, young men, and let your hero get his rest. You, too, Selim!"

Selim frowned and pouted.

"Benyamin," Halvar called out. "Take Selim back to the Rabat."

Selim started to protest. Halvar ignored the tantrum in the making and continued to order his troops.

"Padraig, find out what, exactly, Owen's father brought with him to sell at the Feria. Benyamin, after you get Selim to the Rabat, go and talk with Yakub. Find out whether he ever went to West Caster with his father on trading trips. Selim, don't pout at me! I want you to speak with Maya again. Find out all you can about Ochiye's last trading journey, the one that took him to West Caster. And make sure Maya gets to the Grand Divan tomorrow."

"Why? She couldn't have killed Owen; she was at the Rabat all yesterday."

"She might know something that will tell us who did," Halvar said. "And while you're at the Rabat, tell your father that I want to see him before he gives judgment at the Grand Divan. Tell him to meet me here, at the Gardens of Paradise."

"He won't like it, being given orders."

"Remind him that I carry the calif's seal. Tell him to bring Flores and the Town Guard. Isai, come to the Gardens of Paradise tomorrow, and bring your mother and Lady Tekla and Yakub with you. If they don't come willingly, Tenente Flores will make sure they are here."

He stopped for breath, and Dani Glick took over.

"Do what he says," she told them. "Let the poor man rest."

167

31

DANI HELD THE DOOR OPEN FOR THE CROWD TO LEAVE.
The madrassa lads filed out, leaving her in charge of their fallen hero.
Padraig and Benyamin reluctantly followed. Selim refused to leave,
planting herself in the open doorway, her heavy eyebrows nearly
meeting over her nose in a familiar scowl.

Halvar could smell the enticing odors of cooking meats, and the
headier scent of incense and burning hemp from below. His eyes
fell on Selim as she stood glowering at Dani from the doorway.

"Another of your literary efforts?

"Not me. Benyamin. He said you should be able to explain why
you didn't heed our warnings about the sekonk. And since you don't
write verses, he did it for you. And Padraig had a tune that he thought
might go with the verses."

"You allow the thing to be performed?" Halvar glared accus-
ingly at Dani.

She had changed from her respectable attire to her working clothes
of heavy silk trousers that draped across her shapely rear and legs,
revealing as much as they concealed; a fine kutton shirt under a
brief velvet bodice decorated with silk embroidery and glittering
glass beads. Her hair was unbound, covered by a silk scarf. Gold
chains filled the gap between the neck of the shirt and the edge of
the bodice, gold bangle bracelets jingled at her wrists.

"It's a good follower to 'The Stranger and the Sekonk.' People
like it. And after your performance at the Peace Game, you're some-

thing of a notable person in Manatas. If they didn't know who you were before, they do now."

Dani nodded towards Birgit, who placed the crock on the stool vacated by Selim. Farrah placed the small oil lamp next to the crock. The two attendants stepped back to flank the doorway on either side of Selim, waiting for further orders.

"More of your grandmother's broth?" Halvar eyed the bowl, recalling the crock of nourishment Dani had sent during his previous illness.

"It works," Dani said. She turned to Selim. "My servants will take you downstairs. Your escort is waiting to take you back to your father."

Selim glared at the older woman.

"I should stay here."

"Get back to the Rabat," Halvar ordered. "You have to talk to the Maya girl. She's in the harem, I can't get to her. Ask her whether she went on Ochiye's trading journey into West Caster, and if she did, find out if Ochiye talked with any of the Locals there."

Dani held the door open. "Out, Selim. Leave this poor man to heal."

Halvar made one last effort before he succumbed to fatigue and bruises. "Get back to the Rabat, and do as I ask!"

"What about Noam?" Selim still hesitated.

"Don't you worry about him," Halvar assured her. "Now, for the last time, Go! I'll drink your broth, Dani Glick, and assume you left the poppy juice out of it this time."

"Nothing but chicken and a few carrots," Dani promised him. "I'll see that the child gets back to the Rabat."

"Leave me the lamp," Halvar asked. "And where are my breeches and coat?"

"Afraid of the dark? Or are you cold?"

"I may need the piss-pot. Or the jakes."

"Danic lout!" Dani said, with a smile that took the sting out of the words. "I'll leave you the light. You'd probably flood the place if I didn't."

The flame of the lamp flickered in the breeze from the tiny window set high over the bed.

"I've had your breeches brushed, and the coat is clean, for a change. You'll get them in the morning. I hope you will do as Frater Iosip said and stay put, but if you must used the necessary, the stairs to the garden are at the end of the gallery."

With that, she swept out, shooing her attendants and Selim ahead of her. Halvar was left alone with the soup and his thoughts.

The soup was hearty, and he slurped it up eagerly. His thoughts were not so tasty. He was convinced the deaths of Ochiye Aboutiye and Owen MacAllan were somehow related, but how? What connection could a young Bretain who had never been out of his own settlement have with a well-traveled Afrikan trader? Where did the wily Noam fit in? And who did Owen recognize when he played the Peace Game with the Mahak?

Halvar went over the events of his stay in Manatas. From the moment he'd landed, he had felt something was subtly wrong, something going on he was not supposed to know about. He was always being distracted from his sworn duty, lured into investigating murders and other mischief and mayhem, his attention drawn away from the finances of the Feria.

He fell into an uneasy doze. Images flickered through his brain— a painting of an Old Roumi goddess, mysteriously vanished from Leon's old rooms; a folded note found in the lining of a Franchen assassin's coat; a scrawled message on a piece of coarse paper. He considered the things he had heard—the old saws of his mentor, Old Sergeant Olaf; the orations of the Local sachems; hints dropped by Leon di Vicenza.

He went over everything he knew about the running of Manatas. Of the three tenentes of the Manatas Town Guard—Gomez, Ruiz, and Flores—two had turned out to be murderers and one a thief. Had he made another mistake, allowing Flores to be promoted? The guardsman was too fond of using force for its own sake.

The lamp flickered again. Halvar's eyes popped open.

"That's it!" he said aloud. "That's what this is about! Now, to prove it!"

She's taken my boots and my breeches, he realized. *But that won't stop me.*

"Oh, Dani Glick, you've outsmarted yourself this time," he murmured. "You forgot just how stubborn we Danes can be.

"Dani Glick, Leon di Vicenza, you're going to wish I'd never come to Manatas!"

32

THE NOISE FROM BELOW DRIFTED INTO SILENCE AS THE
patrons of the Gardens of Paradise left to seek their beds, some in
the rooms along the gallery, others in their own houses across the
common ground. Halvar listened to the drunken farewells, heard
the doors slam shut, and the groans of the tired staff.

Along the gallery, doors opened and closed. He eased out of
the bed, hissing as his injuries reminded him he was not quite as
resilient as he had been ten years before, but he was used to pain.

"Where did she put my breeches?" he mumbled, fumbling around
in the dark. He didn't like the idea of creeping around a strange place
in his braies and shirt, but a thorough search made it clear there was
no other way he was going to find what he was looking for. He secured the cord that held his braies tight around his middle, picked
up the tiny lamp, and slowly opened the door.

He looked down into the large central room of the Gardens of
Paradise. A row of lanterns hung from the balcony, the candles within
sputtering as they burned down to the ends of their wicks, throw-
ing eerie shadows on the walls but allowing him to see where he
was going. From behind the closed doors along the gallery came
sounds of enjoyment, lust, or just exhaustion. Halvar's lips twitched
under his mustache. Under other circumstances, he might be the
one making those sounds, but that could wait. He had a mission
to complete.

Stairs led down to the main room and a door that would take him
outside to the garden and the small houses at the end of it, but that
was not the exit he was certain would lead him to his goal.

171

He moved carefully to the left end of the gallery, which ended in a painted wall.

"Leon's been at it again," Halvar murmured as he scanned the lush pastoral scene. A djinn with the face of Mullah Abadul, the leading Islim cleric in Manatas, leered at a scantily clad nymph, possibly one of Dani's more popular attendants. The scene was framed by oak trees and birches.

Halvar smiled to himself. He had dealt with secret stairs in Corduva; the Calif's House was fairly riddled with them. He lifted the lamp to examine the wall. Sure enough, there was a nearly invisible seam, barely a crack, in the wooden surface.

"No hinges," he muttered. "Swings in."

He tapped the wall gently and heard a satisfying echo within.

"Has to open inward," he repeated. He tapped along the seam, testing it for a hidden spring. "Oaks mean acorns," he told himself.

He held the lamp closer. Sure enough, tiny acorns were hidden amongst the painted leaves at the edge of the picture. He pushed them at random. Suddenly, there was a tiny click, and the wall swung open, revealing a stair leading upward.

Halvar stepped into the dark stairwell and listened intently for sounds from above. When he heard none, he lifted the lamp and mounted the stairs.

The third floor of the Gardens of Paradise ran the length of the building, an open space filled with odd furniture and odder-looking apparatus. As his eyes adjusted to the flickering light, Halvar was able to distinguish the outline of the printing press, with its huge screw, platform, and plates on which the type could be set. A high cabinet held the aforementioned type and jars of ink. Next to it, a crate held sheets of the same coarse paper on which the *Gazetta*, the broadside ballads, and the mathematics book had been printed.

He carefully picked up a sheet of the stuff and rubbed his fingers over it, holding the lamp well away from the crate. He didn't want to set the place on fire...not yet!

He moved from the printing press to explore the rest of the attic. He grinned under his mustache as he recognized the tools of Leon's trade—a table where inks and paints were neatly lined up, with much finer paper than that near the printing press.

Another table caught his eye.

"Oho!" He lifted the lamp to observe the tiny clay model, and the pages of the open book next to it. "Leon, you may be a gifted

172

painter, but you are also an engineer. This is why you are so sure you will get off this island."

One more item drew his attention. Leaning against wall at the far end of the attic was the painting he had seen in Leon's rooms the first time he had visited the Mermaid Taberna. Was it only a month ago? So much had happened to him, it seemed as if he had spent a lifetime in Manatas.

Halvar nodded and stepped carefully back to the stairs. He had seen enough.

Dani Glick was waiting for him at the bottom of the staircase, with Donal behind her. She held a pistoia pointed at Halvar's heart.

"I should have known you wouldn't stay put," she said. "Why can't you do as I ask, Halvar Danske?"

"Because I'm a stubborn Dane," Halvar retorted. "What now? Do you let your tame Bretain beat me senseless again? Do you shoot me? It's no use, Dani. I've found what you all have tried to keep hidden, although I don't know how much longer it will be before someone notices there's a bridge connecting West Caster with Manatas. You can't hide a thing like that. It's like the story of the fellow who stole a carthorse, and when the constable asked how he came by it, he just said, 'What horse?'"

Dani sighed and lowered the pistoia.

"If you had only done what you were supposed to do and stayed in the Rabat while the sultan took care of Manatas. If only you hadn't insisted on solving that first murder. Why couldn't you just accept the dead frater as Leon and leave it at that?"

"If?" Halvar shrugged. "Like Old Sergeant Olaf used to say, 'There's no point in moaning about 'if.' If this, if that. If Grandma'd had balls, she'd be Grandpa; if Grandpa'd had tits, he'd be Grandma. If Lovis hadn't decided the world should be Roumi Rite Kristo, it would be a more peaceful place, and if Episcopus Innocente hadn't decided to back him, we'd be left alone to pray as we feel like.

"But the world is as it is, and I am what I am. I questioned whether the dead man was Leon, and the rest just happened. So, Dani Glick, where does that leave us?"

"Back in your room, Halvar, at least until morning. I'll get your breeches and coat to you, and you will remove yourself from my house."

"I'll remove myself, but I still need your building for a meeting," Halvar said, "I've sent for Sultan Petrus and the Ochiye family to join me here."

"Why should I allow you to take over my establishment?" Dani asked. "I owe you nothing."

"You are in possession of stolen property," Halvar countered. "How much did you pay Emir Achmet and his Scavengers to get that painting out of the Mermaid Taberna?"

"That painting was mine by right," Dani snapped. "I sat for it. Leon was going to give it to me when it was finished."

"Then call it a gesture of good will. And one more thing. I need someone to get me to the Mahak village at first light. I have to talk to Firebrand and get into the Cherokee camp to get Noam Vizier before he kills again."

"How many has he killed, this Noam?"

They had reached Halvar's assigned chamber.

"At least three that I know of. Maybe more that I don't. He's a bitter man, and a desperate one, and that makes him dangerous. I don't know how far you've gotten with that bridge, but if he crosses it, he'll be in Bretain territory, out of my hands. I'm assuming he won't go anywhere until daylight, so I have to be at the Cherokee camp as soon as possible. Get me my clothes, and some mokka, Dani Glick, and I'll be gone."

"The clothes and the mokka are yours, Halvar Danske, but you won't go. You'll stay here on Manatas Island until you finish what you started, you stubborn Dane!"

With that, Dani and Donal marched down the stairs to the main room, leaving Halvar to the comforts of his bed.

33

THE FIRST STREAKS OF LIGHT WERE VISIBLE OVER THE
nearly leafless branches of the trees when Halvar left the Gardens
of Paradise. One of Dani Glick's halfling servers guided him through
the woods, along the path next to the beaver pond where he had been
shot.

The Mahak village was already stirring by the time he arrived.
The pungent aroma of boiling maiz wafted over the palisade that
surrounded the longhouses. Dogs barked, warning the inhabitants
of the village of approaching enemies.

"Firebrand!" Halvar called out. "I need you!"

The Mahak slid out through a small gap in the palisade.

"Good cheer to you, Don Alvaro. What do you need me for?"

"No time to be polite," Halvar snapped. "We have to get into the
Cherokee camp. Noam the Afrikan is getting away!"

"Why should that interest me?"

"Because he is the one who killed Owen MacAllan," Halvar said.
"If you want your name cleared, he's got to admit it. Get some of
your watchmen and get me to the place where the Oropans are
building their bridge. Don't bother to deny it's there, I know all
about it. And leave your bow behind. I want him taken alive!"

Firebrand muttered something in Munsi Halvar assumed was
a slur on his ancestry and possibly his destination in the Afterlife.
Then the Mahak vanished, only to appear a few minutes later accompanied by two watchmen.

"The Cherokee are not going to want to give him up," Firebrand warned as they trotted along the path to the clearing where the visitors had pitched their temporary quarters.

They were met by a party of Cherokee, led by Red Knife, in full war-paint, carrying lethal-looking war-clubs.

"What cheer?" Firebrand greeted them in Munsi.

"There has been a killing," Red Knife told him in the Cherokee dialect of that language. "One of our men has been stabbed in the back. The Afrikan is gone."

"He's getting desperate," Halvar said in Arabi.

"We gave him shelter. He betrayed us," Red Knife stated in halting Arabi. "We find him, we kill him."

"We're after him, too," Firebrand assured the Cherokee.

"He go to square-houses," Red Knife declared, pointing toward the smoke starting to rise from the fires of Manatas Town.

"No," Halvar said. "He won't go there. He's headed for the bridge. The one your sachems and Sultan Petrus are so worried I'll find. That's where he's going, and he'll get over it while we stand here gabbling! Where is it?"

Firebrand wasted no more time in chatter. He loped forward with his watchmen close behind, away from Manatas Town, heading north. Halvar followed, trying to match his long stride to the Mahaks' easy lope. Red Knife consulted with his own men then took up the pursuit with the rest of them.

They followed a narrow path that ran up the center ridge of the island. To the west of the path, birches and alders filled spaces between huge piles of rocks. Something growled in the rocky cliff, and Halvar hoped it wasn't a bear. On their right were cleared fields, where groups of women gleaned the last of the maiz, escouash and beans, followed by flocks of birds that pecked at the insects stirred up by the harvesters.

A sudden noise drew Halvar's attention. A massive flock of birds rose ahead of them, so dense that it nearly blocked the light of the rising sun. The pursuit stopped while Firebrand and Red Knife consulted in Munsi.

"Wood-birds," Firebrand said. "They are good to eat, but small. Only a bite apiece, not worth hunting."

"Old Sergeant Olaf used to say, 'Many bites make a meal.' Something frightened those birds. Noam must be ahead." Halvar breathed deeply, ignoring the pain of his bruised ribcage.

"So is the bridge," Firebrand said. "There!" He pointed to the East Channel, where a cloud of dust marked a building site.

"You go too slow, Oropan!" Red Knife sneered. "We go faster!" He sprinted down the path toward the bridge.

"I'll get there," Halvar panted. He plodded forward, grimly gaining ground until he rejoined the Cherokee and Mahak.

The sun was fully up by the time they reached the bridge. Carts loaded with bricks were drawn up at the edge of a cliff, where a mixed crew of Afrikans, Andalusians, and Oropans worked feverishly, loading the bricks onto a platform that could be lowered into the channel cut by the rushing water between the island of Manatas and the mainland of West Caster. On the other side of the channel, a similar gang of workers did the same. Planks were stacked, ready to be nailed together to form a scaffold for the workers to lay bricks on either bank of the river.

Between the banks, masons plied trowels, and mixers stirred barrels of mortar while a broad barge shuttled between the two towers slowly rising from the river. The pilings must have been put in last year, Halvar guessed. The bricks were already a few feet above the rushing water, and rough-cut planks had been placed between the rising towers so that workers could make their way between them and the surveyors could judge the evenness of their height. *At this rate, it will take at least five years*, Halvar guessed. *But it will be a marvel when it's done.*

Some of the bricks had been used to make huts for the workers. Noam stood in front of one of these, loudly arguing with an Andalusian who seemed to be in charge of the construction. He waved a Cherokee tomahawk at the foreman.

"Get me over. Now!" he ordered.

"Not yet! You cannot cross! Too dangerous!" The bridge-builder pointed at the planks. "Won't hold a man, only a boy!" he added, in broken Arabi with the lilt of Erse."Take the ferry, if you have to get across. This bridge won't be finished for many a year! You can't use it now."

"I must!" Noam's voice was shrill. "They will kill me!" He gestured wildly at the Locals, who had reached the edge of the site.

"You kill player from Choctaw." Red Knife and his men dodged the donkey carts to get at Noam.

"And Owen." Firebrand joined the Cherokee.

"And Ochiye," Halvar added. He was winded, aching, and heaving for breath, but he stepped forward to confront the Afrikan. "With mal-chinee poison," he added for Red Knife's benefit.

"I did not put the mal-chinee in his basket," Noam spat out, edging toward the bridge.

"No, you made the Maya girl do it," Halvar said, stepping closer.

"Why kill the Bretain boy?" Firebrand asked. He moved forward, edging to the right while Halvar moved left.

"Because he recognized someone," Halvar answered for the fugitive. "You brought someone back with you from West Caster, Noam. Someone who wasn't known in Manatas because he wasn't Mahak. He wasn't one of the Algonkin from the Long Island, either. I suspect he was Huron."

"Huron!" Firebrand exclaimed. "But I know all of my players. None are Huron!"

"Nor mine," Red Knife stated.

"What about those others, the Choctaw? How well do you know them?" Halvar took another step toward Noam.

"Don't know them. They don't mix with Cherokee," Red Knife said.

"I'll wager one of them isn't Choctaw. He's Huron. Placed there by Noam, so he could go back to the south with you."

"What for?" Red Knife asked.

"I'm not sure, but I suspect it's to get something the Cherokee are guarding. You found where the gold comes from, Noam, and you drew a chart, a map, so that someone else can find it. And you were going to use that gold to buy…what? Guns? Men to shoot them?"

Halvar took two more paces forward. Noam stepped backward, his hatchet held before him.

"Who would get these guns?" Noam jeered. "Afrikans already have gold. They already have guns."

"What about the Cherokee?" Halvar turned to Red Knife. "Did this man come to you? Is that why you protect him?"

"He promised our sachem guns for gold," Red Knife admitted.

"So you can make jihad on the Afrikans," Halvar said. One more step, and he'd have Noam. "Hold him!" he ordered the workmen loading bricks onto the platform.

Noam swung his hatchet, and the workers backed away. He stepped backward onto the narrow path that led to the ferry landing.

The Locals hesitated. Halvar did not. The Afrikan spun around and stumbled down the cliff to the rickety wooden bridge that jutted over the channel to the barge waiting for its next load. Halvar slid down the path after him, clutching at shrubby stems to break his descent.

Noam reached the riverbank and looked wildly about him. There was the pier, which did not go all the way across the narrow channel, and there was the single plank used by the bricklayers to get to their scaffolding.

"Don't try it!" Halvar shouted.

Noam started to cross the shaky span.

"Stop him!" Halvar called out to the bargeman at the end of the pier.

"What? Who?" the bargeman sputtered.

Noam waved the tomahawk.

"I must get across!" He put one foot onto the plank, then another, eyes focused only on the possibility of escape. The bricklayers were caught between their work and the madman advancing on them with his tomahawk.

"He's killed once today," Halvar called out. "Noam! You can't get away! Not this time. You've worn out your welcome with the Cherokee, you've killed a Choctaw, the Mahak won't have you, and your Huron allies are far away. You must face the justice of Al-Andalus!"

"Never! Al-Andalus is finished, the old ways are gone. The Cherokee gold will buy guns and men. Afrika will rise up, and I will rise with it. Ochiye was a fool—he would not see what was before his eyes. This is Nova Mundum!"

"Guns are no good without men who know how to use them," Halvar said. "You didn't kill Ochiye because of his politics, or because you back the Cherokee over the Afrikans. You killed him because you hated him for taking Maya from you." He stepped carefully onto the wooden planks, feeling them bend under his weight.

"He had Yona!" Noam howled. "He only took Maya because I wanted her!" He shook the tomahawk again. The plank shook with him.

"Get back here, Noam, and face the sultan at the Divan," Halvar pleaded.

"I will die first!"

Noam stepped back. The thin plank shifted under his feet. With a howl, he plunged into the rushing water below. The current swept him onto the rocks at the base of the cliff. Noam fought fiercely against the current, but to no avail. He was dashed against the rocks. His body twisted and bent, then lay still. His blood stained the water red.

Halvar frowned. Once again Chance had taken his prey from him, but this time there was no doubt the man was dead.

"Get him out of the water," he told the bargemen. "Carry him up to the builders"

Firebrand and Red Knife looked on as the sad burden rose from the channel.

"Not my fault," Halvar told them. "He fell into the river."

The two Locals muttered together in Munsi. Firebrand turned to Halvar.

"The Cherokee is satisfied that justice has been done. They will not demand blood-money from his kin," he said in Arabi.

The workers huddled together, horrified, as the body of Noam was hauled up on the platform used to bring bricks down to the builders. The foreman hurried over to Halvar.

"What shall we do?"

"I'll take the body with me in one of those donkey carts when I go back to Manatas Town. I'll tell Sultan Petrus that work is going forward on the bridge. How long do you think it will take before it's done?"

The foreman shrugged. "No idea. No one's ever done anything like it before. It's going to be a wonder when it's finished."

"*If* it gets finished," Halvar mused. He turned to Red Knife. "Will you help me, Cherokee? There's a spy among you, a Huron. Find him. You'll know him because he's wearing macassin with blue porcupine quill decorations. Two quills are missing."

"We find Huron spy. We kill him." Red Knife stated, his expression grim.

"Don't kill him yet," Halvar pleaded. "Bring him to the Grand Divan on the playing field at mid-afternoon. He's the only one who can tell us why Noam was so sure he could get guns for the Cherokee."

Red Knife thought this over.

"I bring Cherokee to Grand Divan. We see how Al-Andalus makes justice."

Halvar mounted a donkey cart as the body of Noam was placed on one of the carts used for carrying the bricks to the worksite and ordered the drive to take him back to Green Village. He had most of his answers, but one question remained. It would be up to Sultan Petrus to give him the final answer,

34

ONCE AGAIN HALVAR APPROACHED GREEN VILLAGE AT THE head of a sad procession. Behind him strode the Mahak watchmen and their Cherokee counterparts. Swift runners had preceded them to notify the Local villages while Firebrand and Red Knife remained as part of the escort. By the time Halvar and his cart got to Green Village, news had reached Manatas that the Calif's Hireling had found and disposed of yet another murderer.

At the entrance to the Gardens of Paradise, a squad of the Sultan's Guards lined the path to the main door of the establishment, where Dani Glick waited, arms crossed. Halvar stopped the cart at the gate and greeted the assemblage in the three languages of Manatas.

"*Salaam aleikum*! God be with ye! What cheer?"

Dani Glick responded with little enthusiasm.

"Hail, Halvar the hero!" she said bitterly. "You've brought me custom, but no gelt for it. The Sultan waits for you inside, along with four sachems, two shamans, two fraters from the fratery and Leon di Vicenza. Oh, and I left out your madrassa lads and the Seekers of Truth. Quite a gathering you've assembled, Hireling. Am I expected to feed all these people at my own expense?"

Halvar carefully descended from the cart, handing the driver a few wumpum for his trouble. Padraig, Benyamin and Selim, the Seekers of Truth, shoved past the armed guards to surround their new leader. All of them started to talk at once.

Halvar held up a hand for silence.

"Inside," he ordered. "Dani Glick, will you bring us mokka? And something to eat—I need more than maiz-cakes."

"What else can I bring, Don Alvaro Danico? A dancing girl for your pleasure? A rendition by Willem of Cos?" Dani dropped a mocking curtsey.

"I've heard enough of Willem's verses for a while, and I don't need a dancing girl," Halvar retorted. "Sweet cider for Selim and the lads would be welcome, though."

He herded the Seekers of Truth into a corner of the great room, which had been cleared of debris from the previous night and was now ready for customers. Sultan Petrus had taken the most prominent place in the room, a seat on the raised platform usually occupied by the entertainers.

"Who do you think you are, Hireling, summoning me to this place of sinful entertainment?" the sultan roared, thumping his ivory leg on the floor in his fury. "First you order a Grand Divan, now you prevent me from delivering justice! What is going on here?"

"All will be explained, excellent Sultan," Halvar assured him. "I bear the Calif's Seal, and it gives me authority to override anyone in Andalusian territory, including you. I have to consult with these worthy young people—"

"Worthy? Selim? A child! And this Yehudit, who has barely grown a beard? And this...this..." The sultan could not think of anything insulting enough to describe Padraig.

"Mokka for the sultan," Halvar ordered grandly. He turned to the sachems, ranged against the wall. "Noble sachems, I ask your indulgence. Once these young people tell me what they know, I will be able to explain what has happened here in Manatas during this fall Feria."

Gray Goose-feather settled onto the floor, legs folded under him. Mahmoud did the same. Se-Kwa-Ya and Te-Cum-Sa growled together then joined the other sachems.

Halvar found a table and stools for his Seekers of Truth.

"Sit," he told them. "Report. Selim, you first. What did Maya have to say?"

"Not much," Selim said. "She was with Ochiye when he went to West Caster. As far as I can make out, he stayed on the barge that carried them to the villages on the coast across from the Long Island. Noam would go ashore, do business, bring back goods."

"Ochiye didn't leave the ship at all?" Halvar mused over this. "Noam did all the talking?"

"I don't think Ochiye spoke Erse very well," Benyamin put in. "Isai was fluent, enough to talk to the Bretains and Franchen at the madrassa, but one of the reasons he said his father allowed him to come north was to learn more Erse. What Isai had was the sort that sailors use, not very polite, and his accent was terrible, of the lowest sort."

Halvar turned back to Selim.

"Do you still have that paper we took from the Franchen assassin, Robert Mortmain?" he asked.

"I put it into my notebook," Selim said with a puzzled frown. She flipped pages and found the document. "But you saw for yourself, it's useless. The image is so blurred you can't tell who it is."

She handed it to Halvar, who examined both sides carefully.

"It doesn't matter," he said, carefully folding the paper according to its original creases and putting it into his inside coat pocket. "I was wrong about Mortmain. I was wrong about a lot of things."

"But he *was* a Franchen spy, wasn't he?" Selim asked.

"Oh, that he was, and an assassin—no doubt about that. And he came to a bad end, as all such do. I was just wrong about what he was after. Padraig!"

The Bretain lad sat up, attentive.

"You don't have to be coy about the printing press, I've already seen it. What's important is the paper and ink. Where does it come from? Who makes it, and how does it get to Manatas?"

Padraig shrugged. "I don't know who makes it, but Fru Glick does. She's the one who owns the printing press. Simon Singer works for her."

"Who doesn't?" Halvar muttered Aloud, he called out, "Benyamin!"

"Yes, Don Alvaro?"

"Have you learned anything more about Isai and his family?"

"They are Afrikan, Islim. Ochiye came twice a year, to the spring and fall Ferias. Isai is passionate about two things—languages and the stick-and-stone game. Yakub is the one who runs the business, with his mother Tekla. There's some talk about him and Samuel Igbo's daughter. She comes to his shop in the souk. No one buys that many bracelets."

Halvar sat silently, tugging at his mustache, deep in thought.

Dani Glick appeared with her female guardians, leading a squad of servers bearing jugs of cider and pewter mugs.

"Food and drink, as ordered," she stated. "Tabac for the Locals, at their request. And Sultan Petrus is getting angrier by the minute. Do something quickly, or we'll have another death on our hands. The man will go off into apoplexy from sheer rage."

A burst of noise at the door drew everyone's attention. Flores marched in with Yona and Tekla, followed by Isai and Yakub. Last in was a Town Guard, dragging Maya behind him.

"They're here," Flores announced. "What do you want me to do with them?"

Halvar rose, straightened his cap, and marched to the center of the room.

"Bring them in," he ordered. "Seat them here, in front of the sultan."

Tekla marched into the room, sneering at the gaudy décor, and seated herself with great dignity, spreading her draperies about her. Yakub stood behind her, daring anyone to molest his mother.

"I do not need to be here." Yona turned to leave. Farrah, the Afrikan attendant, blocked her way.

"You, sit!"

Yona sat, with Isai hovering over her protectively.

Halvar took a position in the center of the room, turning slowly to face each of the dignitaries as he spoke their names and titles.

"Attention!" he called out. "By your leave, noble sachems, excellent Sultan Petrus. I thank you for coming, at my request.

"I have sad news. Noam, who called himself vizier, is dead. He tried to escape Manatas over the bridge, which is still a long way from being completed. He fell into the water below and was dashed on the rocks."

Yona gasped once, then recovered her serene demeanor. Only her trembling lips gave her away.

"That was all I had to know," Halvar said. "Yona, wife of Ochiye, I accuse you of poisoning your husband. Maya, concubine of Ochiye, I accuse you of poisoning your master." He turned to Flores. "You were right, Tenente, and I was wrong. Ochiye's death was a harem quarrel."

Flores flushed under the scrutiny of many eyes.

"I know what's what, Don Alvaro. I may not be as clever as Ruíz, or as tough as Gomez, but I know a harem quarrel when I see one."

"A man's dead because his wives can't get along?" Petrus said. "And what has this Noam to do with it? He wasn't involved in this harem quarrel, was he?"

"Not directly. What we have here are two people working at cross-purposes, but with the same target. Ochiye was Noam's shield, so to speak. Ochiye stood in front, Noam worked behind him. "

"To what end? What does this Bretain lad have to do with Noam?"

"Young Owen is dead because Noam had schemes that went far beyond a mere harem dispute between wives. True, he had hated Ochiye for a long time, but it was only when Ochiye took Maya from him that he decided it was time for action. He already knew about the gold in Cherokee territory."

"Gold?" Sultan Petrus's eyes narrowed then widened as he took in the glittering ornaments on the chest of the Cherokee sachem and the knob on the end of the Choctaw's staff.

"Selim, the chart!" Halvar held up the coarse paper with Isai's symbols on it. "Ochiye had gold nuggets among his goods for sale, and his jewelry was made of gold. This chart shows how to find the gold. These are mountains, these are the stars that make up a picture in the sky—we call it the Sky Giant in the Dane-March.

"Look for these mountains and the three stars; there is a river that runs between the mountains. I don't know what the numbers mean, maybe days of travel, maybe leagues of distance; but if you follow this river, it will lead you to a place where the gold is. Am I right, noble Cherokee?"

Se-Kwa-Ya rose.

"It is so," he said in halting Arabi. "Noam come to me. He say he get guns, powder, if I give yellow stones. We take back land from Afrikans." He turned to Yona. "Not good to kill Ochiye. Not Cherokee way." He sat down, having said all he wanted to say.

"Gold for guns," Petrus said. "Where did Ochiye fit into this scheme?"

"He didn't," Halvar said. "It was all Noam and Yona."

"No!" Isai leaped forward. "My mother knows nothing of this!"

"Sit down, lad, and listen. Your mother is at the heart of this conspiracy. Don't go down with her." He turned back to Sultan Petrus. "I don't know who started it, but Yona knew that Noam loved her and wanted Ochiye out of the way. Noam knew that Yona was Cherokee, through and through. She went back to her people every summer, taught Isai Cherokee ways. Noam is gone, so I can't ask which of the two came up with the scheme first, but the plan was to bring a Huron down from the north to teach the Cherokee how to use guns against the Afrikans and their Oropan soldiers."

Tekla glared at Yona.

"You always stay in Savana Port! This year, you came north. I wondered why you did so. Now I know. You spent the whole summer at the Local camps, with the Local women."

Yona sat silent, alone in the center of the room, her face blank. Only Isai dared to approach her.

"Mother, is this true?"

"Noam wanted to rule where Ochiye ruled," Yona said coldly. "But he would be gone when the Cherokee took back what was theirs. The Mahak women would convince their men to join the fight."

"So, noble sachems, excellent sultan, this was Noam's scheme. He had planned it carefully. He could speak Erse to the Bretains of West Caster, who knew him from previous trading journeys he'd made. He told them he would get guns and black powder, saying that he would sell them to the Oropans being hired by Afrikans to protect the kutton that was sold to the Bretain manufactories, which employed the spinners and weavers. They would agree to this to keep the supply of kutton coming to their mills. Then he would bring the guns and powder to the Cherokee, in return for…What? Honor, a place at the council?"

He turned to the Cherokee sachem.

"True. We promised him a place at the council," Se-Kwa-Ya stated. "How do you know this, Hireling?"

"It makes sense," Halvar said. "At first I thought it was Ochiye who was planning the revolt. He blustered, talked against Don Felipe, may he rule long. But Ochiye spoke no Erse, so he couldn't bargain with the Bretains. He stayed on his barge with the goods. He depended on Noam, he trusted him, because that is the Afrikan way, to have your servants for life. And Noam was more than Ochiye's servant, he was his brother. Brothers can hate each other worse than strangers."

"But what about Owen?" Benyamin burst out. "Why kill him?"

"Because he recognized the person Noam brought with him from West Caster," Halvar said. "Guns are no good without someone who knows how they work. Imperator Lovis has sent guns to Kibbick. The Huron of Kibbick are armed with them. They come into Mahak territory to raid. Fru Dani Glick can tell you better than I about that."

Dani stepped forward.

"That's true. It's no secret that I was taken by Huron. They killed my husband, kept me as a slave. Their leader had a gun. Only trouble was, he had no powder, and he didn't keep it clean. He couldn't use it."

"But he had it," Halvar said. "Noam found a Huron who could teach the Cherokee how to use a gun. He knew the Cherokee and Choctaw were coming to Manatas. He knew they would play the Peace Game. His plan was to introduce the Huron into the visiting team. He counted on the suspicion between the different clans and tribes to hide this man's true tribe. The Cherokee would think he was Mahak or Algonkin, the Choctaw would think he was Cherokee.

"The Huron would then travel back with him to Cherokee territory. What he couldn't know was that there would be a Bretain lad who was so taken up by the game that he knew anyone and everyone in West Caster who played it. A real fanatic."

"Bad luck for Noam," Padraig said.

"And worse luck for Owen," Halvar said. "Because Noam didn't dare take the chance that his spy would be exposed." He turned once more to the visiting sachems. "The man killed this morning. Was he known to either of you by name?"

Te-Kum-Se frowned and spoke with Se-Kwa-Ya. The Cherokee stood again.

"There was one who played Peace Game. We found his body this morning, killed with tomahawk. No one know his name," he stated. "He play Peace Game with Choctaw, say he Cherokee, talk Munsi. Not Cherokee, not Choctaw."

"Huron," Halvar said. "And Noam couldn't take the chance that *he'd* talk, either. He sent the Huron to meet with Owen at the back of the Gardens of Paradise. Then, when the two were talking, he struck Owen down with one of the Cherokee playing sticks. Look for one of them with blood and brains on it. That's your weapon. Not a Mahak stick," he added. "I can tell you from my own experience, they bruise, but don't kill."

A titter of laughter seemed to lighten the atmosphere.

Red Knife stood up.

"The man was found dead between the Choctaw and Cherokee camps," he stated. "The Hireling told his messenger to look for one who had blue quill beads missing from his macassins. This man had such macassins. Blue-dyed porcupine quills, two missing."

"Noam must have done it before he made his run," Halvar surmised. "It was this Huron and Yona's Cherokee bodyguards who attacked me at the Mermaid Taberna. They were looking for that chart, but they didn't find it because Selim had it."

"So, Don Alvaro," Sultan Petrus leaned forward in his chair. "If this Noam is dead, and his scheme has come to nothing, what else is there for me to say?"

"There are these women," Halvar said. "What judgment do you pass on them?"

"My mother knew nothing of Noam's schemes!" Yakub cried out. "She has been in Manatas year in and year out. She had nothing to do with his poisoning."

"Except for providing a basket with dried fruit," Halvar pointed out.

"But it was Yona who got the mal-chinee from Noam," Yakub shot back, pointing at the Cherokee woman.

Isai leaped up to defend his mother.

"Ochiye humiliated her! He brought the concubine into our house!"

"And the girl did as she was told," Halvar said. "She put the fruit into the basket, because that is what she was ordered to do. But it wasn't the fruit that killed Ochiye. He'd been drinking sweetened water, laced with a few drops of the poison, for weeks. A jug in the garbage basket had some of the water in it. The dog must have lapped it up, thinking to satisfy its thirst. Instead, it died. Yona, what did you put in your tea?"

Yona said nothing, merely glared at him.

Halvar continued. "Noam knew that Ochiye was the weak link in his plan to turn the Cherokee jihad to his own advantage. I don't know if he knew what Yona was doing—"

"Noam? He was a fool!" Yona spat out. "He thought to rule in Nova Mundum like an Afrikan king!"

"Hatred of Ochiye, jealousy, ambition—all turned the faithful servant into a killer. I should have known from the beginning," Halvar stated. "It was Noam's name Ochiye was trying to say when his mouth was burning up from the mal-chinee. So, excellent Sultan, noble sachems, what is your judgment of the wives of Ochiye?"

"Yona is Cherokee." Se-Kwa-Ya had been following by way of whispered translations from his shaman. "We take her."

"To do what with her?" Tekla asked, her voice full of scorn. "And what about all those halfling brats back in Savana Port? How many of them are Ochiye's?"

"Never say that about my mother!"

Isai leaped at Tekla. Yakub blocked him. The two brothers wrestled until Flores forcibly separated them.

"You, Yakub, sit with your mother. You, Isai, sit with yours!" Flores jerked his head at his guards. "See that they stay there. This is a Divan, not a wrestling match! Order, if you please!"

Halvar grinned. Flores was settling into his new position nicely.

Sultan Petrus held up a hand for silence.

"My judgment in the matter of Ochiye Aboutiye is this. That the woman Yona be taken to her people, who will deal with her in the way that they deal with such matters. That the estate of Ochiye Aboutiye be given to his eldest son Yakub, with a widow's portion to Lady Tekla. That any children now living in Savana Town be under the protection of Yakub, as head of the family of Ochiye. That Isai, as the eldest son of the second wife, should return to Savana Port to care for his sisters and brother, and that Yakub make proper provision for those children. That is the decision of Sultan Petrus, in the name of the Calif Don Felipe of Al-Andalus, may he reign long."

Yakub and Isai glared at each other, but the armed guards kept them apart.

"While we are assembled here, I will give judgment on some other matters." Sultan Petrus harumphed. "In the matter of the ownership of the Mermaid Taberna, although the document giving it to Hannes Zilberstam was signed not by the Pawnbroker Manolo but by his son Jehan, I find the document legal. The Mermaid Taberna may be run by Hannes Zilberstam, who will pay a fee of one silver piece every month into the Manatas Town treasury for its use.

"In the matter of the pawnbrokers' shop, now being run by the wife of the deceased Jehan, said woman may continue to run it, for the same fee as the Mermaid Taberna, that is, one silver piece, paid monthly to the Manatas Town treasury."

"And the matter of Leon di Vicenza?"

Halvar's voice cut through the babble of Erse, Arabi and Munsi as the sultan's decision was discussed by the crowd.

"Oh, I'll take care of that!"

Everyone stared as a slender young man with a badly trimmed beard pushed through the crowd. He strode to the middle of the room with an air of confidence in spite of his mismatched clothing—patched trousers, worn boots, and a black velvet jacket trimmed with tarnished silver braid.

Halvar recognized his own best garment, the one he had reserved for the Grand Divan. He also recognized the wearer. He bowed deeply in an elaborate salaam.

"Welcome to Manatas, Don Felipe."

35

THERE WAS AN EXPLOSION OF NOISE—CRIES OF ASTONISH-
ment, whoops of glee, a clash of arms as the guardsmen stamped
their halberd staffs on the floorboards as they came to attention.
Sultan Petrus struggled to rise from his chair to greet his ruler. The
sachems came forward to look him over. Flores jerked the seated
students to their feet.

"Rise, all! Honor your calif!" Halvar cried out.

He took his place at Don Felipe's side, hand on his knife, ready
to block any attempt at assassination. Once more, he was the Calif's
Hireling and chief bodyguard.

Don Felipe smiled graciously at the group.

"Sultan Petrus," he said in a voice that carried throughout the
room. "You have grown larger since we last met. Manatas seems
to suit you. And I hear you have increased your family, too. Rodrigo!
You have another sister!"

A tall, dark Andalusian shoved through the crowd.

"*Salaam aleikum*, honored father," he said, bowing to Sultan
Petrus. "And you, Hireling. I told you when you left Al-Andalus we
would meet again. I didn't think it would be here."

"We have had adventures, Rodrigo and I," Don Felipe said. "But
we are safe, in spite of Lovis and his allies."

"How long have you been in Manatas?" Sultan Petrus sputtered.
"You should have come to the Rabat! We would have welcomed
you properly."

191

Don Felipe shrugged. "We didn't know whether we would meet with friends or foes. I've learned to be more cautious in my choice of companions. Rodrigo got me off Jebel Tarik and made certain my mother was taken to a place of refuge in a certain mountain estate."

"Where she continues to plot against Imperator Lovis," Rodrigo added with a wry grin.

"Meanwhile, I have plans for Al-Andalus-in-exile," Don Felipe said. "Have you finished here?"

"Not quite," Halvar advised him. "There is the reason you sent me, Don Felipe. Leon di Vicenza now calls himself Frater Leonidas. He's in the fratery here in Green Village, and he's determined to stay there."

"Then, as the old tale has it, when the mountain did not go to the Prophet, the Prophet went to the mountain," Don Felipe said. "I will go to this fratery and speak with Leon myself."

Halvar started to say something, but Don Felipe went on.

"Now, I think it is time that the people of Manatas knew their calif by sight. Have you a horse, Sultan Petrus? I don't think one of your donkey carts is quite suitable. I will meet you all at the Rabat. I do not mean to put you out of your rooms, Sultan, but I hope you can find someplace where your son and I may stay while we are here."

"You will not remain?" Sultan Petrus could not conceal the eagerness in his voice.

"I must meet with Sultan Penina in Salaamabad, and Sultan Calvero at Terra Mara," Don Felipe said. "And I have other work for my Hireling than traipsing through the forest with me. Rodrigo has taken care of me very well for the last three months, he can continue to do so."

Halvar felt a twinge of resentment. After all he had been through to get Leon, he was being shunted off again!

"One thing more," Sultan Petrus announced. "It has been decided that the entire island of Manatas is to be administered by Al-Andalus, according to its laws and customs."

"Decided by whom?"

Donal, with Cormack MacCormack, emerged from the crowd.

"Decided by myself and sachems Gray Goose-feather and Mahmoud," Sultan Petrus told them.

"We were not consulted!" Donal shouted. "Green Villagers are free Bretains! We do not bow to this calif! Why should we obey your customs and laws?"

"Because it is expedient to do so," Don Felipe said before Sultan Petrus could speak. "In the short time I've been on Manatas, I've heard and seen enough to know that this island is too small for three sets of laws. Men like Noam think they can hide in places like the Local camps, where different rules apply. In one thing Lovis is right. There has to be one law, and that law must apply everywhere in Al-Andalus, even in Al-Andalus-in-exile.

"Therefore, I, as your calif, declare this—that all of Manatas will be under the laws of Al-Andalus, which are based on Sharia, and that these laws shall be administered by your excellent Sultan Petrus, who has ruled well in my name these five years.

"However, I am aware that circumstances sometimes demand revisions in Sharia, and that there are always exceptions to certain regulation. Therefore, Green Village may continue as a separate entity, although under the rule of Sultan Petrus. I strongly suggest that Sultan Petrus take the advice of a council, similar to the example set us by his colleague Sultan Penina. And that said council should include representatives of the many peoples who come to this island, including at least one of the Afrikan merchants, one of the Yehudit, one of the Locals, and someone from Green Village.

"That is my decision, as calif. Does anyone dispute it?"

He looked around the room, expecting no reply. Gray Goose-feather surprised him by answering.

"Don Felipe, you are wiser than your years, but you have forgotten something. There are persons of wisdom you did not include in your council. The Mahak have always allowed women to have a place at our council fire. Therefore, I suggest that you include three women who have proved their wisdom at yours. Those are my clan-sister Nokomis, who has advised me well for many winters; Eva Hakim, who knows the people of Manatas; and the Yehudit woman Danela Glick, who escaped from the Huron and must have the spirits of the forest with her."

"Me!" Dani Glick shrieked. "On the Manatas Town Council?"

"A Yehudit woman? A dispenser of alcohol and whores!" One of the drably clad Bretains was equally appalled.

"A woman of much courage and wit," Gray Goose-feather countered.

"It is not our custom to allow women an active part in our councils," Don Felipe said slowly. "But my mother, may she live long, has always been my chief adviser. We will allow these three women

193

to attend the meetings of the Manatas Town Council and offer such advice as they see fit to give. Will that suit you?"

The Mahak and Algonkin sachems conferred in muttered Munsi. Then Gray Goose-feather nodded.

"It is agreed. The Peace Game will be played tomorrow. After that, we go to our winter villages. We will not return until the spring Feria. We wish you well, young man. Good cheer!"

With that, the Locals stalked out of the Gardens of Paradise, taking Yona with them.

"Now," Don Felipe said, "I will ride to the Rabat. Rodrigo, you come with me. Halvar…"

Halvar stepped forward, eager to resume his place at the calif's side.

"I think you'd better give me back my seal." Don Felipe held his hand out.

Halvar removed his cap. He slid one finger into a gap in the stitching of the embroidered band around its edge, the stitching that held the boiled leather in place. He withdrew a bulky folded scrap of parchment sealed with a blob of red wax. He handed the parchment to the calif.

"That's what you were looking for, Dani Glick," he said.

"I should have known," Dani murmured. "There had to be a good reason for you to keep that dreadful hat on, even if you are going bald."

Halvar put his cap on and faced his patron.

"Have you any more orders?"

"One more. If Manatas is to be under one rule, someone will have to see that all the rules are obeyed. I want you to organize one group—call it what you will, guardsmen, constabulary, watchmen, whatever you like—and make sure the laws of Al-Andalus are enforced properly. I hereby appoint you Capitán Halvar Danske, and I wish you well."

With that, Don Felipe strode out of the Gardens of Paradise, leaving Halvar speechless.

194

36

IT WASN'T EASY FOR DON FELIPE TO GET OUT OF GREEN VIL-
lage.

Word had spread through the settlement that the Calif of Al-Andalus had crossed the Storm Sea and come to their shores. Daoud
the News-crier had carried the information to the Feria grounds,
where petitioners waited for the sultan and sachems to begin the
Grand Divan. News-criers ran to Manatas Town to announce the
coming of the calif, who had been given up as lost, dead or taken
prisoner.

Dani Glick nudged Selim.

"Make a drawing, Selim! Benyamin, write something! Padraig,
you're needed upstairs! We have to get out a *Gazetta*! Quickly!"

Noises from above alerted Halvar to the inevitable news-sheet.
Soon, everyone on this island would know that Calif Don Felipe was
here. His job as bodyguard would be made more difficult. Too many
people wanted this young man dead.

By the time Don Felipe had mounted the horse brought to him
by Sultan Petrus's Andalusian guards, the path from Green Village
to the Feria was blocked by humanity. The guards had to use their
halberds to clear the way, and the procession moved slowly through
the people. Andalusians cheered; Afrikans did not. Locals observed
the young leader with detachment.

The parade wound around the Feria grounds to the town wall,
where the waiting Town Guards had formed an honor guard to es-

cort the calif to the Rabat. Sultan Petrus had to be satisfied with a seat in a pony cart next to his son Rodrigo. The Locals followed, Mahak and Algonkin, Cherokee and Choctaw, with their warriors behind them. Halvar brought up the rear, in a donkey cart, with Selim and Benyamin beside him. Padraig was left in Green Village, toiling in the attic of the Gardens of Paradise under the stern eye of Simon Singer.

Once inside the walls of Manatas Town, Don Felipe's triumphal procession halted at the Grand Muskat, where Mullah Abadul stood, waiting to give the blessings of Ilha and a warning to observe all the Prophet's teachings. Across from the Grand Muskat were the instructors and students of the madrassa. Don Felipe bowed graciously to both clerics and professors and went on his way, giving no sign of preference to either. His face was set in a smile that could easily have been a grimace.

He's learned how to be a king, Halvar thought. *He doesn't need me anymore. He's got Rodrigo to watch his back, he's left his mother behind.*

He didn't know whether to rejoice in the young man's new maturity or grieve for the loss of his job.

They had reached the safety of the Rabat. Once the gates closed behind him, Don Felipe sagged in his saddle. Rodrigo leaped out of the pony cart to assist him down from his horse before Halvar could maneuver his aching body out of the donkey cart.

"My rooms are yours, my lord Calif," Sultan Petrus offered. "I will summon food and drink. You must refresh yourself."

"I thank you for your generosity, excellent Sultan. It's been a long and difficult journey. I spent last night in a taberna, and many nights before that on the sea."

"You must tell us of your adventures."

Sultan Petrus puffed his way up to his lair, with Halvar and Selim one on either side to hold him steady on the stairs. He headed for his favorite chair, then remembered that he was no longer the most important man in Manatas, and that the calif had precedence over him.

"Forgive an old man, my lord. I am used to sitting."

"By all means, rest yourself," Don Felipe said, easing onto one of the cushions that had been placed near the sultan's chair and motioning for his new bodyguard to sit beside him. "Rodrigo, you will have to wait to greet your father properly. I want to find out what my Hireling has been up to. Halvar! What is this I hear about you turning into a crazed killer of Franchen?"

196

Halvar stepped forward, tugging at his mustache in embarrassment.

"It's been like this, my lord. From the time I got here, Sultan Petrus has been trying to keep something from me. At first I thought it was because he'd been holding back money from the Feria tariffs, keeping it for himself. Then I saw the town wall, and I thought it was because he was reenforcing the island's defenses. But after a while, I began to wonder about some other things."

Sultan Petrus' face reddened with indignation.

"If I withheld funds, it was for the good of Manatas!"

"Indeed it was," Halvar said. "How long did you think you could hide something as big as a bridge?"

"A bridge!" Don Felipe exclaimed.

"One that will join this island to the mainland," Halvar continued. "Built in the manner of the Old Roumi, like the ones in Al-Andalus, especially the one near the river. Do you recall, Don Felipe, that day when Leon di Vicenza took you and your companions to the river? Selim! Show us the image that was cut from Leon's notebook. The one the Franchen assassin kept."

"Selim?" Rodrigo frowned at the youngster; then recognition dawned.

"Your brother Selim!" Sultan Petrus's voice held a note of warning.

"It's been a long time. You've grown considerably since I last saw you...brother." Rodrigo ended with a sarcastic smirk.

Halvar took over, before any more attention fell on Selim.

"You see this?" He held out a sheet of paper. "This was part of Leon's notebook. The Franchen Robert Mortmain carefully cut it out and folded it, thus." Halvar followed the creases. "He put it into the lining of his coat, where it got dampened during a great storm that wracked this island two weeks ago."

"We got caught by that storm," Rodrigo said. "Ilha was surely with us. The dhow nearly foundered!"

"But you were saved, by Ilha's grace," Sultan Petrus said. To Halvar, he said, "What has this paper to do with the bridge? I thought we had decided it was useless. The image of Don Felipe was quite destroyed by the wet."

"So it was," Halvar said. "But I was wrong about why the Franchen wanted it. It wasn't for the image of the young men embracing. He couldn't have cared less about naughty pictures. If he wanted to preserve that, he'd have folded it to the inside, not the outside, where it would get wet.

"No, what Robert Mortmain was taking back with him to Kibbick was this. What was on the other side of the paper." He displayed a drawing of an arch, with numbers on either side. "This is what Leon was interested in that day. Oh, he drew the portraits of the young men he taught, including you, Don Felipe. But what he was really doing was making a study of how the Old Roumi built their bridges, and built them so well they still stand, all over Al-Andalus, and people use them to this day.

"Once I was allowed time to think it over, I started to wonder just what Leon had been doing all this time. Five years? Someone like Leon wouldn't sit in the Rabat teaching basic mathematics and literature to children for five years. He'd be out and about, roaming this island, and he'd see the need of a bridge. And, being Leon, he'd want to do something about it.

"How did he approach you, excellent Sultan? Bribery? Dreams of glory?"

"Practicality," Sultan Petrus said. "I've seen the world. I know how troops move. This island is at the center of Nova Mundum, but it's also isolated. In winter, the seas are rough, the rivers full of ice. Some days, no one can bring food or water or fuel. Getting goods on and off is hard, with only one place for safe docking. A bridge would bring more trade to the Feria. That means more tariffs for Al-Andalus. More people to settle on the island."

"And the bridge would give work to all those folk who are coming across the Storm Sea," Halvar added. "I've seen the towers starting to take shape. I don't know much about bridges, but I do know that to build them over water, you have to sink piers—great logs—to hold the towers up in the water. This bridge must have been started at least a year ago, about the same time that Leon was removed from the Rabat and took his rooms at the Mermaid Taberna. Which was being run by the Franchen Taverniers, who must have suspected what was going on at the other end of the island. That's why they wanted to get Leon's notebooks, that's what Robert Mortmain was after."

Halvar stopped for breath. Don Felipe nodded thoughtfully.

"I will have to have a very long talk with Leon," he said slowly. "As for you, Halvar Danske, you are still my Hireling. Just because I've found another companion doesn't mean I don't need you. That is why you are now Capitán of Guards for Manatas."

198

"I'm a soldier," Halvar protested. "I've never organized anything. I can't even write a report."

"That's what I'm for," Selim said, with a defiant toss of her head as if daring her brother to reveal her true identity.

"And Tenente Flores will make sure the Manatas Town Guards follow your orders," Sultan Petrus stated.

"I'm sure Fru Glick will do her part in maintaining order in Green Village," Don Felipe said. "So you see, Halvar Danske, you still have work to do for your calif. You are still my Hireling."

"You've paid me, in gold," Halvar admitted. "*Semper fidelis*, always faithful to my employer. Very well, Don Felipe. I'll do what you ask. I'll enforce the laws of Al-Andalus on this island of Manatas."

"It's a new world, Don Alvaro, and a new job. Do it well!"

Halvar bowed. He didn't want to be there, he didn't want to do this; but he'd been given orders, and he would follow them. It was what he did.

END

GLOSSARY

AL-ANDALUS	Spain
AL-LARGATO	Alligator
ALGONKIN	Algonquin/Lenape Indians
ARABI	Arabic
ARAGHOUN	Raccoon
BATATAS	Potatoes
BIRDIE	Homosexual (direct translation of Yiddish *faygaleh*)
BRETAINS	British
BURNWEED	Poison ivy
CHESU	Jesus
CRUX	Cross
CONVIVENCIA	Tacit Agreement Of Tolerance, By Which Islam, Judaism And Christianity Co-exist Peacefully In Al-Andalus
CORDUVA	Cordova
CRANE-BERRY	Cranberry
DANE-MARCH	Germany
DANES	Germanic people (includes Denmark)
DANIC	German language (written in Rune characters)

GLOSSARY

DAY OF BEGINNINGS	Rosh Ha-Shanah
DAY OF REPENTANCE	Yom Kippur
EAST CHANNEL	East River
ERSE	Gaelic language (written in Ogham characters)
ERSE RITE	Christianity as practiced in Northern Europe, under Celtic influence
ESCOUASH	Squash
FERIA	Commercial gathering/fair
FRANCHEN	French language (written in Roman characters); a native of Franchenland
FRANCHENLAND	France
FRATER	General term for a Kristo cleric
FRATERY	Monastery
GREAT RIVER	Hudson River
HAMMAM	Communal bath
HEMP	Cannabis, marijuana
HOLY BOOK	Bible or Qran, depending on who is speaking
HOLY MEAL	Mass
ILHA	Allah

GLOSSARY

ISLIM	Islam
IVRIT	Hebrew language (written in Hebrew characters)
KRISTO	Christian
KUTTON	Cotton
KIBBICK	Quebec
LOCALS	Native Americans
MACASSIN	Moccasin
MADRASSAH	School/university
MAHAK	Mohawk/Iroquois
MAIZ	Corn
MAL-CHINEE	Manchinil, a very poisonous tree native to the beaches of South Carolina, Georgia and Florida
MANATAS	Manhattan Island
MECHICANS	Aztecs
MECHICAN SEA	Gulf of Mexico
MOKKA	Coffee
MOTHER MARA	Virgin Mary
MUNSI	Native American trade language (unwritten)
MUSKAT	Mosque

GLOSSARY

NGUBA	"Goobers," peanuts
NOVA MUNDUM	New World, North America
OLD GRECO	Ancient Greece
OLD ROUMI	Ancient Rome, Ancient Romans
OPASSOM	Opossum
OROPA	Europe; excluding Al-Andalus
PARIGI	Paris
PATRI NOSTRI	"Our Father" / Lord's Prayer
PISTOIA	Pistol
POWHATAN	Renamed Terra Mara – Maryland
QUESTIONERS	Inquisition
RABAT	Fortress
RHUM	Rum
ROUMI RITE	Christianity as practiced south of the Alps, centered in Rome
ROUND ISLAND	Staten Island
SALAAMABAD	Philadelphia
SAVANA PORT	Savannah, Ga.
SEKONK	Skunk
SEQUAKNOK	Pennsylvania
SOUK	Shopping Sector / marketplace

GLOSSARY

STUDY HOUSE	Synagogue
TABAC	Tobacco
"TAKE THE WATER"	Be Baptized
THE PEACE GAME	Lacrosse
THE PIZZLE	Florida
THE PROPHET	Mohammad
THE REDEEMER	Jesus
THREE OLD WOMEN	Norns, Fates
WAMUS	A deerskin shirt with a fringed yoke and sleeves, commonly worn by frontiersmen
WEST CASTER	Westchester/New England
WUMPUM	Wampum; Shells used as medium of exchange for small purchases
YEHUDIT	Jews/Jewish

About The Author

ROBERTA ROGOW wanted to tell stories ever since she could hold a pencil, and to sing before she could walk. After a brief career as professional chorister, coffee-house singer, and actress, she combined her love of literature with her love of music during a 37-year career as a children's librarian in New Jersey, where she could promote literacy and entertain youngsters.

In her spare time, Roberta wrote stories for fanzines incorporating historical characters into fictional situations. This led to paid publication, beginning with a story in the shared-universe anthology *Merovingen Nights*, edited by C.J. Cherryh, in 1987.

Since then, Roberta has written four mystery novels in which the Reverend. Mr. Charles Lutwidge Dodgson (Lewis Carroll) teams up with young Dr. Arthur Conan Doyle to solve crimes, and three set in post-Civil War New York City, where a team of waterfront lawyers take on cases that no one else will touch.

Now her love of history has turned in another direction with the Saga of Halvar, set in an alternate universe on what is almost, but not quite, Manhattan Island. *Mischief in Manatas* is the third book set in her re-imagined Manhattan.

About The Artist

Born in Chicago, *WILLIAM NEAGLE* graduated from the University of Tennessee with a BFA. Having done work for the US Department of Energy and other companies, his work has been distributed worldwide. He has done book covers for the writing team of Joreid McFate and for his own novel, *Catching the Ghost*. He resides in North Carolina with his wife and two children.